A MYSTERIOUS AFFAIR OF STYLE

Gilbert Adair has published novels, essays, translations, children's books and poetry. He has also written screen-plays, including *The Dreamers* from his own novel for Bernardo Bertolucci.

by the same author

in the same series
THE ACT OF ROGER MURGATROYD

fiction
LOVE AND DEATH ON LONG ISLAND
THE DEATH OF THE AUTHOR
THE KEY OF THE TOWER
A CLOSED BOOK
BUENAS NOCHES BUENOS AIRES
THE DREAMERS

non-fiction
MYTHS & MEMORIES
HOLLYWOOD'S VIETNAM
THE POSTMODERNIST ALWAYS RINGS TWICE
FLICKERS
SURFING THE ZEITGEIST
THE REAL TADZIO

children's
ALICE THROUGH THE NEEDLE'S EYE
PETER PAN AND THE ONLY CHILDREN

poetry
THE RAPE OF THE COCK

translation
A VOID

A Mysterious Affair of Style

GILBERT ADAIR

faber and faber

First published in 2007
by Faber and Faber Limited
3 Queen Square London WC1N 3AU
This paperback edition first published in 2008

Typeset by Faber and Faber Limited
Printed in England by CPI Bookmarque, Surrey

A CIP record for this book
is available from the British Library

ISBN 978-0-571-23947-4

2 4 6 8 10 9 7 5 3 1

The cinema is not a slice of life but a slice of cake.

ALFRED HITCHCOCK

To My Editor, Walter Donohue

Dear Walter,

When, prompted by your enthusiasm for *The Act of Roger Murgatroyd*, you proposed that I write a sequel, I immediately rejected the idea on the grounds that I've always made it a point of honour never to repeat myself. Later, however, it occurred to me that I had never written a sequel before (to one of my own books, at least) and hence, applying what I acknowledge is a slightly warped species of logic, to write one now would represent another new departure for me. So if, to adapt Hitchcock's metaphor, fiction can also be a slice of cake, I hope you've left room for seconds.

Gilbert

PART ONE

Chapter One

'Great Scott Moncrieff!!!'

That voice!

Chief-Inspector Trubshawe – or, if one is to be a stickler for accuracy, Chief-Inspector Trubshawe, retired, formerly of Scotland Yard – had just stepped into the tea-room of the Ritz Hotel in quest of repose for his feet and refreshment for his palate, and it was while endeavouring to attract the eye of a waitress that he heard the voice which caused him to stop dead in his tracks.

If the truth be told, the Ritz was not the kind of establishment to which he would normally have accorded his patronage, certainly not for the steaming cup of tea which, for the past hour, he had craved. He had never been one to throw his money about, the less so since having had to learn to subsist on a police officer's pension, and a Lyons Corner House would have been more to his unashamedly plebeian tastes. But he had found himself by chance at the posher end of Piccadilly, whose sole common-or-garden tea-room had teemed with secretaries and short-hand typists gabbling away to one another about the trials and tribulations of their respective working days, all of which had simultaneously come to a close. It was, then, the Ritz or nothing; and he thought to himself, alert to the incongruous reversal of values, well, why not, any old port in a storm.

So there he was, in this unostentatiously elegant room – a room in which the dulcet drone of upper-crust conversation clashed harmoniously (if such an oxymoron is possible) with the silvery rustle of the finest cutlery, a room he had never entered and had never expected to enter in his life – and before he had even properly orientated himself, he had run into somebody from his past!

The person who had hailed him was seated by herself at one of the tables located near the door, her face just visible behind a wobbly stack of green-jacketed Penguin paperback books. When he turned his head to confront her, the voice boomed out a second time:

'As I live and breathe! Do these rheumy eyes of mine deceive me or is it my old partner-in-detection, Inspector Plodder?'

Trubshawe now looked directly at her.

'Well, well, well!' he exclaimed in surprise. Then, a note of sarcasm creeping almost imperceptibly into his voice, he nodded, 'Oh yes, it's Plodder all right. Plodder, alias Trubshawe.'

'So it *is* you!' said Evadne Mount, the well-known mystery novelist, ignoring the faint but meaningful modification of his tone. 'And you do remember me after all these years?'

'Why, naturally I do. It's an essential part of my job – I mean to say, it used to be an essential part of my job – never to forget a face,' laughed Trubshawe.

'Oh!' said the slightly deflated novelist.

'Except,' he added tactfully, 'when you and I first met, it was *after* I'd retired, was it not, which must mean that in this instance it's a personal not a professional memory. Actually,' he concluded, 'it was the voice that did the trick.'

Here came that note of sarcasm again. 'And the disobliging nickname, of course.'

'Oh, you must forgive my jollification. "She only does it because she knows it teases", what? Good heavens, it really is you!'

'It *has* been a while, hasn't it?' said Trubshawe dazedly, shaking her hand. 'A very long while indeed.'

'Well, sit down, man, sit down. Take the weight off your brains, ha ha ha! We must talk over old times. New times, too, if you're so minded. Unless,' she said, dropping her voice to a self-consciously theatrical stage-whisper, 'unless you happen to be here on a romantic assignation. If that's the case, you know me, I wouldn't want ever to be *de trop*.'

Trubshawe lowered himself onto the chair opposite Evadne Mount's, his broad boxer's shoulders heaving as he dusted down his trouser-knees.

'Never had such a thing as a romantic assignation in my

life,' he said with no apparent regret. 'I met my late missus – Annie was her name – when we were both in the same class at school. I married her when we were in our twenties and I was just a callow young constable on the beat. We had our wedding reception – a real slap-up do it was, too – in the dance-hall of the Railway Hotel at Beaconsfield. And until she passed away, ten years ago now, I never once looked back. Or sideways either, if you know what I mean.'

Evadne Mount sat back in her own chair and fondly took the Chief-Inspector's measure.

'What a charming, what a cosy, what an enviably conventional life you make it seem,' she sighed, and she probably didn't mean for her approval of that life to sound as condescending as it may well have done.

'And, quite right, I remember now. Last time we met – the ffolkes Manor murder case* – you'd just become a widower. And you say that was all of ten years ago? Hard to believe.'

'And what ten years they were, eh, what with the War and the Blitz and V.E. Day and V.J. Day and now this so-called bright new post-war world. I don't know about you, Miss Mount, but I find that London has changed out of all recognition, and it's not the better for it. Nothing but spivs, as far as I can see, spivs, Flash Harrys, black marketeers, motor bandits and these gangs of nylon smugglers I keep reading about.

* See *The Act of Roger Murgatroyd* (2006).

'And beggars! Beggars right here in Piccadilly! I've just spent the last half-hour strolling around Green Park, but I couldn't bear it any more. I was endlessly pestered by a bunch of grimy street urchins begging for pennies then calling me a tinpot Himmler – pardon me, a tinpot 'immler – when I refused to give them any. Main reason I came in here was for some peace and quiet.'

'Mmm,' agreed the novelist, 'I have to say this isn't the kind of place I'd associate you with.'

'It isn't at that. I was on the lookout for some plain, ordinary, come-as-you-are cafeteria. You, on the other hand, strike me as quite at home here.'

'Oh, I am. I drop in every day at this time for afternoon tea.'

These mutual pleasantries were interrupted by the arrival of a white-haired, white-capped waitress who hovered expectantly over Trubshawe.

'Just a pot of tea, miss. And tell them to make it strong.'

'Right you are, sir. Would you be wanting bread-and-butter with that, sir? Cucumber sandwiches, p'raps?'

'No thank you very much. Just the tea.'

'Right away, sir.'

Glancing at the neighbouring tables, most of which had been commandeered by plump, well-nourished dowagers, fur stoles drowsily curling about their necks like equally plump, well-nourished pet foxes, Trubshawe turned again to Evadne Mount.

'There's a lot of talk about austerity these days. Not much sign of it here.'

She smiled benignantly at him.

'I do know what you mean,' she answered in a voice whose habitual tenor was so stentorian that, even if she said not much more than 'Pass the sugar, please', it made heads turn as far as three or four tables away. 'The War has complicated everything. It isn't only London that's changed. The whole country's changed, the whole world, I dare say. No more manners, no more respect, no more deference. Not the way it was in our day.

'But then, you know, Trubshawe, those grimy urchins you mentioned, those peaky-faced little ragamuffins? Don't forget that, a mere couple of years ago, they were being bombed out of house and home by the Luftwaffe. When they insult you by calling you a tinpot 'immler, well, that's not just a name to them. It's quite possible the Nazis were responsible for the deaths of their mothers or fathers or a half-dozen of their school chums. In these terribly trying times, I do believe we all need to be more indulgent than usual.'

Trubshawe took her point.

'You're right, of course. I'm just a crochety, antisocial codger, a crusty old curmudgeon.'

'Pish posh!' said Evadne Mount. 'It's been ten years since I last clapped eyes on you and you haven't aged a bit. Really, it's most remarkable.'

'Now that I take a closer look,' said Trubshawe in reply, 'you neither. Why, I wager, if I were to run into you again in ten years' time, you still wouldn't have aged. It's almost as though time has stood still – at least for you. For me too, if you say so. And, of course, for Alexis Baddeley. She never appears to age either.'

'Alexis Baddeley, eh? My alter ego – or ought I to say, my alter egoist? Why, Trubshawe, don't tell me you've become one of my readers? One of what I like to call the happy many?'

'Yes, I have. As a matter of fact, ever since we, eh, we collaborated on that nasty Roger Murgatroyd affair, I've read every one of your whodunits. Just the other week I finished the latest. What was its title again? *Death: A User's Manual*. Yes, indeed, I finished it last – last Wednesday it was.'

There followed a not-so-brief silence during which Evadne Mount patently began to feel it a mild discourtesy on the Chief-Inspector's part to have mentioned the title of her most recent book, to have acknowledged having read it, then to have left it at that. Though she tended to be brazen in her relationship with publishers and readers, admirers and critics, it nevertheless was not her style ever to be the first to open up what might be termed the negotiations of praise – she would claim she never had to – but she found Trubshawe's noncommittal response so frustrating that she finally queried:

9

'Is that all?'

'All what?'

'All you have to say about my new book? That you finished it last Wednesday?'

'Well, I . . .'

'You don't suppose you owe it to me to say what you thought of it?'

Just at that moment Trubshawe was served not merely the tea he had requested but a glazed cherry-topped bun he hadn't. But before he'd had the chance to correct the waitress's error, Evadne Mount raised her glass – only now did he notice that what she was drinking was a double pink gin, a drink that, by rights, should not have been available in a tea-room – and proposed a toast.

'To crime.'

Unaccustomed though he was to toasting precisely those nefarious activities he had devoted his professional life to combating, Trubshawe nevertheless decided that it would be both pompous and humourless of him to refuse.

'To crime,' he said, raising his teacup.

He took a deep draught of the tea and, the waitress having already disappeared, an unexpectedly voracious bite out of the bun.

'Actually,' he continued, 'I have to confess that – now this is just one man's point of view, you understand – but I have to confess that I didn't feel your new whodunit would ever become one of my own personal favourites.'

'No?' the lynx-eyed novelist, eyeing him like a hawk, rejoindered. 'May I ask why not?'

'Oh well, it's all very clever and that, the tension building up nicely as usual, so that, as I read on, I was more and more gripped, just as I'm sure you intended me to be.'

'Interesting you should say that,' she immediately cut in. 'It's my theory, you see, that the tension, the real tension, the real suspense, of a whodunit – more specifically, of the last few pages of a whodunit – has much less to do with, let's say, the revelation of the murderer's identity, or the disentangling of his motive, or anything the novelist herself has contrived, than with the growing apprehension in the reader's own mind that, after all the time and energy he has invested in the book, the ending might turn out to be, yet again, an anticlimactic letdown. In other words, what generates the tension you describe is the reader's fear not that the *detective* will fail – he knows that's never going to happen – but that the *author* will fail.'

'But that's just it,' Trubshawe maintained, seizing the opportunity to cut back in. He had been inordinately indulgent with her, considering that she had after all solicited his opinion but, familiar as he was with her old ways, he was well aware that, if he permitted her to digress as freely as she was used to doing, he would never get around to letting her know what he actually thought of her book.

'The suspense, as I say, was building up nicely to the scene in which your lady detective, Alexis Baddeley, re-examines the suspects' alibis. Then there comes that whole bizarre business of the drunken toff who keeps popping up all over the shop and . . . and, well, you lost me, frankly. Sorry, but you did ask.'

'And yet it's really quite simple,' persisted Evadne Mount.

'Is it? I must say I –'

'You do know what a running gag is, don't you?'

'A running gag? Ye-es,' replied the Chief-Inspector, not altogether sure that he did.

'Of course you do. You must have seen one of those Hollywood comedies – screwball comedies I think they call them – in which the running gag is that some top-hatted toper keeps, as you say, popping up in the unlikeliest places and asking the hero in a slurred voice, "Haven't I sheen you shomewhere before?" Am I right?'

'Uh huh,' he said as prudently as before.

'So when the reader encounters the same type of character in *Death: A User's Manual*, he thinks, aha, this must be the comic relief, just as it is in the films. But no, Trubshawe, in my book the toper really has seen the hero somewhere before. Where? Leaving the scene of the crime, of course. Because he's pie-eyed, though, nobody pays the slightest bit of attention to him. Except for Alexis Baddeley, who insists that, inebriated or not, he's a witness like any other and hence has to be taken as seriously as any other.

'I like to think of it as my variation on "The Invisible Man". The Father Brown story, you know.'

After listening to her argument no less patiently than she had presented it to him, Trubshawe shook his heavy head.

'No, no, I'm sorry, Miss Mount, it won't do.'

'What do you mean?'

'Oh, I grant you, now that you've spelt it out for me, I just about get the hang of the idea. But it's not good enough.'

Evadne Mount prepared to bristle.

'Not good enough?'

'I've read enough whodunits now – mostly yours, I have to say, though once I'd exhausted all of those, I found I was so addicted I even dipped into one or two thrillers of the thick-ear school, James Hadley Chase, Peter Cheyney –'

'The adventures of Lemmy Caution, you mean? Ugh, not my thing at all.'

'Nor mine either. Anyhow, as I was saying, I've read enough of them now to know that, in the best ones, the only really effective ones, you don't have to read the sentence or the paragraph or even the whole page twice to understand what the author's getting at, as you might have to do with, you know, the classics. That's not to denigrate whodunits, yours or anybody else's. All I'm saying is that, when the revelations come tumbling out one after the other, their impact on the reader has got to be instantaneous. They've got to hit you – practically smack you – in the face.

'It's like a joke. If you don't laugh at a joke at once, you're never going to laugh at it. And now I come to think about it, isn't that what's really meant by the Perfect Crime, in whodunits at least? Not a crime whose perpetrator goes un-detected – I mean, whose murderer goes undetected, for nowadays people are so bloodthirsty I don't suppose any-thing short of murder will do – not a crime where, as I say, the murderer goes undetected – no, you couldn't have such a book, the reader would ask for his money back – but a crime in which everything fits together perfectly, in which there's neither too much nor too little evidence to digest and in which the revelation of the murderer's identity turns out to be as inevitable as it's unforeseeable. It *couldn't* be him, you say to yourself, yet it *couldn't* be anybody else. That, surely, is the Perfect Crime.'

Trubshawe ended his discourse almost apologetically, as though conscious of his effrontery. Lecturing on whodunits, and at such length, to the Dowager Duchess of Crime herself! As he finally lit up his pipe, after knocking the dottle into a glass ashtray that was at once whisked away from their table by a hitherto unnoticed waitress and replaced by an identical but pristine one, he gave the novelist a wary sidelong glance.

For a moment, she seemed dumbfounded. Then, to his astonishment, she let rip with an explosive laugh.

The detective cocked his head enquiringly.

'Did I say something funny?'

'No,' was her answer, once she had sufficiently calmed down to speak. 'You didn't say something funny, you said something honest. That's what made me laugh – laugh so much I think I've got a run in my stocking!

'I've become such a success, you see, such a star, nobody else dares to be honest to me. My publishers, my readers, my critics – well, most of them,' she qualified, not quite suppressing an embryonic snarl – 'they all tell me that my latest book, whichever it happens to be, is wonderful, is terrific, is the finest so far, though we all know it's a dud. And even if the reviews are a teensy bit less ecstatic than I'm used to, that's not going to stop the publishing house, when it's reissued, from describing it on the cover as "much-acclaimed". I tell you, Trubshawe, there's never been a book published in this country that wasn't "much-acclaimed". Before too long, you'll see, they'll be advertising "the much-acclaimed Bible" and "the much-acclaimed telephone directory", ha ha ha!

'Not,' she went on, switching to her 'serious' voice, 'not that I'm suggesting *Death: A User's Manual* is a dud, you understand. It isn't one of my few, one of my very few, outright misfires. But you're right, it's too clever for its own good. It's what you might call clever-clever, which sounds twice as clever as clever itself but is actually only half.

'So thank you, Trubshawe,' she said. 'Thank you very much.'

'What are you thanking me for?'

'For being so candid. Candid – and interesting. You may be a relative newcomer to whodunits, but you're already quite the theorist.'

'Well, you know, Miss Mount, I wouldn't like you to

think I didn't enjoy it. I did, really, only not so much as your earlier ones.'

'Very nice of you to say so. And you really must call me Evadne. Old pals and allies as we are. Better still, call me Evie. Cut out the middle-woman, what? You will eventually, so why not start now?'

'Evie,' said Trubshawe unconvincingly.

'And may I call you – well, whatever it is your friends call you?'

The detective drew on his pipe.

'Don't have too many of those left, I'm afraid. But if you mean, what's my first name, well, it's Eustace.'

'Eustace? Oh dear. Oh dear, oh dear. I don't see you as a Eustace at all.'

'Nor do I,' grunted Trubshawe. 'But there you are. It's the name I was given, it's the name on my birth certificate and it's the name that makes me turn my head in the street if ever I hear it called out. Which nowadays, frankly, is never.'

Evadne Mount took a moment to contemplate him.

'I say, Eustace,' she said, consulting her wrist-watch, 'do you have anything special on this evening?'

'Me?' he answered dejectedly. 'I've nothing special on most evenings.'

'I take it that means you aren't in Town for some specific reason?'

'I live in London now. Bought myself a semi-detached in Golders Green.'

'Really? You don't any longer have that cottage on Dartmoor?'

'Sold up and moved on six-seven years ago. It became too lonely for me, you know, after the death of poor old Tobermory. You remember, that blind Labrador of mine that was shot on the moors?'

'Of course, of course I do. So there's nowhere you have to be tonight?'

'Nowhere at all.'

'Then why don't you join me? Eh? For old times' sake?'

'Join you?' he echoed her. 'I don't think I understand.'

Evadne Mount ground her ample frame into the defenceless little chair.

'As it so happens, this is a very special evening for me. At the Haymarket tonight – the Theatre Royal, Haymarket – they're giving a Grand Charity Benefit Show in aid of East End Orphans. Everybody in London will be there,' she said, deliberately courting the cliché. 'Bobbie Howes, Jack and Cicely, the Western Brothers, Two-Ton Tessie O'Shea and I don't know who else, all doing their bit for nothing. It's in the best of causes, after all.

'I'm one of the writers – I cooked up a short curtain-raiser, a mini-whodunit – and you'll never guess who's playing Alexis Baddeley.'

'Who?'

'Another of your former acquaintances. Cora.'

'Cora?' repeated a mystified Trubshawe.

'Cora Rutherford. Don't tell me you've forgotten her?'

For a few seconds more he racked his brains. Then, in a rush, it all came back to him.

'Cora Rutherford! Well, of course, I'm with you now. She was also one of the guests at ffolkes Manor, was she not?'

'That's right.'

'So you too are as inseparable as ever?'

'Well, no . . . To be honest, I'd rather lost touch with Cora until this show brought us together again. Oh, we've had the odd natter on the blower, but we never quite manage to synchronise our watches. When I'm free, she's busy; when she's free, I'm busy. You know what they say, though. Our best friends aren't those we see the most but those we've known the longest. Where it really counts, she and I are still bosom pals.'

'Ye-es,' muttered Trubshawe, for whose taste the novelist's choice of words had proved a touch too vividly fleshy. He pronounced the name thoughtfully.

'Cora Rutherford . . . It's true enough,' he went on, 'I was never a great fan of the Pictures, even when Annie was alive. We'd go together because she liked them even if I didn't. Still, I can't say I've heard much about her of late. Cora Rutherford, I mean. She hasn't retired, has she?'

'Oh no,' said Evadne Mount. 'Cora's still gamely hanging in there. Actually, she rang me up just the other day to tell me that she'd landed a part in a brand-new film production. Confidentially, though, she fancies herself as a bit of a recluse, occasionally sighted flitting along Bond Street like a rare specimen of some exotic avian species – the seldom-spotted film star!'

The novelist laughed indulgently at her friend's eccentricity.

'It's all rather preposterous, you know, because, from what I hear, she's as much the woman-about-town as she ever was. But if it helps Cora to grow old painlessly by thinking of herself as the British Garbo, well, who am I to spoil her fun?'

'And you say she's appearing in the show?'

'She plays Alexis Baddeley in the opening sketch, the one by yours truly. After which, there'll be some singing, some dancing, a few laughs, a few tears, and a spectacular grand finale. So why don't you come along as my guest?'

Trubshawe was tempted. It was obvious that, of late, not much singing, dancing, laughter or tears had enlivened his existence. Yet he was as cautious a private individual as he had been an officer of the law and he needed to tot up the pros and cons of any revision to his plans, particularly his immediate plans, before saying yes or no. In short, he definitely wanted to go to the show, but he was also determined to ascertain in advance whether there was any likelihood of his subsequently regretting having done so.

'The question is,' he finally said, scratching his chin, which wasn't even itching, 'will there be tickets left? You've made it sound such a prestigious event.'

'There isn't a single ticket to be had for love or money. The show was sold out weeks ago, even at the prices they're asking. Five guineas for a seat in the stalls, can you imagine? Not to worry, though. I've been given a couple of comps, so that's all taken care of.'

Trubshawe now cast a downward glance at his suit and tie. It was a perfectly respectable suit and tie, the suit grey worsted, the tie belonging to one of London's less well-frequented gentlemen's clubs. But even he, no habitué of Theatreland, was aware that not one of his fellow-members of what promised to be an exceptionally glamorous audience was likely to beg him for the name of his tailor.

A small grey cloud drifted across his stolid features.

'You're fine, absolutely fine!' she said loudly and encouragingly. 'Besides, just take a look at me, will you, and then tell me you're going to feel out of place!'

It was true. She was dressed, as he recalled had been the case those ten years ago, in a shapeless tweed suit that protruded in the places in which she herself protruded but also contrived to protrude in a few places on its own initiative. Lying on the tablecloth, moreover, creased every conceivable way a hat can be creased, and then some, was the matelot's navy-blue tricorne which had long been her trademark in London's literary circles. No, Evadne Mount hadn't changed.

'Well, Eustace,' she said, 'shall we be off? The show starts at half-past seven, which really means quarter-to-eight, so we've just got twenty minutes to make it.'

Trubshawe nodded agreement. He also insisted on picking up the bill not merely for his own pot of tea but also for his companion's order, which turned out to be not one but two double pink gins and pricier than he had bargained for.

Never mind, he thought to himself, as he cast a handful of silver onto the table and his companion, with a nonchalantly maladroit gesture, swept the stack of green Penguins all at once into her capacious handbag. Things happen around Evadne Mount. She had already teased him out of his sulks, cheered him out of his loneliness, half-cured him of what, in his rare introspective, even poetical moments, he would describe to himself as his 'spiritual gout', and here he was, wholly out of the blue, about to join the elite at a splendid theatrical gala. Well worth the twelve shillings and sixpence.

'By the way,' he said, escorting her from the Ritz, its door held open by a resplendently uniformed flunky, who bowed them into the street with the utmost correctitude, 'what's the name of this show we're going to see?'

Pulling the tricorne hat down hard on her head, she gave its middle furrow a vicious bash.

'*Save the Last Valise for Me*,' she answered. 'Oh, I know, it's a daft title, but then, I fear it's going to be a pretty daft evening. Except,' she added, 'for my own little sketch. That, I do assure you, is deadly serious.'

And, with these enigmatic words, in the gathering shades of a Friday evening in early April, they wandered off together towards the nearest bus-stop.

Chapter Two

The shiny red omnibus which had borne them the length of
Piccadilly, and on whose open top floor they had perched as
majestically as on a Maharajah's elephant, deposited them
fifteen minutes later at the far end of the Haymarket, just a
few yards from the Theatre Royal itself.

The Haymarket, it must be said, was but the shadow of
its prewar self. Its pedestrians were threadbare, its under-
aged, undernourished beggars hollow-eyed. Even the lack-
lustre street-lamps served only to intensify the prevailing
gloom. Yet the theatre itself, whose colonnade of six white
pillars was taller by far than the theatregoers who passed
between them, retained most of its faded grandeur. Nor was
it the theatre alone. As though in a concerted protest against
the drab post-war ethos, the cream of the theatrical, cine-
matical, political, journalistic and social world had patently
decided to demonstrate that, in the War's embattled after-
math just as during the conflict itself, London Could Take It!

Furs had been retrieved from vaults, necklaces from secu-

rity boxes, evening gowns and dinner suits from mothballs, and all donned as defiantly as, not so long before, gas masks and camouflage kits. It's true that not a few of the pearls had been born out of wedlock, so to speak, and most of the furs, evening gowns and dinner suits had grown old with their owners, but it was a magnificent spectacle nevertheless. For the crowd of onlookers who gawped at the Rolls-Royces and Bentleys gliding suavely down the Haymarket, the show was as dazzling in its way as that for which the toffs themselves had turned up.

Even Trubshawe, discreetly elbowing his way through *hoi polloi* as he and his companion entered the foyer, couldn't help but feel slightly overawed.

Yes, he had been one of the top men at the Yard and, in his time and in his prime, he had had dealings with the most eminent and powerful figures in the land. Yet he had been born a fretworker's son in Tooting and had clawed his way slowly up through the ranks, a fact which was all to his credit, more so than if he had been afforded entrée to the superior echelons of the Force through some august family connection. But it did mean that he had never quite succeeded in shedding the skin of his modest ancestry. He knew the ropes, in short, but he had never lost his fear of getting himself entangled in them. He had always had, and had always hated himself for it, a touch of deference in his encounters with the great and the good, even when, as had sometimes occurred, he had found himself obliged to caution them that anything they said might be used in evidence against them. And here he was, hobnobbing with Dukes and Duchesses, Ministers and Diplomats, Actresses and Playwrights.

On the steps of the theatre he even caught sight of someone he knew. The man was a former Cabinet Minister, and Trubshawe was on the point of doffing his cap to him when he remembered in time that their acquaintance was founded on his having managed, back in the teens of the century, to recover from the hands of agents employed by a certain Central European power the only complete blueprint of the X-27 prototype, the exploitation of which, had that power ever come to possess it, would undoubtedly have prolonged the Great War by several months, if not years. Realising, then, that if the facts were looked square in the face, the Minister was more beholden to him than vice versa, he merely returned the other's circumspect nod with one of his own and rejoined Evadne Mount.

'Ah, there you are,' she said, waving to this member of the audience and that, indiscriminately, it seemed, as Trubshawe noticed some of those waved-to staring back at her with a doubtful do-I-know-that-woman? expression on their faces.

'Here's your ticket. Why don't you get yourself settled?'

'Oh, but –' replied Trubshawe in alarm, 'where are you going?'

'Don't worry. I'll be with you in a jiff. I just want to tell Cora to break a leg.'

'You want to what?'

'Theatre lingo, my dear,' said the novelist. 'I want to wish her well for the evening's performance. So be a good chap and take your seat.'

Without letting him voice any further protest, clinging for dear life to her tricorne hat, she rushed off backstage. Meanwhile, stifling a sigh, Trubshawe was drawn forward by the garrulously whinnying mob of privileged humanity and immediately found himself inside the auditorium.

He walked down the aisle, kneading his tartan golf cap between his fingers. And it was only when he arrived at the very last – rather, the very first – row of the orchestra stalls and checked his ticket number that he realised with a start that he and Evadne Mount had been allocated seats just under the stage, seats from which they would be practically as visible to the rest of the audience as the actors themselves. Though he had never been a patron of the theatrical arts, he had certainly seen the odd play in his life, but to be seated in the very front row – this was a new experience for him.

He removed his overcoat, folded it neatly across his lap as he sat down, then opened the luxurious silver-embossed programme which had been handed him by an usherette on his entering the theatre. The first item on the bill, he saw at once, was *Eeny-Meeny-Murder-Mo*, starring Cora Rutherford as Alexis Baddeley and bearing the subtitle 'A Lethal Squib by Evadne Mount'. Having scanned the names of the other cast members, none of whom were familiar to him, he took a last lingering glance round the auditorium and waited for Evadne herself to take her seat.

It was just seconds before the curtain rose that she reappeared, racing down the aisle to general amusement after everybody else had been seated. As Trubshawe observed, she was again blowing kisses left and right to various acquaintances. In fact, she made such a dramatic entrance into the hushed, now near-silent auditorium it was almost as though she were deliberately trying to render her arrival as obtrusive as possible.

Finally, she plumped herself down beside Trubshawe.

'I was beginning to think you'd abandoned me,' he said.

'Apologies, apologies. I'm afraid I was detained longer than I expected to be. I was just given some really rotten news. Rotten for Cora, that is.'

'Oh, I'm sorry to hear that,' Trubshawe said under his breath. 'And only a few minutes before she's due to go on stage. That must be the actor's worst nightmare.'

'It is. But she hadn't yet heard the news herself and I forbore to tell her. It can wait till after the show.'

'Not a death in the family, I trust?'

'No, it concerns Alastair Farjeon.'

'Alastair Farjeon?'

'The great film director. It seems –'

But before she had time to elaborate, the lights dimmed. For Trubshawe, too, the explanation would have to keep.

When, a second or two later, the curtain rose, he could

barely make out what was in front of his own eyes, the stage being nearly as dark as the auditorium. There was a hint – albeit not much more than a hint – of ceiling-high bookshelves, an enormous fireplace, two deep leather arm-chairs and, on the extreme left, a closed door under which a narrow blade of light provided the only source of illumination. Behind that door, apparently, some kind of a party was being held. Audible, inside the room supposedly adjacent to the dim, still unoccupied stage, were lots of gay, eupeptically high-pitched voices, the strains of syncopated Negro music and, every so often, the explosive plop of a champagne cork.

'Scenery's a bit underlit, isn't it?' the Chief-Inspector whispered to Evadne Mount. 'Oughtn't you to do something about it?'

'Shhhh!' she replied in a whisper three times as loud as his, her eyes glued to the stage.

At long last something happened. The closed door opened a sliver, causing the music's already high decibel level to be turned up higher still, as brusquely as though on a gramophone. At the same time, a young man in evening dress stealthily tiptoed into the room, followed by an even younger woman in a white satin gown. Silently closing the door behind him, turning to face her, he put his index finger to his Ronald Colman moustache.

For a few moments they stood together on the unlit stage, neither of them saying a word, both of them listening intently to the muffled din from the next room. When it became obvious that, for now, their absence had gone undetected, the young man switched on the light.

All at once, their facial features having suddenly become visible, a tremendous salvo of applause swept through the auditorium, running the gamut from the vigorously genteel (in the stalls) to the downright raucous (from the gallery). If the Chief-Inspector alone failed to recognise either of the two faces, let alone attach names to them, even he could see on those faces that both stars, as he assumed them to be, were positively aching to step out of character, face the audience of their peers and gratefully acknowledge their accolade.

They resisted nevertheless and instead fell into one another's arms.

Then, when she had finally unsealed her lips from her lover's, the young woman cried out:

'Oh, Harry! How perfectly frightful this evening's been! I don't think I can bear it a minute longer!'

'I know, I know,' he said.

He pummelled his right fist into the palm of his left hand.

'He's a brute, a swine! The way he kept taunting you in front of everybody. Oh, I wanted to kill him!'

'What are we going to do?'

'I'll tell you what we're going to do. We're going to run away together.'

'Run away?' she repeated tremulously. 'But – but when?'

'Tonight. Now.'

'Heavens! Where will we go?'

'Anywhere. Anywhere we please. I'm a rich man, Debo, a very rich man. I can take you anywhere you could ever want to go. I can give you anything your heart could ever desire. A Mediterranean villa, a yacht, a stable of polo ponies . . .'

'Now, Harry' – the first hint of a half-smile playing on her lips – 'what on earth would I do with a stable of polo ponies?'

'Debo darling, how naïve you are! How exquisitely naïve! One doesn't *do* anything with polo ponies. One just *has* them. That's what being rich is all about.'

'I don't give a fig about being rich. All I want is to be with you, as far away as possible from that beast.'

Just then – but one had to be paying very close attention, so surreptitious, so nearly invisible, was the stage business – the door behind them re-opened. The five fingers of a male hand slithered, one by one, around the frame, started groping for the light-switch and, finding it, flicked off the light again. Before either of the two characters already on stage had time to react to this new development, a nerve-jangling shot rang out. The door was immediately slammed shut, the woman named Debo screamed, the audience gave out a loud collective gasp and the young man, or rather his dimly illuminated silhouette, collapsed in a heap on the carpet.

All Hell erupted. The off-stage Negro music came to an abrupt halt – one would almost swear to having heard the scratch of a needle as it was yanked off a record – the library door opened once more, opened wide this time, the light was switched on again and, squeezed into the doorway, faces as white as shirt-fronts, cigarettes, cigars and cocktail glasses clutched in trembling hands, were a half-dozen horrified guests – one of them, as Trubshawe remarked, togged out in full kilted regalia.

Another, as he also remarked, was Cora Rutherford. The quintessence of pre-war chic in a long black evening gown and matching elbow-length gloves, she seemed scarcely altered from the woman he had encountered and indeed interrogated those many years before at ffolkes Manor. At once taking charge of the situation, she strode superbly across the stage, bent over the victim's body exactly (in Trubshawe's memory) as he himself had so often done in his career, put her ear to his chest – meanwhile shoving aside an exquisite tear-drop pearl earring as conspicuously as though she actually intended to raise a smile from the audience – felt his pulse, drew down both his eyelids, then looked back up at the others.

'He's dead.'

This announcement caused an even greater commotion. What was to be done? The police would have to be called in, of course; but in the meantime, there being no doubt whatever that the murder had been committed by one of those present, how were they to spend the time in the uneasy truce that would follow?

Now it must be said that even in those of Evadne Mount's

whodunits he had found most satisfying it was the obligatory but, to his way of thinking, faintly tiresome connective tissue that Trubshawe had always least looked forward to; and here too, after such a suspenseful opening scene, his mind began to wander. So it was that he chanced temporarily to turn his attention away from the stage and towards the novelist who, from the very start of the sketch, had been utterly absorbed in the to-ings and fro-ings of her own creations.

As he watched her from the corner of his eye, however, he saw her features suddenly twitch with a spasm of disbelief, of shock, almost of horror.

A moment later, she caught his wrist in a painfully tight grip and, half-moaning, murmured:

'Oh no . . . No . . .'

'Why, what is it?' whispered Trubshawe.

'Look!' she cried out, seemingly forgetting that she was in a theatre. 'The blood! It's wrong! It's all wrong! There's not supposed to be any blood!'

While some spectators immediately attempted to shoosh this blithering female who had had the nerve, so they imagined, to interrupt the show with her own dim-witted chatter, others who had recognised Evadne Mount as the author of the playlet and on whom the ominous implication of her words was already having its effect, began to wonder aloud if there really could be . . .

As for the performers on stage, they were visibly at a loss

to know what to do next. Should they continue to deliver the lines as they had been written? Or should they pay heed to this grotesque if, all the same, anxiety-inducing outburst from the woman who had written them?

Their minds were made up for them by the eventual realisation, on both sides of the footlights at once, that from the 'dead body' of the character who had just been 'murdered' a thin trickle of blood had indeed started to snake its way downstage and was even now dripping into the orchestra pit, right in front of the seat occupied by, precisely, Evadne Mount.

This was too much for her. Without addressing another word to her companion, she leapt to her feet, hurriedly climbed the half-dozen steps leading up to the performing area and, in front of the entire cast, the petrified audience and a Trubshawe who for the moment was too discombobulated to think of taking any rational action, bounded onto the stage.

Like Cora Rutherford before her, she bent over the body. Bracing herself, she gently turned the young actor's face upward. The audience gasped again – except that this was a different type of gasp, the gasp no longer of spectators at a theatrical show but of bystanders at a car crash. Blood was now sweating freely through the snow-white dickey of the actor's tuxedo, forming an ever-expanding circular stain that resembled nothing so much as the Japanese national flag.

Evadne Mount looked up grimly, straight at the audience instead of at the members of the cast.

'Oh my God, ladies and gentlemen, this is real blood. The bullet – the bullet wasn't a blank!'

Hearing these words, one of the actors, a sixtyish, silver-templed gentleman who had been cast as a retired military officer – so at least intimated the lavishly beribboned and bemedalled lapels of his dinner jacket, the pronounced limp with which he had walked onto the stage and, not least, the monocle which dangled from a red ribbon about his neck – at once stepped forward (now minus the limp) and, prompting yet another gasp, held up what Trubshawe recognised as a German army pistol, a Luger.

'I – I got it from props,' he stammered. 'I didn't even take a look inside it. Why should I? I naturally assumed everything was . . .'

Even before he had completed his piece, his fellow cast members could all be seen gradually distancing themselves from him and gathering in a nervous huddle at the opposite end of the stage.

'Oh, come now. You can't possibly suspect me of . . . Look here, I had no earthly reason to murder Emlyn. Not like this. Not in full view of everybody. No, no, no, that's not what I meant to say. I had no reason to murder him anyway – at all! But if I'd *had* a reason – I mean, just for the sake of the argument – if I *had* had a reason – which, I repeat, I didn't have – I certainly wouldn't . . .'

His voice trailed off in a series of inaudible ramblings. The audience sat as though collectively turned to stone. They were so mesmerised by the extraordinary events which had taken place on stage, it hadn't occurred to any of them to propose that the police, the real police, be instantly summoned.

Except that there was a real policeman, a real ex-policeman, in the house. Trubshawe had finally come to his senses. Realising that he alone of all those present in the Theatre Royal was qualified to ensure that the appropriate protocols would be implemented from that point on, he rose up from his seat.

And he was just about to follow Evadne Mount onto the stage by the same half-dozen steps when she herself stared back at him from the supine body over which she was still crouching and, to his stupefaction, *she winked at him!*

Winked at him? *Winked at him???* Could it be . . . ? Surely not? Surely everything that had happened wasn't just . . . ?

Then, for Trubshawe as for the rest of the audience, the penny dropped.

Already, centre-stage, the novelist Evadne Mount and her most celebrated character, Alexis Baddeley, the former played by herself, as it were, the latter played by the actress known to be her oldest friend, were squabbling (exactly as he recalled them squabbling at ffolkes Manor) as to who had priority in investigating the murder of the juvenile lead. Every gibe, every aside, every taunt and twit, was greeted with gales of laughter as, in their turn, the other members of the cast, all of them famous, though not to Trubshawe, also started insulting each other with coded comments about private lives and loves, professional successes and, even more gleefully, professional failures.

'I never smoke. I never drink. I never take drugs,' was the high-minded claim of one cast member who, in real life, had become notorious for trumpeting each of these abstemious virtues of his in the illustrated magazines.

'Blimey O'Reilly,' riposted Evadne Mount, who had naturally given herself the best of her own lines, 'how do you find the time to do all these things you never do?'

Or when, a few minutes later, Cora Rutherford, half-Alexis Baddeley, half-herself, was asked her opinion of the ingenue, a simpering redhead with insufferable freckles, she cattishly replied, 'My dear, I rather fancy that tonight will turn out to be her farewell debut.'

The audience, needless to say, adored all the rudery and ribaldry, all the banter and bitching and back-stabbing. So too did Trubshawe, once he had quietly decided to forget that so irresponsible a stunt, played out in a packed theatre, really ought not to be condoned by laughter or crowned by applause.

What a strange business, he thought, the show business is. The theatre, for example. If people go to a play, it's surely because they take pleasure in being caught up in all the illusions the theatre can offer. Yet, if there's one thing in which they take pleasure even more than these illusions, it's to have them unexpectedly shattered.

It always seems as though the warmest round of applause is reserved for the actor who understudies a role at the last minute and has to go on-stage with script in hand or the actress so decrepit she can hardly remember her lines or the matinée idol known to have served a prison sentence for buying petrol on the black market or the chorus girl whose husband has dragged both her and her swarthy masseur-cum-lover through the divorce courts. As Trubshawe had good cause to know, considering how often she had told him during their former acquaintance, Evadne Mount's plays had all enjoyed lengthy runs in the West End. Yet he would have wagered his last ten-shilling note that not one of them had been so rapturously received as this trivial squib, the whole point of which was to mock the whiskery props and devices by which the same audience would have been enthralled when watching one of her more serious efforts.

And it fleeted across his mind that if the audience knew what he knew – that, the moment the curtain came down, the leading lady was fated to receive some as yet unspecified piece of bad news – they would have adored it even more.

In any case, after a running time that was neither too long nor too short but, like the baby bear's bowl of porridge, just right, the sketch reached its triumphant climax. The 'victim' abruptly sprang to his feet and, turning to face the audience, let his blood-stained dickey roll up his chest like a circus clown's. Beneath it, on his undervest, three words had been scribbled: APRIL THE FIRST.

'Anywhere,' declared Cora, 'but the Ivy.'

It was just after ten-thirty when the three companions stood on the steps of the Theatre Royal and wondered where to have supper together.

'But, Cora,' protested Evadne, 'you adore the Ivy.'

'Used to, darling, used to,' Cora drawled, bundling her pale furs about her neck. 'You seem to forget, I've withdrawn from that frivolous world. No more hugging and mugging and table-hopping for poor lonely little Cora.'

'But I saw you there only last week.'

'Ah yes,' replied the actress defensively, 'but then I was dining with Noël. I mean to say, Noël . . .'

'Oh, very well, have it your own foolish way. The thing is, it's cold and it's late. Do we eat or do we don't? And, if we do, then where?'

'What about the Kit-Kat?'

Cora turned to Trubshawe who, because he suspected that no proposal he might make would cut much ice with his two redoubtable dining companions, had so far refrained from taking part in the conversation.

'You know it?' she queried. 'It's in Chelsea – the King's

37

Road. First it was the Kafka Klub. Then it was the Kandinsky Klub. Then the Kokoschka Klub. Now it's the Kit-Kat Klub. It's one of those places that are renamed a hundred times but never go out of fashion.'

Evadne Mount's answer was pat and to the point.

'I absolutely refuse to go to the Kit-Kat,' she said. 'The food costs the earth – and tastes like it too. But I say,' she changed tack, 'if what you're hankering after is something off the beaten track, I know a simply marvellous Chinese restaurant in Limehouse. There may be table-smashing but I can assure you there won't be any table-hopping. What say you, Eustace?'

The Chief-Inspector looked slightly ill-at-ease.

'What's the matter? You aren't afraid, as an ex-copper, of being caught in such a den of iniquity? You really needn't worry. Frankly, it couldn't be more respectable.'

'No, no, it isn't that at all.'

'What, then?'

'Well, you see,' he explained, 'I ate Chinese food once. When my wife and I took a weekend break in Dieppe. I just couldn't get a grip on those – those whatyamacallums.'

'You mean chopsticks?'

'That's the word. Chopsticks. I couldn't handle them at all. It felt as though I was eating on stilts, don't you know.'

'Well, of course Trubbers doesn't want to have some foul Chinee muck in the East End!' said Cora Rutherford.

With a plaintive sigh she faded further into her furs.

'I can see it's up to me as usual to make the sacrifice. Oh well, if it must be the Ivy, then the Ivy it is. *Allons-y, les enfants.*'

Chapter Three

'I'm simply gasping for a ciggie!'

A short taxi ride later, they were comfortably installed at one of the most enviable of the Ivy's tables. The two women had ordered a couple of exotic cocktails, Trubshawe was hospitably acquainting himself with a whisky-and-soda, and the incipient conversation awaited only the lighting of Cora's first cigarette.

It was a real performance. For the actress, a cigarette represented a sixth finger. Once, indeed, she had languorously informed an impressionable lady columnist from the *Sunday Sundial* that she was incapable of contemplating Michelangelo's image of God breathing life into Adam without transforming it in her mind into an allegory – an allegory, darling! – of the immemorial gesture of one smoker offering a light to another. The columnist was suitably thrilled. So too, presumably, were her readers.

Now, the cigarette extracted from its platinum case, inserted into a jet-black ebony holder, lit up and luxuriously inhaled, she was ready to rejoin the living.

She turned to face Trubshawe.

'This *is* nice, isn't it?' she said. 'After all those years! So much more *gemütlich* than last time around. I think we all prefer a spoof murder to a genuine one – except for Evie, of course. Now this is a question I really don't have to put to you, because I could plainly see you sitting there large as life in the front row, but I'll put it to you anyway. How did you enjoy the show?'

'The show?' replied Trubshawe. 'I haven't laughed so much since – I don't know when I last laughed so much. And watching you two bicker on the stage certainly brought back a few memories. If I still had my hat on, I'd take it off to both of you.'

He hesitated before pursuing his train of thought.

'Even if . . .'

'Even if what?'

'Well,' he said, 'even if it did seem to me you were sailing a wee bit close to the wind. Pulling a stunt like that inside a crowded theatre, you know, it's tantamount to crying "Fire!". Had the worst come to the worst, you could have provoked a stampede. It was all so very believable, at least for the first few minutes, I wouldn't have been surprised if some of the more gullible members of the audience had assumed there really was a murderer skulking about backstage. I don't suppose you bothered to apply for authorisation, now did you?'

'Well, naturally we didn't,' snorted the novelist. 'Imagine how much red tape we would have had spewed out at us. It was in a Good Cause, don't forget. Besides, that was an exceptionally sophisticated audience out front. Did they look to you about to stampede?'

'No-o-o,' said Trubshawe. 'But then, of course, I was sitting in the very first row. I couldn't really see how they were taking it.

'Anyway,' he added in a conciliatory tone, 'no harm done. It *was* hilariously funny. And, as you say, it *was* in a Good Cause. And, after all, I *am* only an ex-policeman. I couldn't have taken official action even if I'd wanted to.'

The next several minutes saw them occupied perusing the menu. When their choices had been made and their orders taken, the subject turned at last to the bad news of which Evadne Mount had already advised the Chief-Inspector.

'I say, Cora . . .' she began hesitantly.

Cora was instantly aware of the change in her friend's voice. 'Yes, what is it?'

'Well . . . I heard some news – bad news, seriously bad news – just five minutes or so before curtain-up. You'll forgive me, I know, but I felt I had to hold it back until after you'd done your turn.'

'All right,' said Cora bluntly, 'I've done my turn. Out with it.'

'It's Farjeon.'

'Yes?'

'I'm afraid he –' she sought to cushion the blow – 'I'm afraid he's joined the Great Majority.'

'What!' cried Cora. 'You mean he's gone to Hollywood?'

Evadne wriggled in a paroxysm of embarrassment.

'No, no, dear. Do try to concentrate. What I mean,' she frowned gravely, 'what I mean is that he's dead.'

'Dead?! Alastair Farjeon?'

'Yes, I fear so. The stage manager heard the news on the wireless and told me, as I say, just five minutes before you were due to make your entrance.'

It came again, like a belated echo:

'Dead!'

Horror and incredulity battled it out for supremacy on Cora's features.

'Good God! Farjeon dead! A heart attack, I suppose?'

'No. I understand why you might think so. As a matter of fact, though, it wasn't a heart attack. It was something much, much worse.'

There was a momentary pause during which neither spoke.

'Well?' Cora eventually said.

'Well . . .'

'Oh, do get on, Evie, for Christ's sake! By dragging it out like this, you're only making it a thousand times worse.'

'Well, as you know – as I'm sure you know – Farjeon owned a villa near Cookham – you did know that, didn't you? – I've heard it was the last word in gracious living – he used to host lots of weekend parties there – were you ever invited?'

'Yes, yes,' Cora nodded impatiently.

'Well, it seems there was the most ghastly fire in that villa of his and he himself was burnt to death.'

'Oh my Lord, how perfectly awful! Was he alone, do you know?'

'Absolutely no idea. All I know are the basic facts. None of the details. It happened this afternoon – late this afternoon.'

Trubshawe intervened for the first time.

'Apologies for butting in. This has obviously been a terrific blow to both of you. But would you mind if I asked who exactly you're talking about?'

Cora stared at him.

'Don't tell me you don't know who Alastair Farjeon is?'

'Well, no, I can't say I do.'

'Cora, love,' the novelist gently broke in before her friend could air her astonishment at the policeman's ignorance. 'You forget. Not everybody's horizons are bounded by Wardour Street at one end and Shaftesbury Avenue at the other. You lot who work in the show business often forget how very distant that world is from most people's ordinary day-to-day preoccupations.'

'Sorry, sorry, sorry. Right as usual, darling,' Cora replied contritely.

She turned again to Trubshawe.

'*Mea culpa*, my dear. I was just so surprised that you'd

44

never heard of Farje – I mean, Farjeon. I quite took it for granted that everyone knew the name, because he's simply – he *was* simply,' she corrected herself – 'the most brilliantly creative artist we've ever had in the British film industry.'

'I don't get to the Pictures too often,' the Chief-Inspector apologised. 'This Farjeon, he was what you call a film producer, is that it?'

'No, he was a film *director*, and please' – here she raised the palm of her right hand in front of his face to prevent him from posing what she knew would be his next question (it was a ploy he recalled having seen before but, since on that occasion the hand had been Evadne Mount's, the actress must have picked it up from the novelist or possibly vice-versa) – '*please* don't ask me what the difference is between a producer and a director. If I had a silver guinea for the number of times I've had that question put to me, I could retire on the spot. Just take my word for it, dearie, there is one.'

'And now he's dead. Such a tragic death, too,' said Trubshawe. 'I'm truly sorry. He was a close friend of yours, I gather?'

'Close friend?' Cora ejaculated. 'Close friend?? That's a good one.'

'Beg pardon?'

'I couldn't *stand* Alastair Farjeon. No one could.'

The Chief-Inspector was utterly befuddled. He knew the immemorial reputation of theatricals for being fickle, flighty creatures, capricious to a fault, but this was ridiculous.

'Then there really must be something I'm not getting here,' he said. 'I had the impression you were devastated by his death.'

'Oh, I am. But for purely professional reasons, you understand. The man himself I abominated. He was a verminous, arachnoid pig, if I may be permitted to mix my animal metaphors, a pompous, puffed-up little swine, a toad to his inferiors and a toady to his superiors. He also had, if you can believe this, the unmitigated brass to flatter himself that he was God's gift to womanhood,' she added, unexpectedly assuming a maidenly archness that would have been comical if the circumstances were other.

'A good-looking man, was he?'

'Good-looking? Farje?!'

Cora gave a harsh, mirthless laugh.

'Farje, you must know, was *fat*. Not ordinarily, forgivably, lovably fat. He was outlandishly fat, monstrously so. Which is why, when Evadne announced the news of his death, I at once assumed it must have been from a heart attack, for he'd had more than one already.

'He was also the vainest, most egocentric man I ever met. A complete narcissist.'

'A fat narcissist?' said Trubshawe. 'H'm, that couldn't have been easy.'

Cora was now talking compulsively, almost convulsively.

'I've always believed it was out of narcissism that he became a film director in the first place. He had this very

46

special trick – a unique trick, you might say. In every one of his films, right at the start, before the plot had got underway, he would have a double, some extra who looked exactly like him, make a brief appearance in the corner of the screen. It became in a way his trademark, like the Guinness pelican, you know, or the golliwog on the marmalade jar.'

'I see . . .' said Trubshawe, though, in truth, he didn't quite.

'Poor Farje. He was famous for falling helplessly and hopelessly in love with his leading ladies. But because he invariably lusted after the sort of frosty blonde, cool and aloof on the outside, scalding hot on the inside, who couldn't possibly have lusted after him, he found himself obliged to pay them vicarious – is that the word I'm looking for? – to pay them vicarious court via the various debonair young actors he tended to cast opposite them in his films. He was like Cyrano de Bergerac, except that it was Farje's belly not his nose that was oversized.'

She allowed herself the ghost of a smile at her own wit.

'Then, when he finally screwed up what little courage he possessed to make a pass at one of them and, inevitably, was repulsed, he'd take his revenge by tormenting, by practically torturing, her on the set.

'He got himself into trouble with the odd husband or boyfriend, I can tell you. I seem to remember he was once seriously duffed up in the lobby of the Dorchester.'

'So he was an unmarried man?'

'Not at all. He's been – I mean, he was – married to the same woman for Heaven knows how many years. Hattie. Everyone in the industry knows Hattie Farjeon. She's one of those unthreatening little wifies insecure men attach themselves to by the proverbial ball-and-chain.

'It's curious. Whenever Farje wasn't around, Hattie was Miss Bossy-Boots incarnate, a whinging fussbudget, a real besom, as my dear old mum used to say, a meddling, scheming know-it-all, physically unprepossessing, to put it mildly, very mildly, and given to stamping her two little flat feet if crossed. When they were together, though, it was obvious just how terrified she was of him.'

'And you say,' Trubshawe enquired, 'that your reasons for regretting his death were purely professional?'

'I had just signed up for a part in his new picture,' she said bitterly.

'Ah . . . I see. The leading role, I assume?'

'Thank you, Trubbers, thank you for being so *galant*,' replied the actress. 'No, it wasn't the leading role. Oh, small as it was, it was a showy part all right, with one big scene where I positively chew up the furniture, but the lead? No. In fact, I wouldn't normally have accepted such a – well, such a petite role. If I did so in this case, it was only because it was Farje.'

'Sorry,' said Trubshawe, 'but I still don't follow. You claim you abominated the man. You also said that he was famous for tormenting his actresses. You even went so far as to use the word "torture". And you've just admitted that the part you signed up for wasn't even the lead. Why were you so eager to play it?'

Even though the tragic gaze that Cora now trained on him had done stellar service, as the policeman was well aware, in a dozen West End melodramas, it was one in which, on this occasion, real pain was nevertheless detectable. There was the barnstorming actress on stage. Waiting in the wings, however, there was also the bruised human being.

'Listen, my dear,' she said, 'in your long and doubtless varied career you must have had to deal with crooks who were as villainous as they come, except that you just couldn't help grudgingly admiring their professional panache. Am I right or am I right?'

'Yes – yes, you are,' replied the detective. 'Yes, I see what you're getting at.'

'That's how we all felt about Farje. He may have been a rat, but he was also a genius, the nearest thing the British film industry has ever had to a Wyler or a Duvivier or a Lubitsch. For him the cinema was not just a job of work, it was a challenge, a perpetual challenge. Haven't you seen any of his films?'

'Ah well, there you have me, I'm afraid. I may well have done. The thing is, I used just to go to the Pictures, not to any one particular Picture. Most of the time, I didn't actually know in advance what it was I was going to see. I didn't go to *Casablanca*, I went to the Tivoli – and if

Casablanca happened to be showing at the Tivoli that night, then *Casablanca* is what I'd end up watching. This whole complicated business of, you know, directors and producers and suchlike is something of a closed book to me.'

'Well, I can only say that, if you're unfamiliar with Farje's work, you've been denying yourself a great deal of pleasure.'

'There was that wonderful thriller of his, *Remains to be Seen*, about a party of English archaeologists working on a dig in Egypt. The "remains to be seen" are the ruins they're excavating – already an awfully clever conceit, don't you think? – but they're also the remains of the victim, whose freshly murdered body is discovered inside an underground tomb which has lain undisturbed for three thousand years! And it all ends with a glorious shoot-out in and around the Sphinx.

'Or *The Perfect Criminal*. You remember, Evie, that was one of his films you and I saw together? Charles Laughton plays a burglar who never, ever robs his victims the same way twice, never helps himself to leftovers in the pantry, never leaves a half-smoked Turkish cigarette smouldering in an ashtray. And that's why he's eventually caught. Because, as you have good cause to know, Trubshawe, there doesn't exist the criminal who hasn't got his own little set of quirks and idiosyncrasies, quirks and idiosyncrasies which you coppers gradually come to identify and actually look out for. So, in the film, when one perfect burglary after another is committed, none of them with the least trace of any known criminal's tics and tropes, the police eventually realise that it must have been committed by him.

'Or *Hocus-Focus*, which takes place entirely inside a jam-packed hotel lift which has stalled between two floors. The whole film, mind you! And not only is a murder committed in the lift itself but the camera never stops panning and tracking in and around that cramped space. Only Farje would have attempted such a folly.'

'I say, hold on there,' Trubshawe interrupted her. 'How in Heaven's name did he succeed in squeezing one of his doubles into that one?'

'Oh, that was typical of him – all part of the fun, all part of the challenge, the devising of new ways to insert himself into his own films. You see, one of the guests trapped in the lift is a slinky vamp of a Eurasian spy who wears a small cameo brooch pinned to the lapel of her Schiaparelli suit. Well, on the cameo, if you looked hard enough, you could just about make out a tiny portrait of Farje himself. It's a visual pun,' she explained. 'Neat, no?'

Trubshawe's perplexed eyebrows mounted his forehead.

'A visual pun?'

'Darling, that kind of fleeting appearance in a film is what we in the trade call a cameo. In *Hocus-Focus* Farje's cameo literally was a cameo – a cameo brooch. Now do you under-stand?'

'Um . . . yes,' came the uncertain reply.

'You haven't seen his very latest?' she went on. '*An American in Plaster-of-Paris*? It opened only last month.'

Trubshawe shook his head.

'Vintage Farjeon. Another absolutely brilliant thriller. The spectator never once catches so much as a glimpse of the murderer, who's brought to book by the hero, a young G.I. in London whose left leg is in a plaster cast from the first scene to the last. He's recuperating in a not terribly well sound-proofed flat in Bayswater and he figures out, from no more than the sounds he hears filter down through the ceiling, that his unseen upstairs neighbour has just bludgeoned his wife to death.

'I tell you, Trubshawe, there's not an actor, not an actress, in this country who wouldn't sacrifice their own left leg to appear in one of his films. I had the chance – and now I've lost it.'

She shivered, even though the room was, if anything, overheated. It was as though the import of the calamity that had befallen her had only just penetrated the fragile carapace of her sophistication. An actress through and through, on-stage and off, she was so intimately at one with her craft that, like a congenital liar, she was no longer capable of judging where make-believe ended and reality began. Yet there had always been moments in her life when the mask would slip and what was revealed underneath was the anguished face of a woman who had just begun to wonder where her next role, like a pauper his next meal, was coming from. This, it had been evident to Trubshawe for some little time, was one of those moments.

Evadne clucked her tongue sympathetically.

'You really, really wanted the part, didn't you, precious?'

The mask was now slipping off altogether. The tears that glittered in her eyes – even when, as on the present occasion, there was nothing affected or simulated about her distress, Cora remained a star to her fingertips, and a star's tears don't just glisten, they glitter – were as distressing to behold as a woman's, as any woman's, tears always are.

'Oh, Evie, you can't know what I was willing to do to get it. You can't know how I pleaded, how I grovelled. I had my agent ring Farje's office every single day, morning and afternoon. He turned me down twenty times. Said I was too old, too old-fashioned, mutton dressed as lamb, jumped-up trash.'

'Jumped-up trash? He actually said that?'

'To my face, Evie, to my face!'

'Oh, my poor darling,' murmured the novelist, swiftly glancing around the restaurant to check whether anybody had chanced to catch Cora in her moment of panic. Needless to say, everybody *was* watching her, for the Ivy itself had already begun to buzz with the news of Farjeon's death.

'And we weren't even alone.'

'No!'

'He was with his latest discovery, Patsy Sloots. Patsy Sloots! What a name! He apparently plucked her from the chorus line in the new Crazy Gang revue.

'Now that *is* jumped-up trash. You remember Dorothy Parker's quip? "Let's go watch Katharine Hepburn run the gamut from A to B." From what I hear, little Patsy's gamut doesn't even stretch to B. Her speciality is bottoming bills rather than topping them. But she's just the sort of skinny blonde ninny Farje always did fall for. And there she was, draped over his desk at Elstree, looking as though her whole body, not only her face, had been lifted, while he was telling me that my number was up. I couldn't believe how he enjoyed humiliating me!'

Evadne had more than once been witness to her friend's vulnerability, but it had always been when they were *tête-à-tête*, in the privacy and intimacy of either woman's flat. That Cora should be on the point of breaking down here, the cynosure of the Ivy, was a vivid indication of what losing out on such an opportunity meant to her.

'And yet,' she said softly, 'you *did* let yourself be humiliated.'

'It was my very last chance. Such a role – I know I could have been superb in it, I just know! That's why I was ready to grovel before him. And the horrible irony of it all,' she said, the words choking in her throat, 'is that I believe, I truly believe, he always did mean to give the part to me. My agent assured me that no other actress had been tested. Farje simply couldn't resist torturing me anyway, just for his own perverted amusement. And, yes,' – she turned to an embarrassed Trubshawe, who had tried during her tirade to render

54

himself as inconspicuous as was possible for the large, hulking man that he was – 'actors will do anything to land a half-way decent part, *anything*.'

'As I already told you, I know nothing about the picture business,' Trubshawe replied, 'but Farjeon was only the director, after all. If the script has been written, can't they just find somebody else to direct the film?'

'You're right,' Cora replied coldly.

'Well, I did think –'

'I say you're right. You *do* know nothing about the picture business.'

'Now now, Cora,' said Evadne, 'I realise how terribly upset you must be, but it's unfair to take it out on poor Eustace. He only means to be kind.'

Cora immediately took Trubshawe's right hand in her own and squeezed it.

'*Mea culpissima*,' she said, dabbing at her eyes with the folded tip of her napkin. 'Oh dear, I've been shedding so many tears my cheeks are rusty. Sorry to be so beastly. Forgive me?'

'Course I do,' he said magnanimously. 'I quite understand.'

'And what you just suggested, well, I wouldn't like you to think it was totally beside the point. If it were any other film director who had suddenly died, that's exactly what would happen – the studio would simply hire somebody else to take his place. The problem is, there *is* nobody else who can take Farje's place.'

For a moment not one of the trio spoke. Then Evadne delivered herself of one of those edifying truisms which sometimes do succeed, in the short term, in easing an uncomfortable situation.

'Darling Cora,' she said, 'something's bound to turn up. It always does. You know better than most that Life is more like the Pictures than the Pictures are like Life – if you take my meaning – which, to be frank, I'm not at all sure I do myself.'

Little did she know how true these trite, unsingular words of hers were destined to prove . . .

Chapter Four

The very next morning, as Trubshawe was tucking into a breakfast that consisted of one pork sausage and two thin slices of fried bread (an egg had become a once-a-fortnight treat, if that), he heard his *Daily Sentinel* thump onto the door mat. He stood up, padded along the hallway in his dressing-gown and slippers, picked up the newspaper and scanned its front-page headline.

'Famous Film Producer Dies in Fire!' is what it screamed at him.

Back in the kitchen, he took his place once more at the little oblong table tucked away in a cosy, windowless corner, stirred his tea, treated the bundled-up newspaper to a noisy, impatient straightening-out, started mechanically to chew on a modest mouthful of sausage and turned his attention to the article in question.

Even before he had read a line of it, however, his eye was drawn to the two portrait photographs between which it was sandwiched.

The first was of a man in his mid-forties with a face so puffily corpulent it looked as though a twinned pair of thinner faces had been rolled into one and a double chin so fat and fleshy it spilled onto his white shirt-collar like a soufflé oozing out over the top of a cooking-pot. This, according to its caption, was 'Alastair Farjeon, the world-famous producer, familiarly known to those in the film business as Farje'.

H'm, said Trubshawe to himself, so he wasn't alone in having a problem distinguishing a producer from a director.

The second was of a poutily unsmiling young woman. Despite her faintly beady piglet eyes and an elongated slash of a mouth that her lip rouge accentuated to near-freakish proportions, she was an undeniably attractive specimen of feminine allure, except that hers was a kind of chilly, standoffish, inaccessible beauty – 'marmoreal' was the fancy adjective that came to mind – by which he personally had never felt aroused. The caption to her photograph read: '22-year-old Patsy Sloots, Mr Farjeon's ill-fated discovery'.

Trubshawe now turned to the article itself.

Shaken to its glamorous foundations, the British cinema world was in mourning today following the tragic death of Alastair Farjeon, the celebrated producer of such classic pictures as *An American in Plaster-of-Paris*, *The Perfect Criminal*, *The Yes Man Said No* and others too numerous to mention.

The 47-year-old Mr Farjeon perished in a fire yesterday afternoon while week-ending at his luxurious and secluded residence in Cookham. A second fatal victim of the flames which swept uncontrollably through the wooden chalet-style villa was Patsy Sloots, the 22-year-old dancer and promising motion-picture actress whom Mr Farjeon, widely regarded as the British cinema's foremost discoverer of new talent, had spotted in the chorus line of the Crazy Gang revue, *You Know What Sailors Are!*, currently in its second year at the Victoria Palace.

It was at exactly 4.45 pm that the Cookham police and fire brigade were simultaneously alerted to the conflagration by one of Mr Farjeon's neighbours, a Mrs Thelma Bentley, who reported to them of having seen, as she stepped into her garden to mow the lawn, a 'wall of flames' rising out of the villa's living-room windows . Unfortunately, by the time three separate fire-engines had arrived on the scene only a few minutes later, the fire was too far advanced to be immediately extinguished and the villa itself proved impossible of access, or even of approach, so intense was the heat given off.

The priority of the eighteen-strong team of firemen was therefore to get the blaze sufficiently under control to ensure that it would not spread to adjacent residences, all of whose occupants were speedily evacuated. At the height of the conflagration, a heavy pall of smoke was visible from a distance of up to thirty miles away.

At 6.15 firemen were finally able to gain entry to what was now no more than a smoking, skeletal carcass. There the horrific discovery was made of two badly burnt corpses. These have still to be officially identified, but the police have already let it be known to this reporter that there would seem to be no doubt at all that they are Mr Farjeon, the film producer, and his young protégée.

Asked if there was any suspicion of foul play, Inspector Thomas Calvert of Richmond C.I.D., the officer in charge of the case, confined himself to stating that the circumstances of the catastrophe would be thoroughly investigated but that every indication so far suggested that it had been a tragic accident.

Later, interviewed on the telephone, the well-known film-maker Herbert (*I Live in Grosvenor Square*) Wilcox paid a warm and heartfelt tribute to Mr Farjeon. 'His death,' he said, 'is a tragedy for the post-war revival of the British film industry. He was a true artist who brought clever ideas and bizarre angles to a medium which has never been more sorely in need of them. One did not have to approve of all his work to sense that one was in the presence of genius.'

Maurice Elvey, whose many popular pictures have included *The Lamp Still Burns* and *Strawberry Roan*, declared, 'I doubt we shall see his like again.'

The investigation continues.

Trubshawe then turned to the newspaper's necrological page. There was, as he noted at once, a lengthy, laudatory obituary of Farjeon himself but none at all of the far less celebrated Patsy Sloots. Her name, indeed, was mentioned only once in Farjeon's own obituary, as the actress who had been selected to play the leading female role in the producer's (as the obituarist also insisted on describing him) new project, *If Ever They Find Me Dead*, alongside Gareth Knight, Patricia Roc, Mary Clare, Raymond Lovell, Felix Aylmer and – 'At last!' muttered Trubshawe – Cora Rutherford.

He laid the newspaper down and began to mull over what he had just read. Burnt to death! What a ghastly way to go! Puts you on a par with Joan of Arc and – what was the name of the Italian scientist condemned to death for heresy? – Giordano somebody? – Bruno! – Giordano Bruno! We all shudder inwardly whenever we read of how these martyrs were roped to the stake and the faggots piled up around their bare feet and everything set alight and how long did it take before they were asphyxiated and surely the fact itself of asphyxiation couldn't quite mean that they wouldn't have started to feel the flames creeping up their legs? It didn't bear thinking of . . .

Yet, after all, both Joan of Arc and Giordano Bruno were long dead, centuries long dead, ghosts who belonged to a dim, unknowable past and who have survived into the present as not much more than musty illustrations in a schoolboy's history-book. What about all those ordinary what's-their-names who simply had the misfortune to be caught inside a blazing building? Not Alastair Farjeon, of course, who certainly wasn't a what's-his-name and, from all accounts, couldn't have been further from ordinary. No, think instead of those decent, hard-working, God-fearing

East End folk who, bombed out of their beds in the Blitz, some of them at least, suffered no less hideous a fate than Joan of Arc or Giordano Bruno, except that *their* names will never ring gloriously down the ages. Yes, it did make you think . . .

He thought, as well, of the news, the slightly startling news, that the case had been assigned to Inspector Thomas Calvert of Richmond C.I.D. Well, well, well. Young Tom Calvert, already an Inspector. And in Richmond, too – a pip of a posting, if he wasn't mistaken. He had known Tom's father well and had followed the son's progress when he was just a policeman on the beat, down Bermondsey way, he seemed to recall. He had been the kind of fair and friendly bobby everybody warmed to. Always had a gobstopper or a digestive biscuit for the poorer kiddies, always greeted the regulars at the Horse and Groom with a cheery 'Evening all!', never laid too heavy a hand on the shoulder of some bedraggled old biddy who'd had a tawny port or three over the limit. And now he's an Inspector, if you please.

His reflections turned next to Cora Rutherford. It was a queer experience meeting up with her again after the passage of so many years – years, he couldn't help feeling, that had taken their toll on her once flawless façade. She was still, to be sure, the epitome of sheen and self-assurance, still enhaloed by that lustrous aura of the ethereal and the unapproachable that, against all the odds, theatricals and – what would you call them? cinematicals? – somehow manage to preserve, more or less intact, into their dotage, their anecdotage, as the old joke has it. There could be no doubt, though, that she no longer possessed the bubbly vivaciousness of old, quite that potent mixture of film-star poise and spoilt-child petulance that had made her, a decade before, so distinctive a personality. And the fact that she was the very last to be cited among the players who had been cast in Farjeon's new picture, coupled with the equally telling fact that, when she realised that it was no longer going to be made, she had let herself go to pieces so rashly and recklessly – and in the swankiest restaurant in London, too – only confirmed that she wasn't nearly as confident now of her – what's the word? magnetism? – as when they had first met. It was sad, of course, it was really dreadfully sad. But, after all, just what was the woman's age? Fifty? Sixty?

Trubshawe remembered how Evie had revealed, during his interrogation of her at ffolkes Manor, that she and Cora had once shared a minuscule flat in Bloomsbury when they were both barely out of their teens and – no, no, try to forget what else she had inadvertently let slip about that cohabitation of theirs! At any rate, it all did seem to imply that actress and novelist were pretty much the same age, and the latter, he knew, was certainly no spring chicken. No summer chicken either. Autumn, he said to himself, autumn was the season, late autumn at that. Poor woman, he mused, and he did feel a genuine sympathy for Cora's plight. Life was assuredly no sinecure for an actress past her prime.

And Evadne Mount herself? Quite a character, she was. It's strange. If he had been asked, Trubshawe would unquestionably have answered that he hadn't given her more than a passing thought in the decade since their initial encounter. Even when he read her novels (and had taken the trouble to catch up with her long-running stage play, *The Tourist Trap*, whose murderer had turned out, to his naïve surprise and obscure resentment, to be the investigating police officer), he had found them so absorbing that it simply hadn't occurred to him to attribute their qualities to a woman he had actually met – just as a mother, watching her offspring grow up, soon forgets that these autonomous and increasingly independent little beings were once the inhabitants of her own womb.

Yes, he was a fan of Evadne Mount's work; nor was he in any way ashamed to admit it. Yet he almost never spoke to his cluster of acquaintances of his enthusiasm for her whodunits and, on the very rare occasions he did, it was not at all his manner airily to brag of having struck up an acquaintanceship with their author.

By chance, however, she had walked back into his life – or rather, he had walked back into hers, as into a lamp-post – and, less than twenty-four hours later, here he was thinking of her and Cora Rutherford and Alastair Farjeon and Patsy Sloots and young Tom Calvert and all. Like her or loathe her, impossible as she often could be, things did tend to happen around Evadne Mount.

And that was the crux of the matter. Nothing much tended any longer to happen around him. After years of serving the Law, years of being universally respected as one of the Yard's top men, here he was, what, a codger? Yes, a codger. An old geezer.

He owned a pleasant, comfortable, semi-detached house in Golders Green in which he lived a pleasant, comfortable, semi-detached life. He had a thriving little vegetable garden in which he would grow his own leeks and radishes and carrots. He had an ever-diminishing circle of friends from the old days whom he would meet for a congenial pint in his local hostelry. And he had an occasional, these days extremely occasional, lunch in Town with a few pals from the Yard.

When it was with former colleagues of his own generation that he lunched, it was a real treat. He enjoyed reminiscing with his peers about the curiously, paradoxically, *innocent* criminals whom they had all dealt with at one time or another over the years, criminals for whom, by virtue of an unvarying, even comforting, routine of arrest, charge, trial, sentence, release and re-arrest, they had all acquired a certain fondness.

But every so often, or every so seldom, he would be invited out to lunch by one of the younger crowd, somebody whose mentor he'd once been or flattered himself he'd been – and that tended to prove something of an ordeal.

It wasn't just the mortifying impression they left, however

kindly disposed they seemed to be towards him, that, compared to their methods, his generation's had been almost comically outmoded; that, far from having advanced the science of criminology, as he secretly prided himself he had done, he and his contemporaries had actually set it back a couple of decades. It was also the fact that they all appeared to be engaged on fascinating cases which, just to hear about, caused his mouth literally to water.

He felt old and irrelevant, a back-number. If he offered a suggestion as to how they might proceed on some ongoing case, they would listen politely enough until he had finished speaking, then simply pick up where they had left off as though he himself had never opened his mouth. Contrariwise, if he pointed out some striking resemblance between that ongoing case and one with which he himself had been involved several years back, they would shake their heads with ill-concealed amusement, as though to answer him would merely be to humour him, and they would end by remarking, unfailingly, 'You know, Mr Trubshawe, things have changed since your day . . .'

Ah yes, things *had* changed since his day . . . But if it wouldn't be true to say that he had got definitively used to his becalmed way of life, at least he had, if one can phrase it so, got used to not getting used to it. Until, that is, he had idly wandered into the tearoom of the Ritz Hotel and heard the unforgettable – and, he realised, never quite forgotten – voice of Evadne Mount, his old sparring partner.

How that same voice, ten years before, had set his false teeth on edge! And how, yesterday, he couldn't deny it, how it had positively rejuvenated him! As had everything that followed. After tea at the Ritz, a visit to a grand West End theatre, a marvellously funny hoax of which he was just as willing a victim as anybody else in the audience, dinner at the Ivy with Evadne and Cora Rutherford, and finally the shock, but equally (admit it, Trubshawe) the secret thrill, of hearing, before the news hit the headlines, of the death of a famous film director whose name had meant nothing to him just the day before. All that, a good deal more than had happened to him in the past ten years, squeezed into just sixteen hours!

He sat there, at his oblong kitchen table, sucking on his unlit pipe. He had never really looked forward to retirement but had had to resign himself to what was, after all, the ruthless way of a ruthless world. You worked hard for forty years – work, in his case, which he loved unreservedly – and then you retired. Or, as again in his case, you *were* retired.

His own luck, however, had run out almost at once. His wife, with whom he'd looked forward to sharing his retirement, had passed away only a few months after he quit the Yard. His loyal old Labrador, Tobermory, had been shot dead on the moors near ffolkes Manor. Just one exciting thing had happened to him in all the years that followed – meeting Evadne Mount again. Would there be, he wondered wistfully, any more to come?

Naturally, he would never have contemplated ringing her up, even had he known her telephone number. But then a sudden remembrance came to him. What was it she had said? That she could be found at the Ritz every day at teatime. So what if he, Trubshawe, 'just happened' to stroll into the hotel one day at around five o'clock and what if he 'just happened' to run into her? Oh, not today, not tomorrow, not even the day after tomorrow. Towards the end of the week, perhaps? Or at the beginning of next?

He shook his head sadly. That wouldn't do at all.

What troubled him wasn't that Evadne Mount would get 'the wrong idea' – considering their respective ages, appearances and dispositions, nothing could be more improbable – but that she would get the right idea. That she would realise at once he'd become a lonely old man whose need for company was such he actually hoped she would accept the terminally lame excuse that he had chanced to drop, yet again, into the poshest hotel in London.

No, forget it. The novelist had re-exited his life as swiftly and casually as he had re-entered hers.

Ho hum. Might as well spend an hour or two in the garden . . .

Chapter Five

It was five uneventful weeks later, one Sunday in May, as Trubshawe was preparing to wash his car, a chore he performed every dry Sabbath, that the doorbell rang and he discovered, standing on his doorstep, Evadne Mount.

He had spent those five weeks much as he had spent the preceding five years. He had read his *Daily Sentinel*, pottered in his garden, drank his daily pint at his local before returning home to his solitary supper. And, every evening, on his way to and from that local, rain and shine alike, he had walked his imaginary dog.

It should be understood, though, that if the dog was imaginary it wasn't because the former detective had reverted to a state of infantile senility in which he'd started consorting all over again, as in childhood, with a companion who lived exclusively inside his head. It was simply because, when Tobermory had died on Dartmoor, he couldn't bring himself to replace him.

Tobermory had been his excuse – his alibi, as he affected

to call it – for the constitutional he took virtually every evening and his death hadn't struck him as a good enough reason for giving it up. The passing of his wife, with whom he'd shared his entire adult existence, had already familiarised him with the mildly throbbing, toothachy pain of solitude, never quite intolerable but never, ever fading away altogether. Fond of Tobermory as he had been, he was not prepared to be made twice the grieving widower. He had taken his walks before ever acquiring Tober and he refused to discontinue them now. His sole concession to a dog-lover's sentimentality was that, as before the Labrador's killing, he would absent-mindedly pick up its lead from off the hallway table and swing it along with him on his walk, like a soft, rubbery cane. Yet even that habit really couldn't be put down to sentimentality. He had swung Tobermory's lead in such a fashion for so many years now, he just wouldn't have felt right, dog or no dog, without it.

For a few days into the five weeks he had scoured his newspaper in the hope of gaining further information concerning the blaze at Alastair Farjeon's villa. Once or twice he'd even bought a couple of rival rags as well, his interest in the case being, of course, all the greater in that the investigating officer was his own former protégé, Tom Calvert.

But there was less about Farjeon's tragically premature death than he might have expected from Cora Rutherford's effusions. Film directors, geniuses as they may be in the eyes of those who do their bidding, are of significantly less concern to the great unwashed. As for the woman in the case, Patsy Sloots, yes, she was apparently blessed with 'oodles of S.A.' (whatever that was) but, he also surmised, she hadn't been so much of a star as what is termed a starlet, one of Farjeon's innumerable 'discoveries'.

From the scant evidence that could still be sifted through the ashes of the conflagration, it seemed that Mr Farjeon and Miss Sloots had been alone in the villa. And though nothing any longer could be ascertained with assurance, it was now pretty obvious that the fire had been started by a cigarette which one or other of the victims – both of whom had now been positively identified by their next of kin – had either dropped onto the floor, while it was still not properly stubbed-out, or else which had been so casually finger-flicked that it ended up missing the fireplace that would have been its target. Whichever it was, the cigarette had almost certainly rolled across the polished parquet flooring and brushed against the lace curtains of the living-room's big bay window. These curtains would have caught fire at once, the flames immediately spreading to the gauzy chiffon 'exclusive', as wispy as a cobweb, which Miss Sloots had been photographed wearing when she was picked up earlier that same day by Farjeon in his silver Rolls-Royce. Most probably, too, in attempting to rescue her, the film director himself had been engulfed.

There was, in short, precious little to go on, but it had

clearly been nothing other than a tragic and, as is frequently said on such occasions, stupid mishap.

A late postscript in the *Daily Sentinel* made delicate mention of the Sloots family's grief, in particular that of her mother, who was still under sedation. There was no mention at all, however, in any of the newspapers he scanned, of how the tragedy had affected Alastair Farjeon's 'tame little wifie'. And then the news, like the world itself, moved on.

Which is just about when Trubshawe's doorbell rang and he heard someone impatiently hallooing him through its letter-box even before he had time to open the door.

'Eustace, hello!' it boomed.

That voice again!

On this occasion, though, as he owned up to himself, hearing it thrilled him to the core.

She was standing on the doorstep in one of the hairiest and tweediest outfits he had ever seen worn, voluntarily, by a woman.

'Miss Mount!' he boomed back. 'What a very pleasant surprise!'

'I rather thought it might be,' she replied complacently.

'But wait,' he said, just as he was about to invite her in, 'how is it you know where I live?'

Like most of his colleagues at the Yard, Trubshawe had always kept his home number off-limits, even into retirement, as there were just too many ex-convicts at large who would have been delighted to learn, merely by turning the pages of the telephone directory, the current whereabouts of the copper who had been responsible for putting them out of commission. Thrilled as he was to encounter Evadne Mount again, a policeman he had always been and, if only by virtue of his own sense of self, a policeman he still was, and it was as a policeman that he was mightily interested in discovering how she had contrived to track him down.

'My, but aren't you the suspicious one!' she laughed, wagging a podgy finger at him. 'You might have said how glad you were to see me instead of subjecting me to an instant interrogation.'

'Of course I'm glad to see you, Evie,' said Trubshawe, made aware of how rude he had been. 'Very glad. That goes without saying.'

'Yes, but it would have been nicer if you'd said it. I haven't come to nit-pick, though. How have you been these last few weeks?'

'Oh, well, you know . . .' came the policeman's characteristically wary response. 'Much as ever. I've been doing a bit of gardening now that the Spring's here and, if I say so myself, it's all beginning to look –'

He interrupted himself.

'Very neat, Evie, very neat.'

'What is?' she asked, all innocence.

'Changing the subject the way you just did. I asked you how you obtained my home address.'

'If you must know, I got it from Calvert.'

'Calvert?'

'Inspector Thomas Calvert? You remember him, don't you? You ought to. According to him, you took him under your wing when he was just a bobby on the beat.'

'Of course I remember Tom Calvert. Most promising newcomer to the Force I ever came across. But how do you happen to be acquainted with him?'

'You may or may not have heard, but Calvert was the copper assigned to that dreadful business at Alastair Farjeon's villa. The fire? We talked about it with Cora at the Ivy, but you've probably forgotten all about it by now.'

'No,' said Trubshawe, 'I haven't forgotten' – and, in his heart of hearts, he somehow knew that Evadne Mount knew he hadn't forgotten.

'Well,' she went on, 'he was investigating the affair and he questioned a few of Farje's acquaintances to discover whether they might be able to throw some light on the subject and Cora was one of those questioned and it so happened that I was in her Mayfair flat when she was being interviewed by him and, in short, that's how I met him. A sweet young man, very bright, very sharp. He'll go far, I fancy.'

'He certainly will,' replied Trubshawe gruffly, 'as soon as he learns not to give out confidential information, like the addresses of former Scotland Yard detectives, to complete strangers.'

'Oh, don't be such a fusspot. I told him how you and I had met again after so many years and how we'd had a lovely blether at the Ritz and then gone on to the theatre and how I now needed to get in touch with you. I must say, he couldn't have been more obliging.'

'H'm, well, all right, fair enough. But where are my manners? Come in, will you, come in.'

'Both of us?'

'What do you mean, both of you?'

'For a detective,' said Evadne, 'you're not very observant, are you?'

She jerked her head behind her.

'Look who's here.'

Trubshawe shot a swift glance over the novelist's shoulder. Parked in front of his house, the object of admiration by a throng of street urchins, an admiration bordering on slack-jawed, gap-toothed awe, was a powder-blue Bentley motor-car. Inside it, at the steering-wheel, gaily waving at him, was Cora Rutherford.

'Why, it's . . . it's Miss Rutherford,' he said, waving back.

'Coo-eee!' called out the actress, to the uncontainable ecstasy of her tatterdemalion public. Even if not one of them appeared to recognise her, since not one of them asked for her autograph, they all knew a copper-bottomed star when they saw one. The girls had given up their hopscotch, the boys their soccer, and all of them started crowding about and practically clambering over the car, which was probably more of an attraction to them – to the boys at least – than its bewitching occupant.

'Are we coming in,' asked the novelist, 'or aren't we?'

'Of course, of course you're coming in,' Trubshawe replied.

He strode down his front drive, good-humouredly shooed away the pack of urchins, opened the door of the Bentley and ushered the actress back into his house.

A few minutes later, after he had returned from the kitchen bearing a bottle of Dubonnet and three glasses, they were all seated together around his living-room fireside.

'Now listen, Trubbers,' said Evadne Mount, not bothering with the conventional pleasantries, 'can I take it you're no busier tomorrow morning than you were the other afternoon when you popped into the Ritz?'

'Ah, well . . .'

He hesitated for a few seconds – it's never easy affording others a glimpse of how empty your own life has become – before deciding that, whatever the novelist and her friend had come to offer him, it couldn't but be more eventful than what awaited him if he declined.

'No, I'm not,' he reluctantly conceded. 'Same old dull routine. Why do you ask?'

'Because a truly wonderful thing has happened. You recall our little supper *à trois* at the Ivy?'

'Naturally I do.'

'And my having to bear the bad news to Cora about Alastair Farjeon's death?'

'How could I forget?'

76

'Ah, but do you remember that, because of his death, his new film was due to be shut down?'

'Yes, I remember that very well.'

'Well, it has, so to speak, been opened up again.'

Trubshawe's first thought was to offer the actress his congratulations.

'Well, well, well, that's extremely good news for you, isn't it? I can't tell you how happy I am.'

'Thank you, darling,' she said. 'How very sweet of you to care.'

'Oh, I do, I most sincerely do,' he insisted. 'But explain something to me, please.'

'Yes?'

'When we talked about the situation, Farjeon dying and all, you made it clear to me – in no uncertain terms, as they say – that it would be impossible for the picture to be made by anyone else because he was – irreplaceable, I suppose the word is. Yes, irreplaceable in some sense I couldn't really follow.'

'Except,' she replied, 'it turned out in this case that, because the preparations for the film were so far advanced, because the sets had already been built and the actors had all signed their contracts, that kind of thing, the studio bosses were horrified at the financial loss they were liable to incur if the thing never got made. But they just didn't know who, if anybody, would be capable of stepping into Farjeon's shoes.

'Well, then, Hattie – you recall, Farjeon's wife? – Hattie was apparently rummaging through his papers in their

London flat and – what do you think? – she unearthed this rather curious document. It was written in his own hand and it stated that, if, for whatever reason, he was unable to direct the picture, the person it should be assigned to was his assistant – what we in the trade call his First Assistant. And that's precisely what's happened.'

'H'm,' Trubshawe muttered pointedly. 'Queer, that . . .'

'Oh? What makes you say so?'

'Well, it sounds almost as though Farjeon had already suspected he might be prevented from directing it.'

'Oh, you ex-policemen!' exclaimed Evadne. 'You can't stop seeing underhand motives wherever you look. Forget Farjeon. What's important is that the filming started last week and Cora, as you can imagine, is over the moon.'

'Yes, yes, I repeat, my congratulations,' said Trubshawe to the actress. 'I couldn't help observing how badly you took the news of the man's death.'

'The point is,' said Cora, 'the picture is being shot at Elstree and, as I think I told you, I don't actually have all that many big scenes, but one of them is to be shot tomorrow afternoon and, because I've let Evie share in everything I've done since we were both knee-high to a brace of grasshoppers, I naturally invited her down to watch it.

'Then the same idea occurred to both of us at once – as it still sometimes does, I may say. Since dear old Trubbers was present at the bad news, why shouldn't he also be present at the good?

78

'Besides which, I've got to be at the studio at some ungodly hour and Evie, who's never been a morning person, would naturally prefer to make a later appearance, only she doesn't drive, but I assume you do. You do, don't you?'

'Yes, I do. A Rover. So,' he concluded, 'as I understand it, you're inviting me to become Evie's chauffeur for the day?'

'Ingrate!' Cora pretended to snap at him. 'Must you always be so officious and stiff-necked and policeman-y? I just thought, as we'd all met up together again, it would amuse you to accompany Evie. I can't believe you've ever visited a picture studio before, so you ought to find it terribly interesting. What do you say?'

It was without the least hesitation that Trubshawe replied in the affirmative. Truth to tell, he couldn't believe his luck.

'And so, Miss Rutherford,' he asked her, 'Exactly what sort of new film is this?'

'Call me Cora, darling,' she answered airily, and the Scotland Yard man was struck anew by how miraculously rejuvenated she appeared now that, by an unforeseen reversal of fortune, her career seemed to be back on track. He was also, however, a trifle embarrassed, since he was uncertain whether she meant him to call her 'Cora' or 'Cora darling'.

But she gave him no time to call her anything, instantly launching into a description of the film.

'Its title is *If Ever They Find Me Dead*. Good, don't you think?'

'Oh, definitely,' he approved. 'Very enticing. *If Ever They Find Me Dead*, eh? Yes, that's a picture I feel confident I'd want to see. Sounds to me like a jolly exciting thriller. And may I ask what it's about? Or would that be giving too much away?'

'I'm afraid it just might . . . It's Farjeon's own screenplay, you understand, and, where other directors' thrillers often have twist endings, his have always had twist beginnings.'

The concept was a novel one to Trubshawe.

'Twist beginnings?'

'You never saw his *Semi-Coma*?'

'Sorry. You know, I don't –'

'– go to the Pictures. Yes, you told us already.'

'Then, my dear Miss Rutherford,' he remarked tartly, 'if I told you already, why ask me again? And, while I seem to have the upper hand for once, may I ask you something?'

The actress blinked.

'Why – why, yes,' she replied. 'Please do.'

'*Hocus-Focus. Semi-Coma. An American in Plaster-of-Paris.* Didn't this Farjeon fellow ever give one of his pictures some ordinary, everyday title that actually deigned to tell you a little bit about what was in it?'

'Trubbers, my dear,' said Cora, who had never yielded the last word to anyone, and certainly wasn't about to change the habit of a lifetime, 'I seem to recall, when we first met, that you had a dog, no?'

'That's right. A Labrador.'

'And his name was?'

'Tobermory.'

'What!' she exclaimed satirically. 'Not Fido?'

Trubshawe gracefully accepted defeat.

'You win,' he said with a smile. 'Please go on.'

'Well, in *Semi-Coma* Robert Donat plays a meek, mild-mannered bank teller who, in the film's opening scene, goes to bed in his dingy little flat in Clerkenwell. But when he wakes up next morning – the very next morning, mind you – he finds himself, still clad in the same striped jammies he went to bed in, stretched out in a leafy clearing in the Canadian Rockies, of all places, with a solitary stag – a wonderful touch! – a solitary stag placidly grazing just a few yards away. And, of course, it takes him the whole film to figure out how – and why – he crossed the Atlantic overnight.

'That's pure Farje. At the press screenings of his films, the critics would be handed out little slips of paper advising them not to give away the beginning, which meant, in effect, that the films were critic-proof. The critics couldn't give away the beginning, they couldn't give away the ending, and they certainly couldn't give away the middle. They couldn't give anything away at all.

'Dear, dear Farje,' she sighed. 'Such a genius.'

Trubshawe was on the point of expressing his astonishment at hearing her speak so warmly of an individual whom, only a month before, she had called a verminous, arachnoid pig. But then, he told himself, the poor man himself was dead, and Cora in such high spirits. Why cast a shadow over her euphoria by even bringing up the subject?

'So what,' he asked instead, 'happens at the beginning of your picture?'

'Yes, you old trout,' Evadne Mount piped up, 'don't keep us in suspense. That's the job of the film.'

Cora inserted a new cigarette into its holder and lowered her already husky voice to a conspiratorial level.

'Well,' she said, 'it all starts with these two chums, both of them women in their early twenties, at Drury Lane. They've done some shopping up West, just had lunch, and have a couple of tickets for a matinée – some sort of musical-comedy, I think it's supposed to be. And there they are, in the seventh or eighth row of the stalls, browsing through their programmes, chattering away about this and that – the stars of the show, whether it's had a good or bad press, you know, the sort of thing we all talk about when settling down in a theatre.

'Then, suddenly, one of them starts.'

'Starts what?'

'Oh really, Evie, what an idiotic question. She doesn't start anything. She just starts. She goes stiff and tense. It's called starting. If I remember aright, your cardboard characters do it all the time.

'Anyhow, noticing her start, her friend naturally asks her what the matter is. Nothing, says the woman, nothing at all. But, as she's turned quite pale, the friend insists and the

82

woman finally says, "You see that man sitting four rows down, alone at the end of row C?" The other woman takes a gander, locates the man her friend has just mentioned and says yes, what about him? The first woman doesn't speak for a few seconds. Then she replies, in a deathly quiet voice, "If ever they find me dead" – the film's title, remember? – "if ever they find me dead, that's the man who did it."

'Now, as you can imagine, her friend is well and truly hooked, but all she can see of the chap, unfortunately, is the back of his head. And, just as she cranes for a better view, the lights dim, the orchestra strikes up, the curtain rises, a leggy line of high-stepping chorines comes tripping onto the stage and, of course, in her subsequent enjoyment of the show, she forgets all about him.'

Cora had nothing to complain of in the attention paid her by her two listeners. They were literally hanging on her every word.

'At which point,' she continued, after what Evadne Mount herself, in one of her whodunits, would unreflectingly have described as a 'pregnant' pause, 'we at once cut to the following scene – in which, as I'm sure you've both already guessed, the police are examining the woman's dead body in her mews flat in Belgravia.'

'H'm,' said Evadne Mount thoughtfully, 'I must confess I'm slightly envious of that idea. What happens next?'

'Well, I really don't think I ought to reveal any more.'

'Now, now, don't be coy. Doesn't suit you.'

'Oh, all right. Suffice to say that the friend naturally decides to do a bit of sleuthing on her own account and eventually, at a dinner party, she finds herself sitting opposite the man in row C – *or so she believes*. Except, you see, she just can't be sure. So she ingratiates herself with him, starts flirting madly and, still not knowing if he really is the murderer she believes he might be, falls for him in the biggest way.

'Which, I think,' she ended grandly, 'is all you need to know for the nonce. If you want to learn more, you'll just have to wait till the film comes out at your local picture palace.'

'And you, dear lady,' said Trubshawe, 'you play the glamorous young sleuth, I suppose?'

Cora, uncertain for the moment whether or not her leg was being gently pulled, cast him a penetrating glance.

'No,' she said at last. 'No, Trubshawe, I believe I told you when we last met that my role was not – no, I'd be lying if I said it was the lead.'

'Which role *do* you play?' asked Evadne.

'The mur-' – she hastily bit off the tail of the word – 'I mean, the man's long-suffering wife, long-suffering because, as she's become all too aware, hubby has been conducting a whole string of casual affairs behind her back.

'It was a smallish role to start with, insultingly small – but, only the other day, I managed to get it bumped up quite

84

a considerable bit. Now I have two or three really very juicy scenes where I not only get to chew up the furniture but spit it out.

'Oh yes,' she said in a voice of faintly chilling self-satisfaction, 'if I play my cards right, which I fully intend to do, there's no reason why this shouldn't turn out to be the first stage of my comeback.'

The novelist looked at her sharply.

'Cora?'

'Yes?'

'Just how did you manage to do that?'

'What?'

'Bump up the role?'

'Ask me no questions, dearie, and I'll tell you no lies. Let's just say, little Cora has never been backward coming forward. Whenever a windfall drops into her lap, she knows how to exploit it.'

She turned to Trubshawe.

'The first of these big scenes of mine is being shot tomorrow, which is why I thought you and Evie might like to spend the day at Elstree and watch it from behind the camera.'

'I'd like that very much,' said the Chief-Inspector. 'Things going smoothly so far, are they?'

Cora suddenly turned rather pensive.

'Well,' she replied, 'they are now, thank goodness. For a while there, it was touch-and-go.'

'What do you mean?'

'You understand, I haven't done any filming myself yet. But, naturally, I've had to be at the studio every day. Hair tests, complexion tests, clothes tests, make-up tests, you know the kind of thing. Well, you don't, but I'm sure you get what I mean. And from what I could gather from the back-room boys, in addition to what I myself happened to witness, Hanway was an absolute disaster to start with.'

'Hanway?'

'Rex Hanway. Farjeon's former assistant, now the film's director. And, oh God, was he nervous when he first walked onto the set. Positively quaking in his brogues, he was. Didn't have a clue. Couldn't decide where to place the camera, couldn't give directions to the actors, had no idea what the cameraman was referring to when he asked him about lenses and filters.

'To be fair to him, it's a bloody terrifying job making a film for the first time. All those people on the set, all of them old hands, far older hands than you are, firing a hundred-and-one different questions at you and expecting a hundred-and-one correct answers. Not to mention the constant thought of the cinema audiences who are going to be watching it one day. All those hungry eyes waiting to be fed!

'I studied Hanway myself whenever I had some free time. Oh, he looked perfect, with his dungarees creased just so and his Turnbull and Asser shirt and his Charvet silk tie and his viewfinder dangling on his chest as elegantly as a mono-cle. But when it came to the nuts and bolts of getting the picture made, he didn't know whether he was on his head or his heels. He just couldn't handle all the decisions and indecisions of film production, all the meddling and the muddling you have to cope with.

'It got so bad by the end of the first three days that there was talk all over again of closing down the picture.'

'What happened?' asked Evadne.

'What happened? I'll tell you what happened. On the fourth day – that would have been Thursday – he was a new man. You could almost see the confidence ooze out of his pores. How he overcame his stage fright or screen fright or whatever you care to call it, I have no idea, but that he *had* overcome it there wasn't the slightest doubt at all. Drink? Dope? Medication? Whichever it was, he suddenly seemed to know not only what he wanted but how he'd be able to obtain it.

'The transformation was uncanny. He would bark orders at gaffers and grips, he knew how to talk shop with the technical crew and, as for the actors, he had them eating out of his hand. The studio bosses are delighted with the rushes – don't ask what those are, Trubshawe, I'll tell you some sunny day – the money men never stop rubbing their sweaty palms together, everything is running on rails.'

'You know, Cora,' said Evadne Mount, 'what you've just been describing, I actually don't find so hard to explain. Matter of fact, I've often had exactly the same experience myself.'

'You?'

'Absolutely. I sit at my old Oliver typewriter and I sit and I sit and nothing happens. Then, who knows how or why, all of a sudden I find myself merrily typing away. It's as though my fingers have started to have ideas of their own, ideas they don't even bother consulting me about. And the oddest part of it all is that it usually turns out to be my best stuff.'

None too interested in the metaphysics of literary creation, Cora shrugged her shoulders.

'What can I say? As I remarked to Orson only the other day, that's the business we call show.'

Extracting from her handbag two or three delicate little tools of her trade, she rapidly adjusted her face, a face that had begun to bear an increasingly distant acquaintance with her age, and said:

'*Voilà*. Evie will be waiting for you, Trubbers, to pick her up at her Albany flat – at, shall we say, nine o'clock tomorrow morning? You'll drive down to Elstree, where I'll meet you, show you round, introduce you to some of the cast and crew, the usual drill. Then I'll do my big scene in the afternoon. Right?'

Trubshawe had only to nod his head.

Chapter Six

The next morning he rang Evadne Mount's doorbell at exactly quarter-to-nine.

'Unpunctual,' she scowled, ushering him in. 'I might have known.'

'Unpunctual?' he exclaimed. 'Well, really! What *will* you say next?' He consulted his watch. 'It's just 8.45. I'm fifteen minutes early.'

'Precisely. Being early is also a form of unpunctuality, you know. Now, because I'm obliged to keep you waiting for fifteen minutes, you've made me feel guilty. No, my dear Eustace, if we're to continue seeing one another, you must learn to be on time. And I do mean on time.'

Before he could take umbrage at her Jesuitical logic, she rushed past him onto the landing. Her ancient Sealyham terrier Gilbert (named after Chesterton, as she explained to the Chief-Inspector) had waddled out of the flat as soon as he noticed its open front door and, for the sake of the Albany's lush carpeting, immediately had to be coaxed back in again.

'Like all of us, I'm afraid,' she sighed, 'poor Gilbert has become a teensy bit leaky in his declining years.'

When they were finally off, Gilbert having been safely retrieved, it took Trubshawe less than an hour to motor down to Elstree. The studio itself, however, proved a cruel disappointment to both of them. Imposing as it was, it resembled less the popular conception of a Factory of Dreams than it did some commonplace industrial plant, a tannery, perhaps, or a large brickyard. Architecturally without distinction, being all rain-streaked concrete walls and crude corrugated roofing, it was, as Trubshawe scornfully remarked, a warehouse, neither more nor less. Glamour there was none. No more was there the faintest hint of Romance.

At the main entrance, moreover, an obstreperous gatekeeper, a typical petty tyrant of the *genus bureaucratum*, immediately barred their way.

'Can't let you in,' he said, 'if you don't have an appointment.'

Evadne Mount, naturally, would have none of this.

'An appointment!' she barked at him. 'Good heavens, you silly juggins, do you suppose, do you *really* suppose, that we would have travelled all the way down here from Town if we didn't have an appointment?'

'Show us it, then,' said the gate-keeper suspiciously.

'The appointment was made in person. How can I show you what was never committed to print?'

'In that case, I can't allow you through. It would be more than my job's worth.'

'Nonsense! I tell you, my good man, we've come to pay a call on Miss Cora Rutherford – at her own request. I repeat, Cora Rutherford. If you don't open up these gates at once, I shall make it my business to see that you're replaced by someone who will. You'll find out then just how much your job is worth.'

For a few seconds he nervously agonised over what to do.

'P'raps if I was to phone . . .'

Evadne subjected him to her patented 'How like a man!' expression.

'You'll do nothing of the kind. My fear is that Miss Rutherford is already in a state of anxiety, perhaps wondering if we've been involved in some frightful accident. She'll be furious – no, no, no, if I know Cora, she'll be incandescent! – when she learns that we aren't at her side because you were just too bloody-minded to let us in. Permit us to pass, will you, if you know what's good for you.'

Still hesitant, conscious of setting a precedent he was likely to regret, he finally raised the barrier and granted the two visitors access to the hallowed inner sanctum. When the car entered the studio grounds, Evadne had to chuckle as she peered through its rear-view mirror and observed, decreasing in size as they themselves advanced, the poor gate-keeper now quite visibly appalled at the liberty he'd been gulled into letting them take.

A few minutes later, Trubshawe having parked the Rover, the question arose of locating Studio 3, in which, as Cora had told them, *If Ever They Find Me Dead* was being filmed. An obvious solution would have been to ask their way of some passer-by. There was, though, a problem. Practically all the passers-by who crossed their path seemed to be decked out in extravagant fancy-dress costume. They met Roundheads and Cavaliers, Gypsies and Musketeers, Regency Fops and Pearly Queens, from none of whom they would have felt at ease soliciting so mundane a direction.

As often happens, however, wandering among the prefabricated hangars of which the studio complex seemed to be almost wholly composed, they suddenly and providentially found themselves standing in front of the largest of all. Inscribed on its tall metal door was the legend: *Studio 3.* They were there.

Now literary legend has it that, once he had been interrupted by a 'person from Porlock', the poet Coleridge found himself ever after incapable of recapturing the rapturous inspiration which had produced the first few indelible stanzas of *Kubla Khan*. Heaven knows (was the thought running through Evadne Mount's mind as she contemplated the spectacle which confronted them when she opened the door) how anything of enduring value could be created inside a studio that appeared to be home to Porlock's entire population.

There were technicians unfurling railway tracks, or what resembled railway tracks, over the cable-strewn floor. Others, so high overhead as to be almost invisible, were fixing wires to poles, and poles to wires, and screwing gigantic and, after they had been switched on, eye-dazzling arc-lights onto both. Because of the ubiquitous dust, and the equally ubiquitous cigarette-smoke caught in the criss-crossing shafts of light – for every single crew member had, in defiance of various *No Smoking* signs, a wet Woodbine wedged between his teeth – the air was literally tangible.

In fact, when the novelist sought to communicate her first impression of the cinema world, even she was required to raise her voice's already elevated decibel level.

'You know,' she thundered, 'what all this reminds me of?'

'No, what?' the Chief-Inspector shouted back at her.

'A ship!'

'A what?'

'A ship! A nineteenth-century schooner. Look for yourself. Look at all those decks and sails and masts and rigging. I tell you, it's exactly like a ship that's just about to quit the dockside.'

'Why, you're right at that. Yes, I see exactly what you mean. And you and I are like a couple of well-wishers on the quay waving goodbye to the passengers.'

'For Cora's sake,' said Evadne Mount, 'let's hope it isn't the *Mary Celeste*. Speaking of Cora,' she added, 'I wonder how we ought to go about finding her.'

She didn't have long to wonder. Holding a clipboard in her hand and a script rolled up into a narrow cylinder under her arm, owlish horn-rimmed spectacles propped up on her fore-head like a spare pair of eyes, an oddly elfin young woman at once swept up to them.

'Excuse me,' she said in a calm, matter-of-fact voice, 'but I'm afraid I'm going to have to ask you to leave at once. No outsiders are permitted on the set while filming is underway.'

'I'm sure you're right,' said Evadne Mount, inspecting her with interest, 'but, *primo*, we aren't precisely outsiders and, *secundo*, as far as I can make out, no filming is underway yet.'

'Why, of course it is,' answered the young woman. 'Don't be misled by the fact that the camera isn't turning and the actors aren't acting. That's merely the tip of the iceberg. This is what making a film is all about – preparation. Though why I should be wasting my time explaining the ins-and-outs of the business to you I really don't know.'

Lowering her spectacles down onto her eyes, she gazed inquisitively at them.

'Just who are you, anyway? How did you get into the studio?'

'Well, you see, we're both friends –' Trubshawe began.

'You aren't extras on the Agatha Christie picture which René Clair is shooting on Stage 5, are you? What's it called again? *Ten Little Whatnots*?'

The novelist almost blew a fuse.

'Extras on the . . . ?!' she bridled, incapable of pronounc-ing the name of the rival in whose shadow it would seem she

94

was eternally condemned to languish. 'Certainly not!' she cried. 'Why, the very idea!'

'Then will you please leave at once. I don't want to have to call security.'

'This,' declared the novelist, drawing up the battle lines, 'is Chief-Inspector Trubshawe of Scotland Yard and I, my dear, *I* am Evadne Mount.'

A *soupçon* of interest ruffled the young woman's creepy poise.

'Evadne Mount? *The* Evadne Mount?'

'The same – currently President of the Detection Club and oldest friend of Cora Rutherford, one of the stars of your picture, who, I might add, invited both of us down here today and is, at this moment, no doubt wondering where the Hell we've got to.'

The young woman hastily consulted her clipboard.

'Yes, yes, of course,' she finally replied, giving her scalp a vigorous poke with the sharp end of her pencil. 'Forgive me, we *were* advised to expect you. It's just that, as you can see, everything is so frantic at the moment and I've had so many different things to think about. I do apologise. Let me introduce myself. Lettice Morley, Rex Hanway's personal assistant.'

'Rex Hanway?' said Trubshawe. 'He's the producer of the picture, right?'

'Lord, no!' she fluttered. 'Please never let him hear you call him that. He's the director. He took over after Mr Farjeon –

well, I'm sure you heard about Mr Farjeon's untimely demise.'

'And Cora?' enquired Evadne Mount. 'Has she started filming yet?'

At the actress's name, what had never been more than a polite and perfunctory smile was altogether wiped off Lettice Morley's face.

'Miss Rutherford? Ah well, she is, I suppose, a great artist but I'm afraid, like not a few great artists, she – now how shall I express this? – she can sometimes be a touch inconsiderate of her colleagues' needs. The picture business is, you must know, a collective activity and some of our leading stars, our leading ladies in particular, unfortunately lack what might be called the collective spirit. Films are like trains. If they run at all, they have to run on schedule.'

'You mean,' said Evadne Mount, 'she's late.'

'If you're talking about this morning, forty minutes late. It really is most trying for Mr Hanway. Especially as Miss Rutherford's role is by no means crucial.'

The novelist laughed.

'Cora, I'm afraid, is one of those people who are *always* unpunctual and yet who *always* have an excuse, a different one for every occasion.'

'Yes, well, that's all very charming, I dare say, but on a film set unpunctuality is the cardinal sin, one that's forgiven – and then very grudgingly – only if it's been committed by a major star, a Margaret Lockwood, you know, or a Linden Travers. Whereas Cora Rutherford . . .'

She left the remainder of her comment unaired, not just because she had perhaps realised she was at risk of overstepping the bounds of professional propriety but also because, at that very moment, wearing a trim little cocktail dress, black with mauve linings, and brandishing her inevitable cigarette-holder, the actress herself finally wafted into view.

Evadne and Trubshawe watched from a distance as Cora approached someone seated on a folding canvas chair on whose back was printed, as they now noticed, the words *Mr Hanway*. As with the male character in the opening scene of the film itself, however, such as it had been recounted to them by Cora, no more than his own back, along with a mere pinch of his profile, was visible to them; and it was only when he turned his head to hear what the actress's excuse might be for holding up the proceedings that they were granted a more complete view of his facial features. His age, difficult to judge, could have been anywhere between thirty and forty. His face was somehow both intense and expressionless, with eyes of an unnervingly glassy inscrutability. He was wearing, of all improbable items of attire, a labourer's boiler-suit, but a boiler-suit so flawlessly fashioned that his elegant silk tie seemed not at all a mismatch. And on his lap sat an exquisitely bony Siamese cat, washing its face with those nervy little paw-flicks that are irresistibly reminiscent of the hapless flailings of a punch-drunk prizefighter.

'Rex darling!' cried the actress. 'I know, I know, late

again. But I swear to you, it wasn't my fault. When I'm late, it's always for my art, and surely any artist, especially the kind of perfectionist I am, may be forgiven for that.'

After a brief silence, while starting to caress the cat with such vigour he risked wearing it out, Hanway replied, 'My dear Cora, what I want from you isn't perfectionism but perfection. What was the problem this time?'

Cora tugged heartlessly at her cocktail dress.

'This was the problem. I had to ask Vi to take the waist in again. It was so unbecoming it made me look, well, can you imagine, blowsy. Blowsy, *me*? Wouldn't do at all.'

She leaned over to stroke the silky, sulky cat, now all the sulkier at having her ablutions disturbed.

'Nice pussy,' she cooed nervously. 'Who's a pretty pussy?'

Hanway donned a mask of heroic patience.

'Let me remind you, Cora, you *are* supposed to be playing the dowdy neglected wife. We can't have you looking too alluring.'

The director suddenly snapped out of his languor. Lifting the cat up off his lap, he disengaged its claws from the hem of his boiler-suit as cautiously as a hiker untangling a strand of his jumper from a barbed-wire fence and plumped it down on a canvas chair that was next to his own and on the back of which was printed the name *Cato*. Then, leaping to his feet, he clapped his hands together.

'All right, everybody in place! We're going to rehearse the scene!'

Turning to Lettice, who had been diligently hovering over him throughout his brief exchange with Cora, he said, 'I want all the extras on set.'

Cora, meanwhile, aware of her friends' presence, mouthed a flighty 'Yoo-hoo!' and waved over to them. Raising her kohl-rimmed eyes as though to say 'No rest for the weary!', she then huddled together with Hanway while he presumably gave her a few final instructions on how the scene was to be played. At the same time, the extras had begun to position themselves as ordered. There were a dozen of them, half male, half female, all in smart evening dress. And, bringing up the rear, chaperoned by a spinsterish, stern-faced nanny, were two children, a cherubic boy of about ten, the picture of brattish disgruntlement in his starchy sailor-suit, and a shy little girl less than half his age who, in her beribboned white party frock and miniature ballet pumps, was a Mabel Lucie Atwell postcard teased into dimpled, pink-cheeked life.

Then it was the turn of the film's two leads to walk onto the set. If Gareth Knight was no longer quite the *jeune premier*, yet with his raven-black moustache, his suave throwaway manner and above all his smile, that fabled smile of his that had broken many a shopgirl's heart, he still managed to cut an enviably dashing and devil-may-care figure. As for Leolia Drake, the actress who had been chosen to replace the late Patsy Sloots, she certainly had what is known in the trade as a photogenic physique, being luscious, gorgeous, curvaceous, voluptuous and all those other quintessentially feminine adjectives that end in 'ous'.

'By the Lord Harry!' exclaimed Trubshawe, smacking his lips. 'Now that's what I call a real corker.'

Without for an instant compromising his stencilled-on smile, Knight bowed curtly to Cora and shook Hanway's hand. The director stepped over to offer a few words of encouragement to the two children. The scene was ready to be rehearsed.

And it was a scene, as Trubshawe remarked at once, that bore a striking resemblance to the premise of Evadne's *Eeny-Meeny-Murder-Mo*. The setting was a chic cocktail party and, even if he was still almost totally ignorant of the ramifications of the film's plot, he had soon worked out, from the dry runs which the actors were put through by Hanway, not only that the party was being given by Knight and his wife (Cora's role) but also that the latter, while playing the perfect hostess, was keeping a watchful eye on the rather too attentive court her husband had started to pay to the very youngest and sexiest of their guests, the film's heroine (Leolia Drake's role).

It was when Knight actually went so far as to whisper sweet nothings in Drake's ear, sweet nothings which may not have been audible but were certainly visible, that the crisis erupted. A glass of champagne in her hand, Cora was seen to become so enraged by her philandering better half that she ended by snapping its stem in two. At which point, even though the camera hadn't been turning, the director bawled out, 'Cut!'

In all there were four run-throughs. None of them, however, appeared to satisfy Rex Hanway. Each of his 'Cuts!' sounded more fretful than the last. And, after the fourth and final rehearsal, nearly sliding off his canvas chair in frustration, he cried out:

'No! No, no, no, no, no! This won't do at all!'

Everyone, cast, crew and extras alike, fell silent. No matter how insecure his authority had been in the first few days, Hanway now commanded a silent respect from his underlings.

Lettice got to her knees in front of him.

'But, Rex, it's exactly what we have in the script.'

'What do I care?' said Hanway intemperately. 'The script is wrong.'

'Wrong? But –'

'It isn't *The Brothers Karamazov*, for God's sake. It's just a blue-print.'

'Of course, Rex, of course.'

'No, no, there's something missing, there's definitely something missing. It's boring. It's a big nothing of a scene. It's not even a big nothing, it's a small nothing, it's a nothing nothing.'

He held up a clenched fist hard against his brow in a possibly conscious imitation of Rodin's *Thinker*.

'Perhaps, darling,' ventured Cora, 'if we –'

'Be quiet, please!' he snapped. 'Can't you see I'm think-ing?'

'I was only going to suggest –'

Again, though, she was prevented from completing her sentence. As suddenly and dramatically as he had planted it, Hanway removed the fist from his brow.

'I've got it!'

He stood up and marched purposefully onto the set, led his trio of principals off to one side and began whispering to them. When they had understood his new instructions – Cora fervently nodding in agreement, Leolia Drake beaming up at him, Gareth Knight shaking his head in mute admira-tion – Hanway snapped his fingers for the little girl to be brought over. More whispering – on this occasion, it took her somewhat longer to comprehend his intentions. Yet she too, once light had dawned on her, started to giggle. Then he had a few quiet words with his cameraman, who at once proceeded to make the necessary adjustments.

The scene was now ready to be filmed. Silence was repeat-edly called for – one hapless member of the crew being col-lectively cursed by his mates for sneezing three times in a row – and Hanway, poised expectantly on the edge of his chair, finally shouted, 'Action!'

At first nothing had changed. Holding the same glass of champagne, Cora made the same desultory chit-chat with the same dinner-suited male extra, all the while spying on Knight, who, exchanging the same monosyllabic pleasantries as he zigzagged across the crowded room, neverthe-less made the same circuitous beeline for Leolia Drake. She, meanwhile, as though fearful of the intensity of her feelings towards him, attempted to avoid catching his eye as she slowly sidled away towards the door.

Then, on cue, she walked backwards straight into the little girl, causing her to topple over onto the floor.

The actress at once got to her knees to help her back up.

'Oh, sweetheart, I'm terribly sorry. Gosh, aren't I the clumsy one. Are you all right? No bruises?'

When the little girl solemnly shook her head, Leolia on a sudden impulse kissed her on the right cheek.

And it was at that instant that Knight swiftly stepped for-ward. He too knelt down beside the little girl and, neatly timing his gesture to coincide with Leolia's, kissed her on the left cheek. To anyone who happened to be watching them – and if none of the extras were, everybody behind the camera was – the effect was exactly as though they were kissing each other *through the child*.

Then, just like someone speaking into a telephone, Knight whispered into the child's dainty little ear:

'I love you, Margot.'

'Oh, Julian . . .' a tremulous Leolia Drake answered into the other ear. 'Please don't. Not here. Someone may hear us.'

'How can anyone hear us,' he countered smoothly, 'when we have our own private 'phone? There's no danger of a crossed line.'

The child's uncomprehending eyes darted from left to right and back again.

'Say it, darling,' said Knight, 'please let me hear you say it.'

'Say what?'

'That you love me too.'

'Oh, I do. I do so love you.'

To and fro went the little girl's eyes, like those of a spectator at the centre-court at Wimbledon.

The novelist and the detective watched in fascination as the camera now began to glide backward along its little section of railway track while at the same time, in a perfectly coordinated movement, it rose up into the dank and powdery studio air on an extensible ladder, a ladder that itself gradually stretched out over the entire set until there wasn't a single one of the dozen revellers who hadn't swum into, then again out of, its ken.

It eventually came to a halt directly in front of Cora herself. She was glaring implacably at the flirtatious couple. Her face contorted by spasms of jealousy, she mumbled a curse under her breath. Then, with perfect timing, her fingers snapped into two equal halves the slender, fine-spun stem of her champagne glass.

'Cut!' cried Rex Hanway.

Chapter Seven

Evadne Mount, Eustace Trubshawe and Cora Rutherford were seated at a corner table in the studio cafeteria – what in the picture-making business is known as the commissary. In the real world, the word would have been 'canteen'. Notwithstanding the autographed snapshots, aligned along all four of its walls, of several of Elstree's best-loved players – David Farrar and Jeanne De Casalis, Guy Rolfe and Beatrice Varley, Joseph Tomelty and Joyce Grenfell – a canteen is what it resembled and a canteen is what it was.

Since the room itself was nearly as draughty and cavernous as the sound stage from which they'd repaired for lunch, none of them had felt inclined to remove their heavy outdoor coats. Cora had even kept her gloves on, except that, with her innate stylishness, she contrived to convince everybody else that a gloved canteen lunch was the very latest thing, *le dernier cri*, as she herself would have put it, and this in spite of the fact that, to protect her elaborately mounted pompadour, she was also forced to sport a set of unsightly rose-pink curlers.

The other tables were monopolised by the same gaudily outfitted extras whom Evadne and Trubshawe had already admired when they first entered the studio. At one table a Ruritanian Hussar was lunching in the company of two ladies-in-waiting from Louis XIV's Versailles. At another an elderly bobby with a nicotiny walrus moustache, his helmet posed upright on the table-top like an outsized salt cellar, chatted amiably to the very last individual with whom his real-life equivalent would ever be caught lunching, a wiry cat-burglar clad in a black body stocking. And, sitting alone at a third, a queer, hatchet-faced woman was furiously knitting away at some monstrosity in purple wool. Paying as little attention to her fellow-lunchers in the commissary as they were paying to her, she laid aside her work-in-progress only to swallow the odd mouthful of semolina pudding.

'Psst, Cora,' Evadne finally whispered.

'H'm?'

'Tell me. Madame Lafarge over there? Do you know her?'

Cora turned her head, unconcerned as to whether she might be observed doing so by the target of the novelist's curiosity.

'Why, that's Hattie, of course,' she said dismissively.

'Hattie?'

'Hattie Farjeon. Farje's wife. Widow, I mean.'

'Farjeon's widow? What on earth is *she* doing here?'

'Oh, Hattie's always been present on the set during the making of Farje's films. You would see her, in a corner, sitting and knitting all by herself, never addressing a word to a soul, as mousy and uncommunicative as she is now. Officially, she was Farje's script consultant, but the true reason for her presence, as we all knew, was to guarantee there was no hanky-panky between him and his leading ladies. Hanky-panky or, so I've heard, "wanky-spanky". I wouldn't know myself,' she concluded virtuously.

'But why is she here today? With Farjeon dead and all?'

Cora toyed with her corned beef.

'Who knows? Maybe Levey – Benjamin Levey, the producer of the picture – regards her as a good-luck fetish. It was Farje's series of hits, you know, that made him a millionaire. Or maybe she still has a financial involvement in the project and is keeping a watch over her own interests. Or maybe she just wants to be sure that Hanway is faithful to her husband's script.'

'But that's just it,' said Evadne.

'What's just it?'

'Hanway hasn't been faithful to the script. Just this morning he introduced the idea of using a child's ears as pair of telephone receivers. I must say, I thought it rather wonderful of him to come up with such a clever new piece of business right there on the set.'

'Oh, I do so agree!' the actress replied. 'You don't suppose Farje's genius could somehow be flowing through him? Emanations, you know,' she said vaguely. 'Or do I mean ectoplasm?'

In disgust she shoved away the aforementioned viands.

'God, this is foul muck. Even the bread-and-marge is stale.'

Lighting up a cigarette, she returned to the subject at hand.

'Yes, if he keeps it up, Hanway may well become the new Farjeon. Farje also used to have these brilliant last-minute intuitions. I remember when I popped in to visit dear Ty – Tyrone Power to you yokels – when he was filming *An American in Plaster-of-Paris* – Oh, crumbs!'

Without completing the reminiscence, she picked up her knife and fork again, bent low over her plate and addressed her undivided attention to the meal that she had only just rejected.

'For God's sake, whatever you do,' she whispered, 'please, *please* don't look round! Don't make eye contact!'

'Who is it we shouldn't make eye contact with?' asked Evadne, as, to the actress's dismay, she did proceed to look round, at once finding herself face to face, indeed eye to eye, with an earnest, sallow-complexioned young man who, with his shaven head, rimless dark glasses, neatly trimmed goatee and black high-necked polo jersey, would have seemed more at home in some smoke-infested jazz cellar in Saint-Germain-des-Prés. Bearing a tray of food, he was clearly on his way to join them.

'Now you've done it,' hissed Cora.

The young man coolly returned the novelist's gaze,

stepped up to the table and nodded to Cora. Conjuring an impromptu smile as adroitly as though inserting a set of new false teeth between her lips, she extended her right hand towards him. He held it for a moment, raised it to his own lips and lightly kissed the button of her suede glove.

('How very Continental!' Evadne Mount mouthed to the Chief-Inspector.)

'Ah, Mademoiselle Ruzzerford,' he said in a near-impenetrable French accent, 'you are looking as *charmante* as evair.'

'Why, thank you so much, Philippe,' Cora replied. 'Perhaps you'd care to join us for lunch? As you see, we have a free fourth place.'

'Oh, but that would be most kind,' said the Frenchman, who had in fact already begun circling the table towards the unoccupied seat.

'I don't believe you've met my friends,' said Cora. 'This is Evadne Mount, the mystery novelist. And Chief-Inspector Trubshawe, formerly of Scotland Yard. And this,' she explained to both of them, indicating their new lunch companion, 'is Philippe Françaix. He's a critic,' she added grimly.

Once hands had been shaken and how-d'ye-does exchanged, Evadne turned to Françaix.

'So you're a critic? A film critic?'

'*Mais oui* – how you say in English? – but yes. I am a film critic.'

'How interesting. Tell me, though, isn't it rather unusual

for a critic actually to watch a film being made? I don't think I ever heard of such a thing before.'

Françaix shook his head.

'See you, it is quite usual in France, where many unusual things are usual. In your country, no, you have reason, it does not 'appen much. But this is a special case – a long story.'

Cora was quick to intercede.

'That's right, darling. Philippe has been writing a book on Farjeon. A book of interviews, isn't it? The French admire Farje enormously. They don't just regard him as an entertainer, a confectioner of stylish thrillers, but as a – a – *do* tell me yet again, Philippe, what the French regard him as.'

'Where to begin?' he sighed. Then, having always known where, he duly expatiated:

'For us, the French, Alastair Farjeon is not just the Master of Tension, as you call him here. He is above all a profoundly religious artist, a moralist but also a metaphysician, the illegitimate offspring, if you like, of Pascal and Descartes. He is – how you say? – a chess master who plays blindfold against himself. A poet who decodes the messages which he himself has sent. A detective who solves the crimes which he himself has committed. In brief, he is – *mille pardons*, he was – a supremely great *cineáste*, one who has been cruelly – how do you say? – *sous-estimé*?'

'Underrated?' ventured Evadne Mount.

'Underrated, *mais oui*. He has been supremely underrated by you English.'

'But, darling, I keep telling you, we English actually like –' Cora began to say, before being interrupted.

'Like! Like! It is not a question of "like".' He held the verb up as distastefully as though he were handling somebody else's stained underwear. 'The man was a genius. You do not "like" geniuses. Do you "like" Einstein? Do you "like" Picasso? Do you "like" Poe? No, no, no! You worship them. You idolise them. Just as we French idolise Farjeon.

'Of course,' he ended with startling abruptness, 'he was a *crapule* – a *cochon* – a peeg – of a man. Ah, but there you are. Bad manners, the infallible sign of genius.'

'If you say so,' the novelist politely demurred. 'But still, Monsieur Françaix, considering that Farjeon is dead and the picture is being directed by Rex Hanway, there's surely no longer any point in your hanging on?'

Was it a trick of the light or did an almost imperceptible shadow cast itself across Françaix's face?

'I 'ave my reasons,' was all he replied.

Perhaps afraid of saying something he might regret, he continued in a more equable tone:

'*D'ailleurs*, this picture, it was Farjeon's project. It will 'ave his fingerprints on it, no? It is Hanway who directs, but the result will be *totalement Farjeonien*. And because I nearly finish my book, I will add the shooting of this last – alas, *posthume* – work of his as an appendix.'

'It certainly does seem,' said Evadne, 'that young Hanway has learned from his mentor. The scene we watched this morning, with the two leads exchanging kisses through the little girl? I'm told it wasn't planned at all, yet everybody felt that it was as brilliant as anything in the original script. Worthy of Farjeon himself.'

'That is true. It was *definitely* not in the original script,' said Françaix, laying an audible stress on the adverb.

An awkward moment followed. Then the novelist, whose hatred of a vacuum was possibly even greater than nature's, remarked for want of anything more pertinent to say:

'So you're a French film critic, are you? How amusing. We don't see too many French pictures in this country. Not too many foreign pictures altogether.'

'Ah no, Mademoiselle, there you are wrong, very wrong. In my experience, you English, you like to watch nothing but foreign films.'

'Why, Monsieur Françaix,' she protested, 'only a very few foreign films open in London, mostly at a cinema called the Academy. And what a godsend it is for us devotees of the Seventh Art.'

'Mademoiselle, I was making allusion to the films of 'Ollywood.'

'Hollywood films? But those are American.'

'*Précisément*. They are not British. So they are foreign films, no?'

'We-ll, yes,' she said uncertainly. 'It's a funny thing, though. We somehow don't really think of them as foreign.'

'Perhaps you should, as we do,' replied the Frenchman with a brusqueness which succeeded in remaining just this side of insolence.

There followed another awkward pause, before Trubshawe, who hadn't said anything up to that point, finally spoke.

'I saw a French film once.'

Françaix stared at him, nakedly, offensively disbelieving.

'You? You saw a French film? I confess you surprise me.'

'I happened to go with a few of my former colleagues from the Yard. After our reunion dinner last November.'

'Really? And which film was it?'

'Bit of a letdown, I'm afraid. It was called *The Dames of the Bois de Boulogne*.'

'Ah yes. That one, it is a classic. A pure *chef-d'oeuvre*.'

'A classic? Is that a fact?' said Trubshawe ruminatively. And he repeated, 'A classic? Well, well, well.'

'You are not in accord?'

'Well, for me and my chums – and, I must confess, the dinner had been a little too bibulous, a little over-lubricated, if you know what I mean – it did seem awfully tame.'

'Tame? What is "tame"?'

'We were expecting something a bit ruder, a bit naughtier – you know, ladies of the night and all that. Of course, it's ironic, if that's what it actually had been like, we might have been obliged to have the cinema closed down, all of us being ex-coppers. But no, under the circumstances, we did feel like asking for our money back.'

After a few seconds spent wondering whether to take umbrage, Françaix threw his head back and convulsed with laughter.

'You English! Your wonderful hypocrisy! I think I like it even more than your famous sense of humour.'

Not quite knowing what to make of this, Evadne turned to Cora.

'Well, dear, it's your big scene this afternoon. Do tell us something about it.'

Cora stubbed her cigarette out in a cheap tin ashtray.

'As I already did tell you, darling, the scene as it's going to be played is quite a lot juicier than it was to start with. I managed to persuade Hanway that it ought to be developed so that the neglected wife – that's me – becomes a more rounded character, psychologically speaking. But there's no need to go into that. All you have to know is that, because of my husband's blatant dallying with Margot – that's the part played by Leolia Drake – I'm about to blow a gasket.'

'That Leolia Drake . . .' murmured Trubshawe appreciatively. 'She can put her high heels under my bed any time she likes. Pardon my French, ladies,' he said to Cora and Evadne with an apologetic twinkle in his eye, while Françaix treated him to a look of bewilderment.

'Men!' sneered Cora. 'It doesn't matter what age you are, you just can't help slobbering over a pair of bee-sting lips and eyelashes out to here. Be warned, Trubbers, don't let little Leolia fool you. She's about as sweet as a swastika. And you should hear the way she talks about herself – as though she were the next Vivien Leigh. The silly cow has only just made it to the first rung of the ladder and already she's dizzy.'

'What a spiteful cat you are,' Evadne grunted at her. 'You were young once, I can just about recall.'

'As I was saying,' Cora went on, declining to rise to the bait, 'I confront my husband after a cocktail party, a horrific row ensues and I end by hurling a champagne glass at his head.'

'Mightn't that be dangerous?' asked Trubshawe.

'Oh well, it isn't actually a proper glass glass, you know. It's made out of something called Plastic. On the big screen, though, nobody will be able to tell it from the real McCoy.'

'Any chance, do you suppose, of Hanway coming up with another last-minute improvement to the scene?'

'Oh, he already has.'

'He has?'

'Just as we were packing it in this morning, he told me that he'd thought of a little gag to add a certain piquancy to the row. That champagne glass I mentioned? In the script it's empty, you understand. Well now, as I raise it above my head, I happen to notice that there's still some bubbly left inside and I polish it off before I actually throw the glass. Isn't that just too brilliant? The fact that this woman is not even prepared to waste a few drops of flat champagne on her wastrel of a husband conveys to the audience, far more effectively than would a dozen lines of dialogue, the depth of her contempt for him. Yes, I really do believe that Hanway could be the next Alastair Farjeon.'

Back on the set, the novelist and the policeman endeavoured more or less successfully to steer clear of the technicians who were scurrying past them, back, forward, this way and that, rushing out of the studio, then back in, then back out again. Cora, meanwhile, was having her forehead, her chin and the tip of her nose softly dusted by a delicate little Chinese lady of indeterminate age. Gareth Knight was silently rehearsing his dialogue while an effeminate young man with a canary-yellow bandanna, one so tightly knotted as to cause the veins in his neck to stand out, was combing his hair back into wavy perfection. Rex Hanway, a copy of the script tucked under his arm, was peering repeatedly and, it seemed, indiscriminately through his viewfinder. And Hattie Farjeon was sitting alone in her own private nook, her own private world, sublimely indifferent to the hubbub surrounding her, still knitting away as though her life depended upon it.

Everything was finally ready for the first 'take'. Hanway settled himself into his chair next to the camera, Cato curling up on his lap, while Lettice, clutching a sheaf of notes to her breast, took her place at his side. The set began to echo to repeated cries of 'Quiet, please!' Then it was just 'Quiet!' Then, finally, 'Will everybody *please* shut up! We're going for a take!'

'Right,' said the director to his two performers. 'This is supposed to be the mother of all marital rows, so I want it to have lots of vigour and vinegar. Don't forget, Gareth, even though you give as good as you get, you do have an under-lying sense of guilt. You *know* that what Cora is accusing you of is all too true. So, when you start shouting back at her, I still want to see, lurking behind those soulful baby blues of yours, a real defensiveness, a real insecurity. At this stage in the picture we don't want you to lose the audience's sympathy.

'And Cora? This may not be the last straw but, for you, it's the latest one and you're not prepared for an instant to let Gareth off the hook. You understand?'

He turned to the camera operator.

'Camera okay?'

The operator nodded.

'Sound?'

The sound recordist nodded.

Now it was his own turn to nod, to everyone and no one at once.

'Okay, let's go. And – action!'

The clapper-boy read out, '*If Ever They Find Me Dead*, Scene 25, Take 1,' and clapped his clapper-board.

It was a juicy scene all right, just as had been promised, and both performers, as they prowled about the set, a sumptuously upholstered drawing-room strewn with cocktail-party debris, played it well beyond the hilt.

Cora, a consummate actress when given the opportunity to be one (as Trubshawe was already saying to himself), contrived to be, all at once, warm and abrasive, sensitive yet as tough as old boots. Like a virtuoso ascending, then dizzily redescending, the scales of human bitterness and resentment, holding in her hysteria all the better to let it explode, she never once delivered two different lines of dialogue with the same intonation, never once repeated an effect.

Knight's performance was almost as thrilling to watch. There were moments when he struck one as no more than an ogreish, drunken, sinisterly jovial bully wearing a fixed grin that could hardly be told apart from a snarl. At others, straining to avoid the gale force of Cora's fury, her shrill voice and jabbing forefinger, he would protest his innocence with such apparent candour and sincerity that one felt forced to revise all one's preconceptions as to which of the two bore ultimate responsibility for the failure of their marriage.

So powerfully acted, so nerve-rackingly tense and realistic, was the row – to the point where it felt almost obscene to be eavesdropping on such an intimate tragedy – that, even if everybody on the set had not been ordered to remain silent, they would surely have done so in any case.

Suddenly Knight, drawing himself up to his full six-foot-two height, loomed over a momentarily cowed Cora.

'Admit it, Louise,' he said, his voice dropping an octave. 'Our marriage is a sham.'

'A sham?'

'Yes, it's always been a sham. Right from the day I proposed to you. I asked for your hand, but, as I see now, all you were willing to offer me was your arm.'

'What on earth is that supposed to mean?'

'You didn't want a husband. What you were looking for was an escort.'

'That's absolutely –'

'As for love, it's something you could never give me, because you don't know what it is. You've never known what it is. Which is why,' he ended sadly, 'I admit it, I did turn elsewhere.'

By some indefinable alchemy, its secret known only to the greatest actors, the anger that had so disfigured Cora's features was abruptly replaced by a brief but vivid flash of self-realisation, when one saw not just the woman's emotional frigidity but also, terrifyingly, that she too had seen it. It was an epiphany which rendered the character, if only for a second or two, sympathetic, even faintly pathetic.

Not more than a couple of seconds later, however, the virago reasserted herself.

'Why, you . . . !' she shrieked, raising the champagne glass above her head. It was at that instant, of course – and everyone simultaneously realised what a brilliant conceit it had been of Hanway's – that she noticed it was still half-full. A queer, misshapen smile on her lips, she swallowed the champagne at a single go and, raising the glass again, prepared to hurl it at Knight.

Then it happened.

Time itself was suspended. One moment Cora was holding the empty glass above her head, the next she had let it fall onto the floor. With both hands at once she clasped her throat so tightly that her bulging eyes appeared about to pop out of their sockets. Whereupon, straining to scream but managing only to moan, the colour draining from her face, she collapsed in a heap on the floor.

Not again!

The two words resonated in Trubshawe's brain. It seemed only yesterday that he'd watched a similar scene being played out on the stage of the Theatre Royal, Haymarket. That one turned out to be an April Fool's hoax. Would this scene, too, prove to be some sort of tasteless practical joke?

He shot a swift glance at Evadne Mount. If it were a joke, she would be in the know. But she was mesmerised, petrified. For the novelist this was no hoax.

Nor for anybody else. The entire studio resembled a *tableau vivant* of a type one would ordinarily expect to see on the cover of a cheap thriller. No one spoke, no one moved, no one was capable of taking any action whatever. No one, that is, but the Chief-Inspector himself. Despite his age, despite his bulky frame, he rushed forward onto the set, tripping over wires, shoving technicians out of his way, until he was standing directly over the body.

He at once knelt beside Cora, lifted her arm, felt her pulse and laid his head sideways against her chest.

Though he was, of course, a stranger to every member of the cast and crew, not one of them disputed his authority to examine the actress or questioned his right to be there at all. And if many of those watching him already knew what he was about to say, they all waited tensely to hear him say it.

A few seconds later he said it.

'She's dead.'

PART TWO

Chapter Eight

'Steady, old girl . . .'

Trubshawe crouched in front of Evadne, who was sitting at one of the empty commissary's Formica-topped tables, her forehead glistening, her pince-nez also glistening, her face still as chalky-white as when she had witnessed the spectacle of Cora's death.

An hour had elapsed. The police had immediately been alerted, and had undoubtedly already arrived, and on Trubshawe's own advice none of those present on the set when the murder was committed (and, perhaps influenced by the type of picture they were making, everyone had at once assumed it couldn't be anything but murder) had been allowed to leave. But, seeing how distraught Evadne was, he had also made the suggestion that he might absent himself to take her somewhere less crowded, somewhere more private, somewhere, in short, where she would be able to compose herself away from public scrutiny.

No objection had been raised. The memory of authority

exerts nearly as powerful a pressure as authority itself and, even had anyone wished to, no one was tempted to contradict an ex-Scotland Yard officer.

'How do you feel, Evie?' he now enquired in a surprisingly tender voice. 'Bearing up, are you . . . ?'

She eked out a wan smile.

'Eustace, you're wonderful.'

'Wonderful?' he echoed her. 'Me?'

'Yes, you. I never realised that great big burly police officers could have such perfect bedside manners. Certainly none of those in my whodunits ever had and I realise I've been libelling you all. Without you I don't know what I'd have done. Made a right Charley of myself, I dare say.'

'Chut! Chut! You've pulled yourself together wondrously well, in my opinion, considering what close friends you and – and Miss Rutherford were.'

Though he and the actress had eventually made it to first-name terms, he felt awkward about being posthumously familiar with her.

'You know, Eustace,' replied the novelist, 'I've spent the last twenty years blithely killing off my characters, devising the most picturesque forms of death for them, and somewhere in the deepest recesses of my mind I suppose I've always wondered how I myself would react if the same kind of fate were to befall somebody I knew. Roger ffolkes was already a test – but Cora! How could such a thing happen to Cora?

'We'd lost touch with each other in the last few years. But you know, as they say of the last breath of a drowning man, when a woman like Cora dies, it's also her friends who see her whole life flash before their eyes. So many good times to remember . . . She was a game old bird and, my God, she'd really been a game young bird. Oh, she had her faults. She could be a proper she-devil when crossed, but she never really meant any harm. She just couldn't resist a bitchy comeback. Half the time she was genuinely surprised to discover that your feelings had been hurt.'

'I understand,' murmured Trubshawe, scouting the idea. 'Of course I barely knew her, but I do believe I recognise her in what you've just been saying. With all her badinage it was as though she were acting in a play, if you know what I mean, as though nothing she said should affect you more than it would some actor she was playing opposite.'

'Why, that's it exactly. After all, you don't start booing the actor you've just watched play Iago or Richard III if you meet him afterwards in the street, do you? Cora was simply playing a role, the role she was born to play, the witty, catty stage and screen star. And now she's dead. Poor, dear, glorious, outrageous Cora. Heaven's finally Heaven now that she's there . . .

'It's funny,' she added softly. 'I'm not sure why, but I'd always taken it for granted that, of the two of us, I would be the first to go. It's almost as though she jumped the queue.

'Cora dead . . .' she said again, still not quite able to credit it. And she was just repeating, 'Cora dead . . .' when the door to the commissary opened and Lettice Morley walked in. Behind her was a boyishly handsome young man in a fawn raincoat, a prim black bowler hat held in his hands.

'Here you are, Miss Mount,' Lettice said, holding out a battered silver hip-flask. 'It's Gareth Knight's. Scotch, I'm afraid, not brandy, but it ought to do the trick. Go on, take a swig.'

'Why, thank you, my dear, you really are a very sweet girl.'

She unscrewed the top of the flask, raised it to her lips and took a long, gurgly drink. Almost immediately, a splash of colour suffused each of her cheeks.

'Ah,' she sighed, 'I needed that.'

Sensing that the moment was propitious, the raincoat-clad young man stepped forward and respectfully addressed the Chief-Inspector.

'Mr Trubshawe, sir?'

'Yes?'

Trubshawe shot a keen glance at him.

'I'm sorry. Don't I know you from somewhere?'

'Well, you I'd know anywhere, sir,' said the young man with a hesitant smile, his restless Adam's apple bobbing up and down, 'even if we haven't clapped eyes on each other for longer than I care to remember. I'm Tom Calvert.'

Trubshawe peered at him.

'Why, of course. P.C. Tom Calvert. My apologies – Inspector Thomas Calvert of Richmond C.I.D., so I've been reading. Congratulations, young 'un!'

The young policeman nodded, shyly twirling his bowler.

'Thanks. I owe my success to you as much as to anyone. And may I say, sir, it's quite amazing, but in all those years you haven't changed a bit.'

'I kind of thought you'd say that,' replied Trubshawe with a sardonic smile.

'Oh, why?'

'No reason, no reason at all. So you've been assigned to this case too, have you?'

'Too?'

'Well, I read of how you investigated the fire at Alastair Farjeon's villa in Cookham, and now here you are.'

'You heard about that, did you?'

'I not only heard about it, I've been following it more closely than you'd ever imagine.'

'Well, sir, it seemed pretty logical to have me cover this business. Not that we have any reason to believe there might be a connection between the two – except that, as I'm sure you know, Farjeon, before he died, was to be the producer of the picture they've been making here.'

'Director,' said Trubshawe drily.

'What?'

'Take it from me, Tom, my boy. Director, not producer.'

'Very well, sir. I see you've come to know the patois.'

'I have indeed. You see, I've been spending the day down here with –'

He turned to Evadne.

'– with the well-known mystery writer Evadne Mount.'

'Ah yes, of course,' said Calvert warmly, shaking her hand. 'Very pleased to re-make your acquaintance, Miss Mount. And just let me say how terribly sorry I am. I know that Cora Rutherford was a very old friend of yours.'

'Re-make her acquaintance?' said a baffled Trubshawe. 'What do you mean by that?'

'Have you forgotten, Eustace?' said the novelist, 'When I wanted to invite you down here, it was Mr Calvert who was kind enough to give me your home address.'

Before Trubshawe could reply, Calvert, who had to stifle a smile on hearing the Chief-Inspector's Christian name, explained:

'That's right, sir. I did give Miss Mount your address. I know we're not supposed to do that, even for retired officers like yourself, but she insisted you'd be glad to hear from her and I assumed . . .'

'Not at all, not at all,' Trubshawe answered genially. 'As a matter of fact, I *was* extremely glad. Unfortunately, what started out so very pleasantly has now turned into a nightmare.'

'It's a nasty one all right.'

'She *was* poisoned, I suppose?'

'It's what all the signs point to, sir. Of course, the doctor's only just arrived, and even he won't be able to give us anything conclusive until he's performed an autopsy. Poison, though, would seem to be the obvious bet so far. Which poison is another matter.'

'No lingering aroma of burnt almonds, I suppose?' asked Evadne Mount.

'I wouldn't know,' said Calvert. 'But I'm afraid, Miss Mount, since we're in the real world here, we can't rely on having that kind of clue served up to us on a plate.'

He turned to address Trubshawe again.

'The police surgeon – that's Dr Beckwith, by the way, you probably remember him from the old days –'

Trubshawe nodded.

'Well, he's a cagey one, the type that won't say much till he's two hundred-percent sure of his facts and figures, but I did get it out of him that he thought it most likely to be one of the acid-based poisons. They're quite tasteless and colourless, you see, and, even if they're pretty horrendous things to swallow, it's all over in ten seconds. As I say, though, we won't really know until the autopsy.'

'A tricky case, Calvert,' said Trubshawe, 'with so many people milling around.'

'You can say that again,' replied Calvert with a sigh. 'Between the lunch break and the moment Cora Rutherford dropped dead, do you know that there were no fewer than forty-three people on the studio set? And all of them had an opportunity to administer the poison. We already know when the lemonade was poured into the glass, and by whom, but that's it.'

'Lemonade? I thought it was champagne.'

'Can't have the cast quaffing champagne, you know. No, it was some kind of transparent soda pop. As the doctor was examining the body, this chap came forward – almost in tears, he was – he'd been in charge of props and it was he who, at one o'clock, just as the afternoon filming was about to start, opened a bottle of the fizzy stuff and half-filled the champagne glass, as per his instructions. He wanted to get his defence in before he was questioned, and I can't say I blame him. The first person we would have gone after was whoever actually filled the glass.'

'And he's to be believed, you think?'

'Oh, I really can't imagine why not. No motive, you see. Been in the picture business upwards of thirty years, so he claims. And, above all, he's got witnesses.'

'Witnesses?'

'It appears that his assistant, the chap who brought the bottle of lemonade from the studio canteen, actually hung around long enough to see him unscrew the top.'

'I don't suppose the bottle could already have been tampered with in the canteen itself?'

'Not a chance. It was picked up at random out of a couple of dozen on display. And the top was unscrewed in the presence of this lady here' – he indicated Lettice – 'who also verified that the glass had just enough liquid in it.'

He hesitated, turning to Lettice herself to complete the explanation.

'Tell us again, Miss, what you just told me.'

Lettice answered with characteristic composure.

'The fact is,' she said to Trubshawe, 'I'm responsible for what's called continuity, for making sure that, if there's a red handkerchief in an actor's jacket pocket in one scene, it hasn't turned into a yellow handkerchief in the next, that kind of detail. Well, when Props – his real name's Stan but everybody calls him Props – when Props came on set with the bottle of lemonade, I had to be present to check that there was going to be exactly the right amount of "champagne" in Miss Rutherford's glass. And I can testify that Props opened the bottle in front of me.'

'So that puts him out.' Calvert sighed once more. 'Which leaves us with just forty-two potential suspects, any one of whom could have introduced the poison. I've already gathered – these picture people are a pretty talkative lot, I can tell you – I've already gathered that it takes so long to set up a new shot, as they say, that the glass sat on the table for about an hour while everyone went about their respective jobs, installing lights, laying cables, making up the actors and actresses and I don't know what else. I haven't a clue where we're going to start. In fact, I haven't a clue, full stop.'

'Then may I offer you one?' said Evadne Mount, who had been paying close attention to the exchanges between Calvert and Trubshawe.

'One what?'

'Clue. An important one, if I'm not in error.'

'I'd be grateful, Miss Mount, for even the most trivial of clues.'

'Well,' she said, 'as Eustace here will confirm, we watched this morning's filming together before going off to the commissary to lunch with Cora. And it was during our meal that she mentioned how Rex Hanway, the director, had taken her aside just before the break to tell her about a new idea he'd had for the afternoon's big scene, the idea being that there should be some champagne, or lemonade, still in the glass and that Cora should swallow it before throwing it at Gareth Knight. In the original script, you see, she was simply to pick up an empty glass, which was naturally how everyone expected it to be filmed.

'*Ergo*,' she ended, taking evident pleasure in hearing the Latin word trip off her tongue, 'whoever decided to poison Cora could only have hatched the plot between twelve noon, when Hanway apprised her of his idea, and two o'clock, when she herself drank the lemonade.'

'Curses!' Trubshawe berated himself. 'Why didn't I think of that?'

'Which means, of course,' she went on, once more raising her arm like a policeman to control the conversational traffic, and more especially to warn the Chief-Inspector not to venture down what she regarded as her own private one-way street, 'that the murderer would also have had to belong to what must surely be an extremely select group. That's to say, only those who were actually privy to Hanway's change of plan.'

Both Calvert and Trubshawe instantly saw the justice and relevance of her words.

'My God, Evie!' cried Trubshawe. 'Poor old Cora has just been murdered and already you've come up with an important clue. You're the real thing.'

'Yes, bravo!' Calvert chimed in. 'With that one insight you've considerably narrowed the scope of the investigation. Now all we have to do is draw up a list of everyone whose job would have necessitated their being told of the business with the champagne glass. My word, we're actually getting somewhere.'

'Is there any reason, Mr Calvert, why we don't start right away?' asked the novelist. 'This crime isn't going to solve itself.'

'What do you mean, start right away?'

'Start drawing up a list. It shouldn't take too long. I can't believe that any of the – what did Cora call them? – the ordinary grips and geezers would have been informed of the change. As I said, it could only have been a select few. Indeed, I rather think a couple of the prime suspects may be sitting right here in this room.'

Hearing these last words, Calvert, who had been nodding over each pertinent point raised in the conversation, stiffened almost as though he were immediately preparing to apprehend, with handcuffs if necessary, the two about-to-be-designated suspects.

For his part, however, Trubshawe merely smiled.

'If I'm not mistaken, Tom,' he said, 'she means us – me and her. I'm right, Evie, aren't I?'

When the novelist nodded in agreement, Calvert shook his head.

'You two as suspects? Come now, Miss, let's be serious.'

'Oh, I assure you, I *am* being serious, deadly serious. What would be the point of drawing up such a list if it weren't both inclusive and unbiased? Eustace and I were the very first to hear, from Cora's own lips, of the new bit of business. And even though, this afternoon, not once were we out of each other's sight – also, as mere visitors, practically interlopers, neither of us was permitted to approach the actual performing area – we were nevertheless physically present at the scene of the murder and might well have committed it, singly or in tandem, via some incredibly deft sleight-of-hand. One of those impossible crimes you read about in the anthologies.'

'All right, Miss Mount,' said Calvert, 'we'll have it your way if you insist. You and Mr Trubshawe are Suspects 1 and 2. Now shall we get down to brass tacks? The third suspect – and, as far as I'm concerned, the first in any real sense – must be this Rex Hanway. The idea *was* his, after all.'

'Ah, but don't you see, Inspector, unless I'm very much mistaken, the fact that Hanway actually *directed* Cora to drink from a glass of lemonade which turned out to be poisoned is going to be precisely his alibi.'

'His alibi? Why, it's the very contrary of an alibi.'

'Not at all,' she replied. 'I can just hear how he might respond to any such accusation you level against him. "My dear Inspector,"' she went on in a remarkably lifelike imitation of the director's cut-glass vowels, '"if I'd really planned to murder poor, darling Cora, do you suppose I'd have told her – in public, mark you, in public – to drink out of a glass I already knew to contain poison?"'

'H'm,' said Calvert, stroking his cheek, on which few traces were visible of a razor's coarsening attentions. 'I see what you mean . . .'

It was now Trubshawe's turn to speak.

'Hold on a sec there,' he said. 'Yes, Evie has cleverly shown why we need take far fewer than the original forty-two suspects into serious consideration. Hats off to her, even though,' he added a trifle ungraciously, 'it's a point that one or other of us would have made eventually. But there's something else she seems to have forgotten.'

'Oh,' said Evadne, 'and what's that, may I ask?'

'Well, of course I don't claim to know much about film folk, but I have had a lot of experience of murderers. Now someone who had a premeditated intent to kill might well decide to visit the scene of his intended crime with a pistol or a revolver or even a knife concealed about his person in the hope that a suitable moment would arise for committing it.

But poison? Until just before the lunch break there was no question of Cora drinking out of the champagne glass. Do either of you seriously believe that her murderer has been strolling around the set these past few days – ever since they started making this cursed film – with a flask of poison tucked inside his or her pocket? Eh? And, if not, where would they be expected to lay hands on such a flask in the two hours or so that elapsed between Hanway coming up with his new idea and Cora swallowing the poison? Answer me that.'

Calvert's eyebrows registered the logic of the Chief-Inspector's argument.

'Ye-es, that's certainly another point we ought to consider.'

'I should think it is,' said Trubshawe. 'And what it means is that Hanway surely remains your number-one suspect.'

'All right,' said Calvert, 'that makes three we know of, you two and Hanway. Anyone else come to mind?'

'Philippe Françaix,' suggested Evadne Mount.

'Who's he when he's at home?'

'A French film critic.'

'Nuff said. I don't have much time for critics myself. All they ever do is criticise.'

'He's one of Farjeon's greatest admirers – writing a book about him, or so he claims – and he's here in Elstree to follow the shooting of the picture. He also, pretty much at his own invitation, I should tell you, lunched with Eustace,

Cora and me in the commissary. So he knew all about the champagne glass.'

'Any conceivable motive?'

'Just like that, Tom?' said Trubshawe. 'We met the chap for the first time only two or three hours ago. Give us old lags a chance, will you.'

'What's your opinion, Miss Mount?'

'On this occasion I'd have to agree with Eustace. Except . . . except that there was something . . .'

'Something?'

'A feeling I had,' she replied, momentarily lost in thought. 'Not even a hunch. Nothing worth repeating. Not yet anyhow.'

'So. We have four suspects now. Who else?'

'Me.'

Everyone turned, startled, to face Lettice Morley.

'You, Miss? Are you admitting that you're a suspect?'

'I admit nothing,' she answered with the always slightly off-putting self-possession that seemed to be her defining trait. 'All I'm saying is that, if I accept the criteria by which you're in the process of designating suspects, then I cannot fairly exclude myself.'

'Sorry, but your name is . . . ?'

'Lettice Morley. I'm Rex's – I should say, Mr Hanway's – personal assistant. As such, I naturally have to know everything that occurs to him at the very instant it does occur to him. When he suggested to Miss Rutherford that she drink the champagne, he at once informed me too, and I went off and told Props, so that the half-filled glass would be precisely where it was supposed to be just as soon as Rex was ready to film the shot.'

'I see,' said Calvert. 'Well, thank you for being so candid. It's most unusual, most refreshing.'

'Not for a second, you understand,' she carried on imperturbably, 'am I intimating that I murdered Cora Rutherford. Even if the woman's irresponsible antics exasperated me, there was nothing personal in my dislike of her and, as my professional future is bound up in my making good on this picture, it would have been very foolish of me to jeopardise its own future by bumping off one of the cast members.

'However,' she added, to her listeners' undiminished amazement, 'since you've already hit upon all kinds of clever clues, perhaps I might indicate one of my own before it's turned against me. I've read quite a few whodunits in my day – yours among them, Miss Mount – and, if there's one thing I've learned from them, it's that poison is traditionally a woman's weapon.'

She looked towards Evadne Mount for confirmation.

'Isn't that so?'

'We-ell . . .' said the novelist, close to speechless for once, 'I suppose it *is* one of the conventions of the genre. But it doesn't mean we whodunit writers believe that, every time someone is poisoned, a woman necessarily did it.'

'No?' said Lettice. 'It's certainly the impression you leave the reader.'

'Ah but, Miss, if you *have* read Evie's novels,' said Trubshawe, 'you should remember that, in at least two of them, it turns out that a male murderer used poison precisely in order to lead the police astray – hoping they'd suspect that the crime had been committed by a woman.'

'That may be so, I suppose. I merely mention what Miss Mount called the convention to remind you that, on the face of it, the fact that Miss Rutherford was poisoned would seem to make me an even likelier suspect than the others on your list.'

Her tirade had left them all shaking their heads, both in puzzlement and in open admiration. Calvert finally broke the silence.

'Very well. That would appear to make you Suspect No. 5. And since you've been so admirably frank in expressing your opinions, Miss, since you also know your way about the studio better than any of us, perhaps you yourself would propose a candidate for No. 6.'

'Certainly,' said Lettice with the same unruffled aplomb that she had displayed from the start. 'Not only No. 6 but No. 7. As someone is bound to point this out to you sooner or later, it may as well be me and it may as well be now. Gareth Knight and Leolia Drake will also have to be regarded as potential suspects.'

'Gareth Knight, eh?' said Calvert. 'Don't I know that name?'

'I should hope you do. He's the leading actor in *If Ever They Find Me Dead* and it was I who personally alerted him. He had to know of the alteration to the script because he was due to play the scene in question opposite Miss Rutherford. I told him just before he went off to lunch.'

'And Miss Drake?'

'She and Mr Knight happened to be chatting together at the time. Naturally, she too was made aware of the business with the champagne glass, even though it didn't affect any of her own scenes.'

'Well, thank you again, Miss Morley, you've been extremely helpful, more so, indeed, than I had any right to expect.'

He rubbed his two rosy-cheeked palms together and turned to face Evadne Mount and the Chief-Inspector.

'Look,' he said, 'I'm going to let everybody go home now – no point as I can see in having them hang around much longer – but, and of course I don't know how you're likely to feel about this – you especially, Miss Mount, seeing as how close you were to the victim – but I'd really like to proceed with a preliminary interrogation of these five suspects of ours – if you don't mind, I'm not even going to bother including you two – as soon as possible. Tomorrow afternoon, perhaps, and here, I think, rather than at the Yard. And I wondered, in view of how much ground we've already covered during this little off-the-record parlay we've been having – well, I was hoping you might both agree to be present.'

It was Trubshawe who spoke first.

'Tom, I'd be very pleased to lend you any assistance you need, very pleased indeed. It'll be just like the old days, when I worked alongside your late father.'

'But father's not late yet,' said Calvert. 'I mean, he's still alive, you know.'

'*Is* he?' said a surprised Trubshawe. 'Oh, excuse me, my boy, I'm most terribly sorry!'

Then, attempting to cover up his gaffe, he explained, 'No, no, I mean – I mean, of course, I'm delighted he's alive. Delighted. I can't imagine why I thought he was dead. I suppose I tend to assume that all my contemporaries are dead, since I never seem to hear from any of them.'

Conscious of being already halfway towards committing a second gaffe, he swiftly changed tack.

'I repeat, I'd be very pleased to second you. I can't speak for Evie, though. I imagine Cora's murder has been quite a shock to her system.'

'Yes, it has,' said the novelist, 'which is all the more reason for my insisting on joining you.' She turned to Calvert. 'Many, many years ago, Chief-Inspector Trubshawe and I worked together on another murder case. This time, though, it means more to me, a very great deal more.'

She squashed her tricorne hat down hard on her head.

'This time,' she concluded with a monumental frown, 'it's personal.'

Chapter Nine

Inside the studio the atmosphere had dramatically deteriorated.

The impact of Cora Rutherford's death had been so electrifying that it had struck them all, performers, technicians and extras, as quite legitimate that they would be ordered not to budge so much as a foot from where they had been positioned when the crime was committed. Legitimate, too, that even an excursion to the conveniences had not only to be taken in the company of a uniformed police officer but also to be preceded by a rapid and thorough body-search – presumably to make certain none of them had the bright idea of flushing away some incriminating piece of evidence. In view of the fact, though, that instead of being stabbed, shot or strangled, the actress had been poisoned, a fact that appeared screamingly obvious to everyone present even if it had yet to be forensically confirmed, it was hard to comprehend just what the police imagined they might find concealed about anyone's person.

But time passes, and nothing happens, or nothing seems to happen, and the most innocent of bystanders start to fret and fidget as even the shock of having witnessed a cold-blooded murder eventually subsides. The victim's body had already been removed with professional swiftness and discretion, so what was the point of preventing everyone else from going home? It wasn't doubted for a moment that the film production would be closed down, possibly for good and all, and the minds of many of those marooned inside the studio had begun to concentrate on the question of where and, even more imperatively, when they might expect to land their next engagement.

Some were gloomily forecasting that, of the very few new pictures known to be going into production at Elstree, most of the plum jobs would already have been snapped up, while others were whispering among themselves that, after all – and, yes, they realised that Cora Rutherford was only just dead and her body still warm – but still, it wasn't showing any disrespect to the poor woman to point out that her role hadn't been so crucial that she couldn't easily be replaced. One cynical crew member even ventured to suggest, albeit *sotto voce*, that, for a picture titled *If Ever They Find Me Dead*, the murder, on-set, of one of its better-known actresses would at the very least generate the kind of front-page publicity that couldn't be bought for love nor money.

The reaction, in short, was that of a typical cross-section of fallible humanity when confronted with tragedy, genuine compassion commingling inextricably with naked self-interest.

When Calvert re-entered the studio, however, accompanied by Evadne, Trubshawe and Lettice Morley, everyone wearily stood to attention.

The first thing the young Inspector did was call over the two police officers with whom he had arrived and introduce them to his former superior.

'Just so as you know, sir. These are a couple of colleagues of mine from Richmond, Sergeant Whistler and Constable Turner.'

As the two officers nodded deferentially, Evadne, with a hint of her natural indomitability, couldn't resist quipping:

'Sergeant Whistler? Constable Turner? Heavens! Sounds more like the Tate Gallery than the C.I.D.'

'Yes, Miss,' answered a poker-faced Calvert, 'I believe they've heard that one before.'

'Sorry. Just trying to cheer myself up.'

'I do understand.' He turned to the Sergeant. 'Whistler, what have you got to report?'

'Well, sir, the body has already been removed. And Dr Beckwith left with it. He said he'd be in touch with you when he had something definite to be in touch about.'

'Fine, fine.' Calvert glanced over at the waiting cast and crew. 'Nobody getting too restless, I trust?'

'They're mostly all right,' the Sergeant went on. 'Three or four of them, maybe, growing a bit impatient. Wondering

how long they're going to be held here. And the – the producer of the picture, I think he said he was – he's turned up.
In quite an agitated state, he is. That's him, standing next to
the camera,' he said, pointing to a plump gentleman in his
fifties who was in deep consultation with Rex Hanway.

'Very well. I'll have a few words with him first. Ask him to
join us, will you.'

Almost immediately the producer appeared before them.
He had a set of floridly jowly features, patently not of native
English origin, and wore a double-breasted Savile Row suit
in flamboyant grey pin-stripes from whose breast-pocket he
would repeatedly pull a handkerchief, perfumed and polka-
dotted, to mop his brow with. If he had been wearing a hat
– a Panama by choice – you felt sure he would never stop
fanning himself with it.

Calvert held out his hand to him.

'Inspector Calvert, sir. Richmond C.I.D. I'll be the investigating officer on the case. You are, I believe, the producer of
the picture that was being made here?'

'Yes, yes, that's right.'

He nervously shook Calvert's hand.

'Levey's the name, Benjamin Levey. And what a terrible
thing to happen. So soon after . . . Just terrible! *Mein Gott*,
what have I ever done to deserve this?'

'Benjamin Levey?' said Trubshawe. 'Why, of course, I
remember now. You arrived in this country in – in '37,
wasn't it?'

147

'That is so.'

'There was almost a minor diplomatic incident, as I recall. Even the Yard had to get involved. You left Germany in quite a hurry, didn't you?'

'*Ja, ja,*' said Levey, suddenly wary. 'I was late for the train.'

The Chief-Inspector suppressed a smile.

'No, no, sir, you don't follow. I – well, what I meant was that you had to flee the country because of the persecution you were suffering.'

Levey yanked his handkerchief out and mopped his brow.

'*Ach!* The persecution, yes! Those German critics!'

'No, sorry, I meant –' Trubshawe began all over again, then finally decided to let it go.

Evadne Mount meanwhile asked:

'Mr Levey, didn't you produce *The Miracle*?'

'No, I produced the disaster.'

'The disaster? What disaster?'

'My production of Goethe's *Faust*. In Berlin. You have heard of it, no?'

'Well, apologies, but I'm afraid I haven't.'

'It had a really wonderful twist. A Jewish *Faust*. The Devil buys Faust's soul – what is the English word? – wholesale? But, my dears, what a disaster! The Nazis hated it. The Jews hated it. My mother hated it. Everybody hated it. When the curtain came down, it was so quiet you could hear a pin get up and walk out of the theatre.

'And now this. First my director is burnt to a crisp. Then one of my players is murdered, poisoned right in front of the whole crew. You know, my dear Inspector, I am not a superstitious man, but I start to believe this picture of mine is *verdammt*. But why? Why? For what am I being punished?'

'Well, sir,' Calvert assured the producer, 'I'm going to do everything I possibly can to get to the bottom of it all. And I can tell you, I already have a few interesting leads. But, first, I wonder if you could be of assistance to me.'

'Anything, anything, my dear.'

'I'm going to let your people go home now. Before they leave, of course, the constable will take down their names, addresses and telephone numbers – those of them who are on the 'phone. I'm well aware you'll have all these particulars on file, but there were so many people milling about on the set we have to be certain there was no one here who shouldn't have been – and, conversely, no one who should have been but, for whatever reason, cannot be accounted for. You understand what I'm saying, sir?'

'Yes, yes,' replied Levey. 'You must take all the precautions.'

'That's right. However, there happen to be five of them I should like to question within the next twenty-four hours, if I may. While the details of the event are fresh in their minds. I trust you have no objection?'

'Objection?' Levey weighed the word. 'Have I the right to object?'

Calvert smiled a noncommittal little smile.

'Well, no, you haven't. I suppose I was trying to be polite. But, above all, what I wanted to let you know was that among those I intend to interview are your two stars, Gareth Knight and Leolia Drake. And who else? Oh yes, the director, Rex Hanway. I felt you ought to be forewarned.'

Levey once more mopped his brow.

'Oy! Please go gently, Inspector. If this picture is to have a future, I would not like for my actors to be bullied.'

A hideous thought crossed his mind.

'You are not thinking of arresting one of them, are you?'

'No, no, nothing like that,' Tom Calvert replied. 'As I say, it's merely a preliminary interro-' – he hastily amended the word – 'merely a preliminary chat to establish what occurred and how it occurred. Just a formality.'

Levey dolorously shook his head.

'Just a formality, eh? How we Germans came to fear that phrase. Ah, but this is England, is it not, where such methods are unknown. Yes, Inspector, go ahead. Proceed with your interrogation,' he concluded, without appearing to place any ironic emphasis on the last word.

'Thank you, Mr Levey. And now I'd like to ask one very last favour of you.'

'Please?'

'I intend to summon – shall we say the interviewees? – for tomorrow afternoon. You understand, I'd prefer the questioning to take place before the inquest, which they'll all be expected to attend. I'd also prefer it to take place here, at Elstree. Less intimidating for them than at the Yard and, for all kinds of procedural reasons, I myself have got to come back down here anyway. But I shall need a room, a quiet room. An unused office, perhaps? Somewhere out-of-the-way where I can sit down and chat with them without being interrupted. Could you yourself suggest something suitable?'

'Of course,' Levey said unhesitantly. 'You must take Rex Hanway's office.'

'I was thinking of a more –'

'Nonsense. It's comfortable, he won't be needing it now, alas, and I will make certain you are not disturbed.'

'And you yourself . . . ?'

'*Ach*, I must go up to London. Wardour Street. I have a meeting, you know, an important meeting with my backers.' He suggestively rubbed his thumb and forefinger together. 'To find out if we can still save this *verdammte* picture!'

Chapter Ten

The following afternoon, at two o'clock, Calvert was sitting behind Rex Hanway's massive mahogany desk, its in-box piled high with dog-eared typewritten scripts, its out-box empty. Directly opposite him sat the first of the suspects to be invited to submit to his questioning, Hanway himself. Stiffly flanking the director, to right and left of his own desk, seated on a matching pair of upright chairs of an uncompromisingly metallic and modernistic design, were Evadne Mount and Chief-Inspector Trubshawe. Sergeant Whistler stood discreet guard near the door.

That morning Calvert had given his two unofficial colleagues confirmation that, according to the medical report which he had just received from the lab, Cora Rutherford had indeed been poisoned. The police surgeon had discovered traces, both in the actress's empty champagne glass and inside her own body, of a widely and legally available type of cyanide, one with numerous industrial applications, notably in printing, photography and electroplating. As he had already intimated, when on the set itself, death would have been extremely painful, but also, thankfully, all but instantaneous. The inquest was to be held three days hence, but neither Evadne nor Trubshawe were required to attend. A purely formal stage in the process, it would very speedily be adjourned by the Coroner.

Now the young police officer was ready to direct his full attention to Rex Hanway.

'Well, Mr Hanway,' he said, 'I hope you don't mind my trespassing in this way. It was Mr Levey's kind suggestion that I borrow your office.'

'That's quite all right, Inspector. It's my office only in the sense that I happen – happened – to be working on a picture next door. I can't help feeling that, given the way things have been going, it'll become some other director's office before too long.'

'Yes, yes, I do know what you mean. Thank you, nevertheless. So just let me explain to you what this is all about. I felt it might be useful to put to you – you and a few others, I should add – some preliminary questions about this dreadful business while all the details were still fresh in your mind.'

'I'm not likely to forget them in a hurry. But I can quite see how meaningful to you one's immediate impressions might prove. May I ask, however . . . ?'

'Yes?'

Hanway turned to look at the two other seated occupants of the room.

'Forgive me for being blunt, but who exactly are these people? Surely they're not also police officers?'

'No, they aren't. That's to say, this gentleman' – he indicated Trubshawe – 'is an ex-police officer, Chief-Inspector Trubshawe, formerly of Scotland Yard, and this lady' – he extended his arm in the novelist's direction – 'is Miss Evadne Mount, the author, you know.'

Hanway nodded politely at the novelist.

'Of course, of course. I noticed you on the set yesterday afternoon and actually wondered where I could have seen you before. You were a good friend of Cora's, I believe?'

'I was, yes.'

'My commiserations. This must be especially unpleasant for you.'

Calvert took charge again.

'Since you're wondering why they're here, let me simply say that we three were discussing the case in the cafeteria yesterday and, in the course of our conversation, both Miss Mount and Mr Trubshawe came up with several interesting insights. Which made me ask them if they would accept to be here, in a totally unofficial capacity, while I conducted my inquiry. If you have any objection to their presence, you have only to say –'

'No, none at all. I welcome whatever – or rather, whoever – it takes to solve this terrible crime.'

'Good. Then that's settled. We can proceed. You are Rex Hanway, the director of *If Ever They Find Me Dead*?'

'I am.'

'Which, as I understand, you took over after the death of Alastair Farjeon?'

'Yes, I did.'

Evadne Mount suddenly interjected.

'May I, Inspector?'

Though willing to acquiesce to her request, Calvert was nevertheless slightly taken aback. It's true that it was he himself who had invited the novelist, along with his own former superior, to participate in the questioning, but he hadn't expected that she would be so indecently prompt in taking up his invitation. Spotting a twinkle in Trubshawe's eye, however, one that seemed to signal 'I could have told you . . .', he merely said:

'Please, Miss Mount.'

'Mr Hanway,' she asked, 'is it not true that you took over the picture under somewhat unusual circumstances?'

'When you use the word "unusual",' asked Hanway in his turn, 'do I take it you're alluding to the circumstances of Mr Farjeon's death?'

'Yes, partly so. But I was really thinking of the very singular testament which he left behind in his London flat.'

'Testament?' said Calvert. 'What's this? I've heard of no testament.'

'Perhaps,' said the novelist calmly, 'Mr Hanway would like to explain.'

'Miss Mount is quite correct, Inspector. There *was* a testament. I mean, there was a – queer, I think you'd have to call it – a queer document which Hattie, Mr Farjeon's wife, discovered among his papers after he died.'

'What sort of a document?'

'As far as I'm aware, Mrs Farjeon still has it in her possession and will, I'm sure, be only too happy to hand it over to you. It was written and signed by Farje.'

Trubshawe now took it upon himself to intervene.

'Was it witnessed by anyone?'

'Not to my knowledge. Basically, it stated that, if anything happened to him – that is, to Farje – before he was able to start shooting *If Ever They Find Me Dead*, then I was to be assigned to direct the film in his place.'

A moment of silence ensued while Calvert digested this information. Then:

'That strikes me as a most extraordinary statement.'

'I wholly concur,' said Hanway coolly.

'Is this sort of posthumous delegation or deputation – however you want to define it – standard practice in the picture business?'

'Not at all. It's the first time I ever heard of such a thing. Whenever such a situation arises – like the death of a director in mid-shoot or even before the actual filming has begun – I would have assumed it was exclusively the producer's prerogative to decide how to proceed, if at all. But you understand, Inspector, that's only my assumption, as I really can't remember it ever happening in the business.'

'I see. So you yourself were surprised to learn of the existence of this document?'

'Surprised? I was flabbergasted. I couldn't believe my ears when Hattie told me.'

Now Trubshawe asked:

'Did Mr Farjeon ever confide in you that he feared for his life?'

'Certainly not. Nor does it sound very much like the Alastair Farjeon I knew.'

'Assuming he *had* harboured such a fear, who would he have confided it to?'

'I imagine that, if he confided in anyone, it would have to be Mrs Farjeon. But she never once said anything to me about it.'

'Perhaps,' said Trubshawe to Calvert, 'we should have Mrs Farjeon called in.'

At that moment, prefacing his interruption with a polite cough, Sergeant Whistler announced from the doorway:

'She's already here, sir.'

'What? Farjeon's widow is in the studio?'

'Yes, sir. I saw her arrive. About twenty minutes ago.'

'What on earth is she doing here?'

'It seems she's always here,' said Evadne.

'Always here?'

'So Cora told us. When Farjeon used to make his films here, his wife would always be present in the studio, sitting – also knitting – in a corner all by herself, never exchanging a word with anyone.'

'But what is she doing here *today*?' Calvert insisted. 'Mr Hanway, have you any idea?'

'Knitting as usual, would be my guess. But if you mean, why has she turned up on the set of a film which has just been closed down, I really couldn't say.'

Trubshawe turned again to the young Inspector.

'Whatever the reason, it might make sense for us to question her too.'

'Good point,' replied Calvert. 'Whistler, go find out if Mrs – Hattie, isn't it? – if Mrs Hattie Farjeon is still in the studio. If she is, inform her – politely, now – that I'd prefer her not to leave until I've had a chance to speak to her.'

With a brisk 'Right away, sir,' the Sergeant left the room.

'Mr Hanway,' was what Evadne now said to the director, 'you've just admitted that you were surprised to hear of the existence of this unorthodox document. Obviously you must have been. But were you also pleased?'

Before answering her question, Hanway, as everyone observed, took the time carefully to construct a tiny Indian wigwam out of his crossed hands and fingers. Then he said:

'I beg your pardon?'

'Were you pleased? Pleased that Farjeon had passed on his film to you?'

'Well, of course,' he replied at last, 'of course, I was pleased that he had, as you put it, passed on his film to me. I would, though, prefer to use the word "honoured". It was a great compliment to me from somebody I not only admired, even revered, as an artist but also regarded, on a personal level, as a mentor. A father-figure, almost. And since it's always been my ambition to direct a film of my own, and since I've had to wait a very long time for the opportunity to do so, there was obviously no question of my rejecting that opportunity when it finally did arise.

'I want you to understand, however, that I was extremely close to Farje, I was his collaborator and friend for nearly a decade, and his recent death came as a huge shock to me, a shock from which I still haven't recovered. And I believe I can claim in all honesty that my ambition was never such as to have made me wish that he might die prematurely so that I'd be free to direct my first film. If that *was* the implication of the question you've just asked me – if you were implying, in short, that I was pleased not just that he'd passed on his film to me but that he'd passed on, full stop – then I must say I resent it.'

'Nothing of the kind, young man. Please accept my assurances that I was imputing no underhand motives to you. But tell me,' she continued, affording him next to no time to be mollified, 'and please don't take further offence at how I express this, why would Farjeon propose you, a mere assistant, as his substitute, his heir, rather than another experienced director?'

'Miss Mount, I don't think you realise what it means to be a director's assistant, a First Assistant, as we call it in the picture business. For instance, I have no notion whether you, a writer, have an assistant or not. But, if you do have one, I imagine it must be some efficient young lady who takes dictation from you, types out your manuscripts, helps you with any research you might have to conduct and perhaps even makes your tea. A First Assistant in the film industry, by contrast, is the director's right arm. He offers advice, makes suggestions if a scene is not working properly, even directs the odd shot or two if for some reason the director himself is temporarily unavailable. It's a very important post and, as I say, I've filled it at Farje's side for ten years. He trusted me implicitly and I have to suppose that, in consequence, he trusted me more than anyone else to take over his film.'

'Yet, from what poor dear Cora told us, Mr Trubshawe and me, that trust of his was originally misplaced. You were a pretty catastrophic director, were you not, to start with? You were so hopeless, it appears, there was even talk of closing down the production a second time. Wasn't that the case?'

Though he was still disinclined to step in, Calvert did find himself wincing at the novelist's incorrigibly brutal candour; even Trubshawe, accustomed to her bulldozing style, wondered whether she hadn't overstepped the bounds.

Hanway, for his part, remained unflinchingly calm.

'It was indeed the case,' he replied. 'Miss Rutherford's impression was entirely accurate, as I would be the first to admit. Well, evidently not the first, since she got there before me. I won't deny that those early days on the set were a nightmare for me. I was completely intimidated by the example, by the spectral presence, by the aura, if you like, of the great Alastair Farjeon. I kept asking myself, "What would Farje have done? What would Farje have done?" And the more helplessly I threshed about, the worse it was. A film crew, you know, is not unlike a pack of wild animals. They can sense fear in a director and, when he himself realises that that's what they're beginning to do, the situation becomes untenable. To be honest, I might well have packed it in before the studio did.'

'What happened so suddenly to change everything?'

'It was quite simple. I stopped asking, "What would Farje have done?" and I started asking what I myself ought to do. I cast off his shadow like some hand-me-down suit of clothes. I knew that I had it in me to make a good job of the film and that all I had to do was to get it out of me.'

'Can you tell us, Mr Hanway,' asked Calvert, feeling it was high time he re-asserted his authority, 'exactly where you were when Cora Rutherford was poisoned?'

'Ah, so it *was* poison. There was nothing about that in this morning's papers. Are we supposed to keep the fact a secret?'

'Not at all. If it wasn't in this morning's papers, it's because it was only this morning that I myself was informed.'

'I see.'

'So let me repeat. Where were you when it happened?'

'Where was I? I was sitting in my chair watching her, as we all were. Watching her, I mean, not all sitting in my chair.'

'You didn't have any suspicion of what was about to occur?'

Hanway looked incredulous.

'Are you serious?'

'Just answer the question, sir.'

'Of course I had no suspicion. None whatsoever. How could I have? I was as dumbfounded – and horrified – as everyone else was.'

'And Miss Rutherford herself? What were your feelings about her, your own personal feelings?'

'Cora? Well . . .'

For an instant the director's attention was distracted by the return of Sergeant Whistler, who communicated a message to Calvert by no more than an affirmative nod of the head. Then the young officer faced Hanway again.

'Did you like her? Dislike her? Understand me, I'd prefer you to be completely honest.'

'On a personal level, I had nothing against Cora. Nothing for her either. You've got to realise, Inspector, before I was put in charge of *If Ever They Find Me Dead*, I'd never once met Cora Rutherford. I'd seen her on stage two or three times, of course, but that was it.'

'And professionally?'

'Professionally? Well, from a strictly professional point of view, I can't deny that Cora Rutherford was not, and would never have been, my first choice for the role. I inherited her as I inherited every single other aspect of the film.'

'Except Leolia Drake,' said Trubshawe unexpectedly.

Hanway, for the first time, appeared disconcerted.

'Yes . . .' he answered at last, having taken some time to gather his thoughts. 'It's perfectly true. But, you must understand, that specific decision was forced upon me. The actress who had initially been cast in the role was Patsy Sloots, who died along with Farjeon in his Cookham villa. So, yes, of necessity Miss Drake was my own personal choice of actress.

'You were asking me, though,' he quickly changed the subject, 'about my attitude towards Cora Rutherford. The fact is, she isn't somebody I would ever have cast in the part had I myself been empowered to make such a decision.'

'Oh,' asked Evadne Mount, 'and why not, may I ask?'

The reply came sharply.

'Miss Mount, I know how close you were to Cora. In this interview, however, you've been very candid with me, aggressively so at times, and I can't see why I shouldn't be equally candid with you. Cora was desperate for the role, as I already learned from Farje. She would have done practically anything to land it. Why? Because, quite frankly, she was on her way out. Farje knew it, I knew it, Cora herself knew it and I think you know it too.'

'Whether I know it or not, it surely wouldn't have detracted from her skill as an actress.'

'Excuse me, but I beg to differ. In my experience – which is hardly as great as Farje's was, of course, but it's the only experience I can credibly speak from – in my experience, an actress as desperate to land a part as Cora was is precisely the last actress who ever ought to be offered it.'

'Why so?'

'Because such an actress would have so hungered after the part she simply wouldn't be able to resist the temptation of squeezing out of it more, in fact, than it actually contained. I had several pre-production conversations with Cora and I swear that, for her, the film itself only mattered because, without it, her own part in it wouldn't exist. As far as she was concerned, *If Ever They Find Me Dead* represented above all a comeback for her – to which my film was conveniently attached.

'Well no, Miss Mount, that's not what I look for in an actress. I don't want somebody hogging and ultimately clogging up the screen. Cora's part, after all, was a fairly secondary one.'

'Yet, as I understand it, it was one that you yourself were happy – or at least willing – to enlarge. You "bumped it up", to use Cora's own expression.'

'Only,' he cut in glibly, 'only because I could anticipate the kind of overheated, overblown – in a word, a cruel word but a justified one, *hammy* – performance she was likely to give me and I wanted her character to have a more extended presence on the screen in order to accommodate all the hysterics and histrionics that I dreaded. *That*, I assure you, is the one and only reason I "bumped up" her part.'

'And when you watched her play the scene, just minutes before her death,' the novelist quietly asked, 'did you still think she gave a hammy performance?'

Hanway looked at her for the longest time before shaking his head.

'No, I didn't. I was wrong, hopelessly wrong. She was magnificent. I make total amends. To you – and to Cora too, if she can hear me now.'

There was a moment of silence before Calvert spoke again.

'I have one last question for you, Mr Hanway, and then I'll let you go.'

'Yes, Inspector?'

'As I've been informed, it was immediately *after* the lunch break that Cora Rutherford drank out of the poisoned glass. And that was because, immediately *before* the lunch break, you yourself had told her she'd be expected to do so because you'd just had the idea of improving the scene. Now you do see, don't you, how bad that sequence of events looks for you?'

There was no change in Hanway's expression. It was a question he knew he was going to be asked.

'Inspector, apart from the fact that I had no conceivable motive for killing Cora – indeed, I had not one but two extremely strong motives for keeping her alive, if I may put it that way. One, as I've just told you, I thought the performance she had given me so far was quite magnificent and, two, her death risks seriously endangering the future of this film and my own future with it. Apart from all that, however, let me answer you in this way. Do you really suppose that, if I had wished to kill Cora, I would have requested her – in public – to drink out of a glass into which I myself had just sprinkled poison?'

'I'm sorry, sir, but –' Calvert began, except that Hanway hadn't finished.

'Let me continue, Inspector, since I believe I can predict what you're about to say. You're about to say that such an argument simply doesn't count since, whether I did or did not kill her, I would offer exactly the same response? Am I right?'

'Ye-es, something along those lines,' replied Calvert, who couldn't help smiling at how slyly he had been pre-empted.

'Then I submit, with all due respect, that the question should never have been posed in the first place. I repeat, with all due respect.'

'*Touché*, Mr Hanway,' said Calvert. 'But please consider this. Cora Rutherford was neither stabbed nor shot nor strangled. She was poisoned. Now I've been involved in quite a few criminal investigations and I've never yet had a case in which someone carried poison about him on the off-chance that he was going to feel like committing a murder. The only person who could have poisoned Cora Rutherford was someone who had premeditated the crime, someone who brought the poison into the studio yesterday morning because he knew – he *knew*, Mr Hanway – that she would be expected to drink out of the champagne glass yesterday afternoon. I'm sorry, but I can't think of anyone else who fits that description but you.'

'Aren't you forgetting one thing, Inspector?'

'Am I?'

'Yes. You're forgetting that this is a film studio. It has a laboratory. And in that laboratory, if I'm not mistaken, you will find many samples of the so-called industrial poisons – hydrocyanic compounds, I believe they're called – that are widely employed in the photographic and cinematographic industries. Everyone who works at Elstree will confirm what I've just said. And everyone would have had just as easy access to these poisons as I had. The lab is only a five-minute stroll from here.'

Calvert gazed at him as though at an insect under a magnifying-glass. Then:

'*Re-touché.*'

With a rakish nod of his head, Hanway acknowledged in his turn Calvert's own rueful acknowledgement of defeat.

'Oh, and I don't suppose, Mr Hanway, that you mentioned the idea of half-filling the champagne glass to anyone else before you spoke to Miss Rutherford about it?'

'Do you mean, did I tell someone about my idea before I had it myself? Come come, Inspector.'

'Yes, sir, point taken. Well, thank you for giving me so much of your time. If I need to contact you further, I know where I can find you.'

'Thank you, Inspector, for making it all so painless, so *relatively* painless.'

Bowing crisply to both the novelist and the detective, the director stood up and strode out of the room.

For a moment no one spoke. Then, plugging his pipe with tobacco, Trubshawe said:

'Now that's one cool customer.'

Chapter Eleven

In deference to Benjamin Levey's concern that the film's leading man and lady not be imposed upon more than was absolutely necessary, Calvert decided that the very next person to be grilled would be Gareth Knight, followed immediately by Leolia Drake. As before, it was Sergeant Whistler who escorted Knight into Hanway's office and silently steered him to the interviewees' chair. With a first vague nod at both Evadne Mount and Trubshawe, the actor turned to face Tom Calvert. Then, removing his cigarette-case from the inside breast-pocket of his impeccably cut sports jacket, he was about to ask whether he might be permitted to smoke when, the two men taking stock of one another, an unexpected thing occurred.

Though probably nothing untoward would have struck the untrained eye, for Trubshawe there was no doubt at all. It wasn't that he merely fancied he saw – no, he definitely did see – the actor momentarily flush with apprehension. Clearly, Knight recognised Calvert, and it was that recognition which had caused him to – in Cora's word – start.

Did Calvert, though, recognise Knight? That was less obvious, as the young officer opened the session with a politely neutral, almost sycophantic approach.

'I want very much to thank you, Mr Knight, for agreeing to appear before us and also to assure you that I mean to take up as little of your valuable time as I humanly can. I'd just like to ask you, if I may, some questions about the terrible thing that happened here yesterday afternoon. You don't mind, do you?'

Shifting uneasily in his chair, the suddenly rather waxy-complexioned Knight seemed to have more of a problem lighting his cigarette than one might have expected of so urbane an idol of the silver screen.

'Not at all, not at all. I – I'm entirely at your disposal.'

'Good. Now then, I really don't have to ask who you are and all that. Somebody as well-known as you needs, as they say, no introduction. So we'll proceed directly to –'

He didn't complete the sentence.

'I say, sir, haven't we met, you and I? I know I ought to remember, but . . .'

Knight bit into his lower lip, but so furtively that the gesture was noticed, again, only by Trubshawe, whom years of experience had taught to be eternally on the watch for all such, to others, imperceptible symptoms of disquiet.

The actor decided at once, however, that it would be both pointless and counterproductive to conceal the truth, and replied in a clipped tone:

'Yes, Inspector, you're quite right. We have met before.'

'It was when I was on duty, was it not?'

'Yes, it was.'

'It's coming back to me now. The reason I didn't at first remember where and when we met is that, at the time, you weren't using the same name. Am I right?'

'You are.'

'Would you mind telling me what name you were arrested under?'

As Hanway had before him, Knight edgily glanced back at the novelist and the Chief-Inspector.

'No need for alarm, sir,' said Calvert. 'Everything we hear will remain between these four walls. Mum's the word – unless, of course, it should turn out to have a bearing on the case we're investigating.'

'Very well,' said Knight, struggling to control his nerves. 'It happened about eighteen months ago. On V.E. Day. Or V.D. Day, as I believe some wag jocularly called it. I was arrested by two constables in Leicester Square for . . .' – he hesitated again – 'for soliciting in a Public Convenience. The – the young gentleman with whom I imagined I was having a pleasant and, uh, promising conversation turned out to be – as *you* know, Inspector – a plain-clothes policeman. I must say that did seem to me to take policing a little bit too far, especially on such a joyous and festive occasion.'

'Well, of course, I'm sorry you feel that way, sir, but for me it was an assignment like any other. Our job, after all, is to protect the public from the likes of –' said Calvert. 'Anyway, do go on.'

'As I say, I was arrested in Leicester Square and taken to Bow Street Police Station. Fortunately the sergeant there failed to recognise me and I was able to give another name –'

Calvert interrupted him.

'I'm amazed to hear you brazenly admit that, Mr Knight. That was a most serious offence you committed.'

'You don't understand, Inspector. Gareth Knight is my professional name. For an obvious reason – which is to say, my career would have been killed stone dead if the press had got wind of the arrest – I gave my real one.'

'Which is?'

His cheeks tensing, Knight seemed even more reluctant to confess to his real name than to the offence he had committed.

'Colleano. Luigi Colleano.'

'I see,' said Calvert. 'Luigi Colleano? Doesn't quite have the same ring as Gareth Knight, does it? So you're Italian?'

'As a matter of fact, I was born in Bournemouth. My father, who emigrated just before the First War, earned his living by selling ice-cream cones and wafers on the pier.'

'Uh huh. All very respectable, I dare say. But, well, didn't you also look different?'

'I had shaved off my moustache for the occasion. And wore spectacles.'

Observing Calvert's expression of mild reproof, he added:

'No crime in that, I believe?'

'Never said there was, sir, never said there was. If I'm not mistaken, you were sent to Wormwood Scrubs, right?'

'Three months penal servitude. My war record was taken into account. I'd been an R.A.F. pilot in the Battle of Britain. Shot down four Messerschmitts and one Dornier. Awarded the D.S.O.'

'Only three months, eh?' said Calvert. 'Well, Mr Knight, I really don't think you have too much to complain of. Could have been two years, you know.'

'There is that, I suppose,' agreed Knight drily. 'The essential is that there was no write-up in the papers and my reputation was saved.'

'You yourself might want to put it that way. For us in the police, of course, the essential is that you were made to pay your debt to society. And, since you did, we'll say no more about it.

'Now to the matter at hand. As I understand, you were actually performing alongside Cora Rutherford just before she died?'

'That's right. We were playing our one big scene together.'

'What was your reaction, your initial reaction, when she collapsed in front of you?'

'My initial reaction? To be absolutely honest with you – it's awful to have to say such a thing – but my initial reaction was that she was grandstanding.'

'Grandstanding?' said a puzzled Calvert. 'I don't think I know that word.'

'It's what the French call "pulling the covers over to your own side of the bed",' explained Evadne. 'Isn't that so, Mr Knight?'

Knight turned to face her.

'Yes it is, Mrs . . . ?'

'Miss. Miss Evadne Mount.'

'Miss Mount. Yes, I'd say that was rather a neat definition.'

Then, to Calvert again:

'It means trying to upstage your co-performers. And, well, I blush to think of it now but, before I realised that something deadly serious had happened, that's exactly what I thought Cora was up to.'

'So you disliked her, did you?' the novelist put to him.

'Cora? Why, not at all,' he replied, expressing surprise. 'Oh, I won't pretend she didn't sometimes set my teeth on edge with all her tantrums and taradiddle, and especially her chronic lateness – I cannot abide unpunctuality – but, no, deep down I was really rather fond of Cora.'

This revelation arrested Evadne's head.

'*Were* you?' she said, even more surprised by Knight's answer than he had been by her question.

'Yes, I was. I can't say I knew her all that well, but over the years, you know, we'd run into one another at the Ivy and the Caprice.'

'You had no previous professional connection with her, I assume,' Calvert asked.

'Yes, I did. Just the once. It must have been in 1930. Possibly '31. She and I were in a stage production together.'

'Really?' remarked Evadne. 'Cora never mentioned it to me.'

'I can't say I blame her. It wasn't something either of us felt like boasting about. A play by Eugene O'Neill, but decidedly one of his feebler efforts. *Orpheus Schmorpheus*. Adapted from the French – Jean Cocteau, you know. It closed after five performances. Precisely five too many, in my opinion. O'Neill never had the light touch.'

'But as to Cora,' the novelist persisted, 'you say you really liked her?'

'Well, yes, I rather did. Certainly, when I first met her, about fifteen years ago, she was very special. Unforgettably gorgeous and possessed of an extraordinary presence. Not just on stage but in life. She was one of those actresses who didn't need spot-lights or arc-lights. She didn't absorb light, she herself seemed to emit it.'

'Nicely put, young man.'

'Well, thank you, Miss Mount. And, incidentally, thank you, too, for the "young man". We were two of a kind, Cora and I. She was somewhat older than I, of course, but we both had what she'd have called a "past". We both launched our careers in the theatre before eventually gravitating to the films. And we both knew we were getting on when we stopped lying about what we were going to do and started lying about what we'd already done.

'The trouble with Cora, though, is that she never learned to adapt. Even when she was acting in front of a film camera, she continued to deliver her lines as though she had to pitch them to the very last row of the Upper Circle. And she continued to behave – to misbehave – as though she were a major star, which, these last few years, she was most definitely not. All the same, she had class, real class. She wasn't like one of these fluffy little chits one finds oneself acting with nowadays who not only couldn't play O'Neill but have never even heard of him. And for all her bitchiness – of which, I have to tell you, I was more than once the target – she could be a generous soul.'

'I wholeheartedly agree with you,' said Evadne Mount. 'It's what I was saying to my friend Eustace here. Cora was a good egg.'

'Let's say, rather, a curate's egg,' murmured the actor, adding chivalrously, 'but by Fabergé.'

'So,' said Trubshawe, none too pleased to hear his deplorable Christian name afforded another reckless public airing, 'you didn't object to her being cast in the picture?'

'Object? Certainly not. As a matter of fact, it was I who persuaded Farje that she'd be ideal for the role.'

'Oh, you did, did you?' Trubshawe said pensively. 'Now that *is* interesting . . .'

'Why so?'

'Well, don't you see, sir. Somebody obviously had his reasons for wanting Miss Rutherford put out of commission.

And one way of disposing of her would be to have her poisoned in the middle of a crowded film set. Now we learn that it was you who recommended that she be cast in the picture. Don't you see what I'm getting at?'

Gareth Knight thought this over, then said:

'Well, no, I can't say I do. You seem to have forgotten that there was nothing in the original script about Cora drinking out of the champagne glass. It was an idea the director had on the set, at the very last minute, just as used to happen heaps of times with Farje. Can you actually be suggesting that I knew in advance, by some kind of intimate conviction, that Hanway was going to have that idea?'

'That's one in the eye for you, Eustace!' Evadne Mount almost crowed.

'Besides,' Knight smoothly continued, 'I repeat, I liked Cora. It's absurd to imply that I might have had a reason to kill her. Not only did I not, I simply cannot imagine why anyone else would. There were times I would happily have throttled her – but not killed her, if you know what I mean.'

'Just so,' said Calvert. 'But tell me, Mr Knight, during the ninety minutes or so between the moment when everybody broke for lunch and your own reappearance on the set, what exactly were your movements? Where did you go? And what did you do?'

'I spent the entire hour-and-a-half in my dressing-room.'

'You didn't have lunch in the canteen?'

'The commissary? No, never. My secretary prepares my

177

lunch every day and brings it down to Elstree from my London flat.'

'And this secretary? Was she with you any of the time in your dressing-room?'

'He, Inspector.'

'He?'

'My secretary is male.'

'Aha . . . I see. Well, was *he* with you any of the time?'

'He was with me all of the time. In fact, he and I lunched together. Then he helped me run through the new scene. He played Cora. I mean, he read Cora's lines. He will absolutely vouch for that.'

'I'm sure he will, sir, I'm sure he will.'

Changing tack, Calvert now said, 'This picture – *If Ever They Find Me Dead* – it does appear to be jinxed, doesn't it? Miss Rutherford dying as she did, right there on the set, and of course Mr Farjeon also dying only a few weeks ago. His death must have come as a great shock to you.'

'It *was* a shock, yes,' said Knight. 'A huge professional blow. I've acted in several of Farje's films, you know. I was one of his repertory company, as it were.'

'A professional blow, you say. Not a personal one?'

Knight fell silent. It was patent that he was debating with himself whether to speak out or not. Finally, he said:

'Inspector, I yield to no one in my admiration for Alastair Farjeon as an artist. He was, I need hardly say, a true genius, one of the very few reasons it was still possible for us to take

178

pride in this mostly lamentable British film industry of ours. As a man . . .'

He shrugged his shoulders.

'You weren't close friends, I gather?'

'But that's just it, we were close friends,' Hanway replied with a grimace. 'That's what I found so unforgivably cruel. You understand, I –'

'Yes, Mr Knight?'

'Oh well, in view of what I've already been obliged to confess, I don't see why you shouldn't be acquainted with the whole story. Now that he's dead, it no longer matters. When I was arrested, it was Farje whom I asked to pay my bail and contact my lawyer and so forth. Naturally, that meant he had to be in on the whole sordid business. And, just as naturally, given his twisted personality, he at once realised the implications it held for my future career.'

'He did, nevertheless, continue to cast you in his pictures.'

'Yes, Miss Mount, I grant you, he did that. On the other hand – and, with a man like Farje, there always was another hand – he never once allowed me to forget what he knew. How with a single negligent word from him my reputation would be in ruins. How he'd always had a weakness for the strong stuff and how, when he'd been drinking too much, he had an unfortunate tendency to become a tiny bit talkative – hence it was in my interest to make sure he stayed safely on the wagon – and so on – and so forth. He taunted me and taunted me until I thought I was going to lose my mind. So, you see, it would be hypocritical of me to pretend that, when I heard of his death, I didn't breathe an immense sigh of relief, even as I sincerely bemoaned his loss to the British cinema.

'But to return to what you said a moment ago, Inspector, you may be right at that. There may well be a jinx on this film. I don't want to sound ghoulish but I can't help wondering . . .'

'Wondering what, sir?' Calvert prompted him.

'Wondering who's going to be next.'

Next, as it happened, but only in the sense that she was next up for questioning, was Leolia Drake.

She entered the room wearing a heavy, layered cashmere coat, clutching it to her body as tightly as though it were bitterly cold, which it wasn't, or as though she were naked underneath, which she wasn't. She accepted the chair opposite Calvert's, pulled her skirt down over the top of her knees as showily as though they themselves were showing, which they weren't, and waited for him to proceed with his interrogation.

Since Calvert's preliminaries were much as they had been with both Hanway and Knight, they need no repetition here. The essential point was that the actress duly confirmed what Lettice Morley had already told him, that she had indeed been chatting with Gareth Knight when she'd heard about Hanway's 'super new idea'.

'Then can you describe to me, Miss Drake,' said Calvert, 'at the moment when Miss Rutherford drank from the poisoned glass – poison has now been officially confirmed, by the way – where precisely were you? On the set itself, by any chance?'

'Yes, I was. But nowhere near Cora, you know. I was standing behind the camera. I couldn't possibly have –'

'Why,' Evadne Mount asked, 'were you on the set at all if you weren't playing in the scene?'

'Oh, it's just that Rex is so frightfully brilliant I couldn't bear to tear myself away. I preferred to be there at his side, watching him be clever. It sent all sorts of funny little shivers up my spine.'

'I can see you have a high opinion of him as a film director.'

'Of course I have,' she replied. 'I mean to say, we *are* going out together.'

'Is that a fact?'

'Well, to tell you the truth' – she couldn't resist a naughty-little-girlish giggle – 'we're *staying in* together, if you follow me.'

'Is that why he gave you a part in the picture?'

'What?'

'I asked you if that was why he gave you a part in the picture?'

The actress was outraged by the question.

'What a beastly thing to say!' she finally cried. 'It wasn't my fault Patsy Sloots got hers in that fire. Inspector, I don't know who this woman is, but I simply refuse to stay here and be insulted by her.'

'Yes, Miss Mount,' said Calvert, 'I do have to agree with Miss Drake. I cannot accept there's any call for you to be so systematically hostile to witnesses who, after all, are doing their best to be of assistance to us. If you don't mind, I'll take charge of the inquiry from now on.'

The novelist mutely declining to reply, he began to pursue his own line of questioning.

'Miss Drake, what were your personal feelings towards Cora Rutherford?'

'I really don't know what to tell you.'

'Just tell me what you thought of her. It'll go no further than here.'

'She's not somebody I gave much thought to one way or the other. She was foisted on Rex, you know. He didn't choose her for the film and, if he'd been, well, a free agent, I don't suppose for a single second he would have.'

'That may well be true. Yet, in this very room, just a little while ago, Mr Hanway himself voluntarily admitted to us that he had been wrong. That he'd been tremendously excited by the way her performance was turning out.'

'Did Rex say that?'

'Yes, he did.'

'Oh well,' she replied carelessly, 'that was very handsome of him. But so like Rex. He's such a generous person.'

'You yourself were not impressed?'

'I'd rather not speak ill of the dead, Inspector.'

'You just did,' Evadne Mount muttered under her breath.

There ensued a silence which, even though it lasted only a few seconds, began to seem awkwardly protracted to the young actress, who must eventually have felt it incumbent on her to bring it to an end.

'Oh, Cora was all right in her way, if you like that kind of thing. But really, Inspector, let's face it. I mean, she was a bit – well, quite a lot more than a bit – past it. So p'raps,' she ended pleasantly, 'p'raps what happened was, you know, all for the best.'

'All for the best?!' Evadne let out an indignant snort. 'Do my ears deceive me, you – you – or are you actually suggesting that Cora ought to consider herself lucky to have been murdered?! Is that really what you're saying?'

'Oh no, no, no, that's not at all what I meant! I think it's most unfair of you, taking the words out of my mouth like that. And out of context too. Of course, it's dreadful that Cora was killed, dreadful. All I meant was – well, she didn't really have too much of a future, did she, so it's not so bad – I mean, it's not *quite* so bad – as it would be if somebody like – well, somebody younger and prettier – oh, now you've got me so mixed up I've quite lost track of what I do mean.'

'That's all right, Miss Drake,' said Calvert diplomatically, 'that's all right. It's been a trying situation for you.'

Sensing that it would be futile to prolong the interrogation, he offered his hand to her.

'And thank you so much for coming in. You've been most helpful.'

'I tried to be, Inspector, I really tried.'

'I know you did. And you're free to go. But – this is just a formality – please don't make any travelling plans without first advising me.'

'Oh, I do understand. In any case, now that this picture looks as though it's up the spout, I hope quite soon to start rehearsing a play in the West End. *The Philadelphia Story*? It's by Sir James Barrie, you know?'

'Is it really?' Calvert tactfully agreed. 'Well, I do wish you better luck in your theatrical career than you've had so far in the films. Thank you again and goodbye.'

'Goodbye to you, Inspector,' she mumbled almost tearfully. Then, looking neither at Trubshawe, who had said nothing at all, nor at Evadne, who had said much too much, she once more gathered her coat about herself and hurried out of the room.

A moment later, Calvert turned to the novelist and wagged an emphatic index finger at her.

'Really, Miss Mount, really . . .'

Chapter Twelve

'Sit down. Please.'

Without offering a word of thanks, grasping a bizarre carpet-bag decorated with ornate, cod-Oriental motifs, out of which protruded a formidable pair of knitting-needles, Hattie Farjeon sat herself down in the chair towards which she had been motioned by the Sergeant. Since she accorded only the briefest of glances to Evadne and Trubshawe before turning wordlessly away again, Calvert didn't this time feel any obligation to make the usual excuses for their unorthodox presence or even to introduce them to her by name.

Fiftyish and frizzy-haired, dumpy, frumpy and also, or so it already appeared, permanently grumpy, Hattie Farjeon, it has to be said, was not an attractive woman. Yet there was something perversely frustrating about her physical and sartorial drabness. It was almost as though she had laboured hard to present the least prepossessing image of herself to the world. True, she was never going to win first prize in a beauty contest. Yet, one couldn't help wondering, did her hair *have* to be as unkempt as it was? Did her complexion *have* to be so speckled and blotchy? Did she really *have* to wear a blotter-green two-piece suit fraying at every hem at once? Above all, did she *have* to confront her fellow human beings – human beings who, given encouragement, might well have been prepared to meet her halfway – with such an insulting absence of curiosity?

But that, it seems, was Hattie. Take me or leave me as you will, her ungiving corporeal language seemed to be saying, but don't expect me to care either way.

'I'd like to thank you, Mrs Farjeon,' said Calvert, politely neutral, 'for agreeing to be interviewed. We have met before, you may remember, when your late husband's villa burnt down in that terrible fire.'

There was no response from Hattie.

'And – and, eh, I do assure you, I won't take up more of your time than I absolutely have to.'

Still no response.

Calvert started to feel that, if he didn't ask a direct question soon – the sort of question a refusal to answer which could no longer simply be ascribed to natural taciturnity but would constitute an outright provocation – he'd become too unnerved to be capable of posing any question at all.

'You are Hattie Farjeon, are you not?' he asked.

'I am.'

'The widow of Alastair Farjeon, the film producer?'

'Director.'

'Ah, yes. Ha ha, sorry about that. Yes indeed, I always do seem to get it wrong. For a layman like me, uncoached in these matters, the difference between the two isn't as clear-cut as it might be, but I suppose, for you people in the picture business . . .'

His voice trailed off. Silence.

It was time to come to the point.

'Tell me, Mrs Farjeon, why have you been turning up at the studio every day?'

'I beg your pardon?'

'I asked why you still regularly make an appearance on the set. I mean to say, I realise that this picture was originally your husband's project, but after his tragic accident there would seem to be no practical reason for your presence. Or is it that you see yourself as – well, as they say, the Keeper of the Flame?'

Immediately recalling the literally incendiary circumstances of Alastair Farjeon's death, however, he realised how ill-chosen that last phrase of his had been.

'I do apologise. I'm afraid I expressed myself rather badly. No pun intended, I promise you.'

'And none taken, I'm sure,' she replied sniffily. Then she fell silent again.

'But you haven't answered my question.'

'What question is that?'

'I have been led to understand, Mrs Farjeon,' Calvert said

in a voice now so pitched as to call attention not only to his put-upon patience but also to the fact that it was fast running out, 'that when your husband made his films here at Elstree you yourself would always be present in the studio. But your husband is no longer with us. So why have you continued to journey down here when this film, *If Ever They Find Me Dead*, is being made by someone else?'

'Alastair would have wanted me to.'

'Alastair would have wanted you to? But why would he have wanted you to? Precisely what purpose do you serve?'

'I wouldn't expect you to understand what I'm about to say, Inspector, but Alastair always liked to have me near him on the set as a sort of good-luck charm – he was an extremely superstitious man – and, if I've kept coming, it's because I feel I represent a silent guarantee of fidelity to his vision. After all, it worked in the past. Why shouldn't it work now, even if it's no longer Alastair himself who's directing the film?'

A real answer. Even a rather intriguing one.

'And why are you here today? The picture, after all, has been closed down.'

'Till further notice, yes.'

'Do I take that to mean you don't believe the project has been abandoned?'

'Of course I don't.'

'But Miss Rutherford's murder . . . ?'

'The fact that Cora Rutherford is dead alters very little.

Her part was relatively unimportant. There are dozens of actresses in this country who could play it just as well. If you must know, the main reason for my coming to Elstree today was to discuss with Rex Hanway just who we might consider offering it to.'

'Oh, I see, I see!' Evadne erupted with her habitual precipitation. 'Poor Cora not yet in her grave and already you're thinking of who will replace her!'

'Naturally, we are. This is a business. Our obligation is to the living, not the dead. Upward of sixty people were employed on *If Ever They Find Me Dead*. Surely it would be more humane to try and save their jobs than to spend valuable days, even weeks, mourning Miss Rutherford's death, unfortunate as it is.'

'If I may change the subject, Mrs Farjeon,' said Calvert, nipping back in before the novelist had time to remount her hobby-horse, 'I understand that, if Mr Hanway was commissioned to take over the direction of the film, it was because you found a particular document among your husband's papers?'

'That's right.'

'You wouldn't have that document on you, I suppose?'

'Of course not. Why should I? When I came here this afternoon, I had no idea I was going to be questioned by the police. Even if I had, I doubt it would have occurred to me to bring it along.'

'I trust, though, it's still in your possession.'

'Naturally.'

'And there's no doubt at all that it was written by your husband?'

'None whatever. I ought to know Alastair's handwriting.'

'When you were going through his papers, was it that specific document you were looking for or did you come across it by chance?'

'I could scarcely have been looking for it. I didn't even know of its existence.'

'What *were* you looking for?' Evadne Mount asked.

Hattie Farjeon's withering tone, when she answered, conveyed the impression that she was so utterly undaunted by the novelist's discourtesy she couldn't even be bothered to take offence.

'If it really is any business of yours, I was looking for Alastair's will.'

'Ah . . . his will,' said Calvert. 'Did you find it?'

'Yes, I did.'

'No unpleasant surprises?'

This time the implication *was* visibly upsetting to her.

'Certainly not. Alastair and I drew it up together. And may I say I find that an impertinent question to be asked, Inspector.'

'I'm sorry, it wasn't intended to be. But to come back to this strange document – from what I've been informed, it stated that, if anything were to happen to your husband which might prevent him from shooting the film, the direction was to be handed over to Rex Hanway. Was that the gist of it?'

'It was not only the gist, it was all there was to it. Just that one statement. And Alastair's signature, of course.'

'H'm. Did your husband go in fear of anything, Mrs Farjeon? His life, maybe?'

'What a preposterous idea.'

'Why, then, would he entertain such a queer hypothesis?'

'To be honest with you, Inspector, it wouldn't at all surprise me to discover that Alastair had drawn up a similar document before each and every one of his earlier films. Naturally, I cannot say for sure since, if he had, he'd doubtless have torn it up it once the film was completed. My husband was a brilliant man but, like many brilliant men, he simply couldn't cope with the real world. He was, as I already told you, childishly superstitious. And my own belief is that, by committing such a statement to paper, he was actually hoping to outwit Fate. You know, by what they call reverse psychology? Or perhaps what I mean in Alastair's case is reverse superstition. By pretending to Fate that he feared something dreadful might happen to him, he hoped that Fate, being as contrary as we all know it to be, would then make sure it didn't. I realise how infantile that must sound – but then so, in many respects, was Alastair himself.'

'That's interesting, really most interesting,' said Calvert, who couldn't mask his surprise at having received such a detailed response to one of his questions.

'None the less,' said Trubshawe, taking advantage of the momentary silence, 'it would be useful for us to know if your husband actually did have any enemies. Or, should I say, given his power and prominence, if he had *many* enemies.'

'Childish as Alastair could often be,' his widow replied after a moment of reflection, 'he was at least shrewd enough to make friends of those with power and enemies of those without.'

There was suddenly a faint, thin-lipped trace of menace in her voice.

'I was the sole exception to that rule.'

And on that chilling note the interview was brought to its end.

After Hattie Farjeon's departure the three friends glanced at one another.

'That woman,' Trubshawe eventually remarked, 'knows more than she's prepared to let on.'

'I shouldn't wonder,' said Calvert.

Calvert began his questioning of Françaix, as he already had with his previous interviewees, in a blandly conversational mode. He assured the Frenchman that the interrogation to which he was about to submit himself was no more than a formality, that all he sought of him was that he relate whatever knowledge he had, no matter how trivial it might initially have struck him, of the circumstances surrounding Cora Rutherford's death.

'*Mais naturellement.* I will tell you everything I know.'

'Then just let me first run over a few of the chief points. Your name is . . . ?'

'Françaix, Philippe Françaix.'

'And you are, I believe, a film critic?'

Françaix made a moue of squirming deprecation.

'I'm sorry,' said Calvert, 'have I got that wrong? I was certainly advised you were a film critic.'

'Oh, it is not, as you say, the large deal. It is just that I prefer the term *théoricien*. How you say in English? Theorist?'

'Ah. Well, I don't have a problem with that. But what exactly is the distinction you're making?'

'The distinction . . .'

The Frenchman leaned back in his chair in a manner ominously suggestive to anyone who'd already heard him expatiate on the topic.

'I would say that the distinction between a film theorist – one who writes in the obscure journal, no? – and a film critic – one who writes in the daily newspaper – it is the same as between an astronomer and an astrologer. You comprehend? The first one creates a theory in order to describe the cinematic cosmos. The second concerns himself only with the stars. *Avec les vedettes, quoi.* I think that you in particular will appreciate, Inspector –'

'Actually,' said Calvert hastily, 'What I'd really like to –'

'No, no, you please must let me finish. You and I, we are like a pair of peas. And why? Because we both have theories, *n'est-ce pas*? For what are detectives but the "critics" of crime? And what are critics – true critics, theoretical critics – but the "detectives" of cinema?'

While Trubshawe could be glimpsed mouthing 'Potty! Absolutely potty!', Calvert made a new attempt to stem the flow.

'Interesting . . . So shall we agree that you're a purist and be done with it?'

'A purist, yes, yes, that is the truth, we French theorists are all of us purists. *Par exemple*. I have a colleague who claims that the cinema, it died – it died, you understand – when it started to talk. Pouf! As simple as that! I have another colleague who is such a purist he will watch only films that were made in the nineteenth-century. For him *mil neuf cent*, 1900, it is the end of everything. *Moi*, I specialise in the oeuvre of a single *cinéaste*, the great, great Alastair Farjeon.'

Relieved that Françaix had done him the favour of at long last coming to the point, Calvert pounced on the name.

'Alastair Farjeon, yes, precisely. You're writing a book on his work, I believe?'

'I am, yes. I study his films for many years. He made many *chef-d'oeuvres*.'

'Sorry, I didn't quite hear that,' said Trubshawe. 'He made many what-did-you-say?'

'*Chef-d'oeuvres*. Masterpieces. He was a very great director, the greatest of all British directors. You know, we French sometimes say that there is an *incompatibilité* – what is the expression in your barbaric language? – an incompatibility? – between the word "Britain" and the word "cinema". But Farjeon, he was the exception. He made films that are the equal – *qu'est-ce que je dis?* – that are more than the equal, much more than the equal, of any in the world. Beside Farjeon, the others are so much *vin ordinaire*.'

'Monsieur Françaix,' said Calvert, 'if I may now come to the business at hand.'

'Ah yes, the death – the murder – of poor Miss Ruzzerford. It is very sad.'

'It is indeed. You, I believe, were actually on the set when it happened.'

'That is correct.'

'Then you must have seen her drink from the poisoned glass?'

'Yes, I see her.'

'And collapse on the ground?'

'That too. It is horrible, horrible!'

'Now, before it happened, was there anything at all, anything you observed, that struck you as, well, queer – unusual – out-of-the-ordinary? Think hard, please.'

'Inspector, I have not the need to think. I observe nothing of the kind you say. I am here to watch the shoot. I place myself in a corner and I take the notes.'

'For your book on Farjeon, no?' (The French style, Calvert ruefully realised, risked becoming contagious.)

'Yes. The last chapter is going to be about *If Ever They Find Me Dead*. It will be a very curious chapter – not at all in the style of the rest of my book . . .'

As his answer died away rather inconclusively, Evadne seized the opportunity to put one of her own questions.

'Monsieur Françaix,' she began, 'you will remember, I'm sure, that yesterday we lunched together in the commissary.'

'*Mais naturellement*. I remember it very well.'

'It was during lunch, was it not, that you told us about the interviews you'd been conducting with Farjeon for your book?'

'Yes.'

'And, above all, about your admiration for his work, an admiration which you've just reiterated?'

'That is so.'

'But you also told us, practically as an afterthought, that you considered him to be a despicable human being. If I may quote you, "a pig of a man". Am I right?'

'Yes, you – you are right,' he replied, his eyes indecipherable behind his thick dark glasses.

'Well, my question to you is this. Why? Why was he a pig of a man?'

'But everybody knows why. It is *dans le domaine public*. It is public knowledge – his reputation – I repeat, it is a known thing about him.'

'That's quite true,' Evadne continued. 'Yet I had a feeling, a very distinct feeling, that when you spoke about him, the violence of your condemnation was based not just on public knowledge but on private experience, personal experience.'

Françaix pondered this for a moment, then shrugged his shoulders.

'*Qu'est-ce que ça peut me faire enfin?*' His dark glasses looked the novelist directly in the eyes. 'Yes, Miss Mount, it was based on personal experience. A very unpleasant experience.'

'Will you share it with us?'

'Why not? You see, I devote my life to Alastair Farjeon. I study his films, I watch them many, many times, and each time brings new discoveries, new and fascinating details I never notice before, the films are all so rich and strange. Then, at last, I take the courage in my two hands to write to the man himself, here at Elstree, and I propose something completely *inédit* – how you say? – untried? A book about him, but not a monograph, no, no, a book of interviews. To my surprise, he agrees. I at once catch the boat-train to Victoria and we sit down together, not here but at his splendid villa in Cookham, now alas no more – and he talks and I listen. He talks and he talks while I listen and I take notes. It is *extraordinaire*, what he says, it is *tout-à-fait époustouflant*! I am so very happy. I begin to think I will publish the greatest book about the cinema that there has ever been.'

His baldness was glistening with minute beads of sweat.

'But there is something else. Inside every film critic is a film-maker who cries to get out, you comprehend? And I am no different. I am so *impregné* with Farjeon's work I myself start to write a scenario – with his style in my mind. I work on it for many months till I feel it is ready for him to read. Then I send it to him with a nice, timid letter in accompaniment. And I wait. I wait and I wait and I wait. But I hear nothing, nothing at all. I cannot understand. I think maybe I must telephone to ask if he receives it. Then I read in the newspaper that he prepares a new film. Its title is *If Ever They Find Me Dead*. And I do understand – *enfin*.'

'What do you understand?' asked Evadne Mount quietly.

There was a brief pause. Then:

'My scenario, it is called *The Man in Row D*. It tells about two women who go to the theatre and one of them points out a man who is seated in front of them and she says to her companion –'

At which point of his narrative he and Evadne chimed in together:

'"If ever they find me dead, that's the man who did it . . ."'

'"If ever they find me dead, that's the man who did it . . ."'

'Snap,' said Evadne gravely. Then she added, perhaps unnecessarily, 'He stole your script.'

'He stole my script, yes. That is why I say he is a genius but he is also a peeg.'

'Curious . . .'

'What is curious?'

'The way Cora described the plot to us, the man was sitting in row C.'

Françaix allowed himself a mirthless laugh.

'So there is at least one thing he changed.'

'That, and the title.'

'And the title, yes.'

'Was there nothing you could do about it?' asked Calvert.

'Nothing. I had no proof. No copyright. Nothing. I was so avid that Farjeon is the first to read it, this scenario I write for him, that I do not show it to my friends or my colleagues or speak about it to anybody. And all that, see you, I write in the nice, timid little letter I insert inside the manuscript. I was – how you say? – the perfect sap.'

'You can't blame yourself,' Evadne Mount maintained. 'After all, how were you to know he would be so unscrupulous?'

'But yes, I was to know!' Françaix exclaimed, slamming his fist down hard on the desk.

'But how?'

'It is all there – in his films! I see it again and again, but I do not comprehend what I see!'

'You know,' said Evadne pensively, 'I really must try to catch up with a few of those pictures myself.'

'Ah yes? You are curious to discover Alastair Farjeon's work?'

'Well, of course I am.'

'Then you must permit me to escort you. Tonight, if you are free. It will be a great honour.'

'Escort me? Tonight? Heavens, where?'

'To your Academy cinema. At midnight there is an all-night show of his films. An *hommage*. You did not know?'

'No, I didn't. Well, I hardly dare recall how long ago it was I stayed up all night, but this *hommage* is too important for me to miss. Monsieur Françaix, you have a date.'

The last of the sessions, that with Lettice Morley, was equally the briefest, in part because she had so impressively presented the case against herself in the commissary the day before and in part because she struck them all as far the least likely of the five suspects. Calvert's questions, then, were mostly routine, her answers no less so. She had seen what everybody else had seen and had reacted much as everybody else had reacted. It was, in fact, only when the proceedings were drawing to a slightly anti-climactic close that she added anything of value to her questioners' store of knowledge.

Just prior to that, however, there had taken place an odd little diversion. So monotonously repetitive had Evadne Mount begun to find the alternating sequence of questions and answers, she'd actually nodded off. "Nod" was indeed the word as, to Trubshawe's amusement, when doziness eventually shaded into unequivocal slumber, the novelist's head would tip over to left or right before at once jerkily righting itself. Then, a few minutes later, even as she was attempting almost manually to prop up her eyelids, it would happen all over again. And then again.

The fourth time it happened, she did somehow contrive to prise her eyes open before actually sitting upright. And what she saw at that instant, what proved to be directly in her line of vision, was a small wastepaper basket tucked away out of sight under Rex Hanway's desk. It was stuffed to the brim with assorted papers – presumably old letters, obsolete contracts, pages from rejected scripts and suchlike. On top of them all, though, poking out of the basket, was an oblong strip of paper, badly singed on both sides, which had clearly been ripped from a much wider sheet. Her sleuthial instincts stimulated by the sight of one of those trifling but, as invariably turned out to be the case, vital scraps of paper, discarded if not quite destroyed, which had so often figured in her own whodunits, she shot out an arm as deftly as an ant-eater its tongue, clasped the paper between her fingers and took a few moments to peruse it before sticking it unobserved (so she imagined) inside her handbag. Then she drew herself up erect on her chair and endeavoured to give her full attention to Calvert's interrogation.

'Come now, Miss,' she heard him saying, 'you must have been sickened, to put it mildly. A famous film director invites you down to his villa to discuss plans for his latest picture and then, without warning, attempts to – well, to ravish you. What respectable woman would not be sickened by such reprehensible behaviour?'

'At least in the film business, Inspector,' Lettice answered, 'only a very foolish woman would be sickened by it. A real namby-pamby. Oh, I see how shocked you are and, I assure you, it's not because I treat rape lightly. Yes, I repeat, rape. What Farjeon tried to do was rape – not, as you coyly put it, "ravish" – me. He tried to rape me, just as I'm certain he tried to rape Patsy Sloots. Unlike poor Patsy, though, I know how to handle men, especially when, considering Farje's reputation, I suppose I'd half-expected it to happen in the first place.'

'How *did* you handle him?'

'I tore myself away from his clutches – and, incidentally, tore a new and rather pricey Hartnell frock in the process – I ran from the villa, found a half-decent B & B in Cookham, where I spent the night licking my wounds, and caught the first train back to Town next morning. More or less in one piece.

'Naturally, after my rejection of him, I was convinced I was off the film – I had been Rex Hanway's assistant – and that I'd better start looking around for another position. Then I read, first, about the fire at Farjeon's villa and, three or four weeks after that, about Rex himself being assigned to direct *If Ever They Find Me Dead*. I rang him up and – not surprisingly, considering how long and how well we'd worked together – he offered me his own old job.

'So no, Inspector, to answer your original question, I was not at all devastated, as you put it, by Alastair Farjeon's death, for the reasons I've just given you.'

Sitting back in his chair, Calvert almost fondly contemplated her.

'Well, I think that's all I wanted to know. I'd like to thank you once more for coming in, Miss Morley. If I may say so, you've made a remarkable impression on us all. Almost unnerving. I only wish all the witnesses I'm obliged to question were as lucid and level-headed as you.'

'Well, thank you too, Inspector.'

She stood up and unaffectedly smoothed out her skirt.

'Goodbye, Miss Mount. Mr Trubshawe. It's been an interesting experience meeting you both. I do mean that.'

As soon as she had closed the door behind her, Trubshawe said:

'There's one young woman who's got her head screwed on tight.'

'She certainly has,' agreed Calvert. 'I've come rather to admire her. What say you, Miss Mount?'

'What say I? I say I need a drink. Especially if I'm going to spend the whole night watching pictures at the Academy Cinema.'

'Then, my dear Evie,' said Trubshawe, 'let me offer you, in the first instance, a lift back to Town, *mais naturellement*, and, in the second, a brace of double pink gins in the Ritz Bar.'

'Both offers, my dear Eustace, gratefully accepted.'

'Good, good. How are you fixed, Tom? You won't be needing a lift, I suppose?'

'No thanks, I've got my own car. But just let me say how grateful I am to you and Miss Mount for agreeing to participate in this little experiment of mine. Also for putting some very germane and' – he couldn't resist stealing a mischievous glance at Evadne – 'trenchant questions. What I would ask you to do now is let your minds dwell on everything we've heard this afternoon and, if and when you have any new ideas you feel you ought to communicate to me, please don't hesitate to ring me up. I meanwhile will let you know how things go at the inquest.'

'As a matter of fact,' said Trubshawe with an enigmatic half-smile, 'I fancy I already have an intriguing new slant on the whole case. If you've no objection, though, I'd like to let it simmer awhile before running it past you . . .'

Chapter Thirteen

To begin with, on the journey back from Elstree in the Chief-Inspector's Rover, neither he nor Evadne appeared to have much to say to one another. Yet, notwithstanding the policeman's phlegmatic temperament, coupled with his aversion ever to declaring his hand prematurely, doubtless a product of his years of service at the Yard, she couldn't help observing in his demeanour a barely repressed excitement that was most unlike the Trubshawe she already felt she knew of old.

'Eustace, dear?' she finally asked after having been driven by him in silence for about twenty minutes.

'H'm?'

'You're awfully quiet. There isn't something you're concealing from me, is there?'

'Yes,' he was forced to avow, 'there is. I swear to you, though, "conceal" isn't really the right word. All will be revealed when we get to the Ritz. I'd rather not talk about it and drive at the same time.' Then he added, 'But, Evie, what about you?'

'What about me?'

'Only that I have reason to believe you're concealing something too.'

'Am I?'

'I think you are. Out with it.'

'Out with what, pray?'

'You know what. Thought nobody noticed, did you?'

'Eustace, will you please stop speaking in riddles. If you have something to say, then for goodness' sake say it.'

'That scrap of paper you snatched from Hanway's waste-basket. Oh, you were very nimble, very sly. Quite catlike, in fact. But you didn't fool old Inspector Plodder. We're partners, aren't we? Is there any point in not letting me in on the secret?'

'No point at all,' she replied. 'Unlike you, I don't play Hide-And-Seek.'

Whereupon she opened her handbag, extracted the crumpled-up piece of paper and flattened it over her knees.

'Shall I read it out to you?'

'If you will.'

'All it says – and all of it, mark you, in block capitals – is: "SS ON THE RIGHT".'

The ex-policeman mulled this over.

'SS ON THE RIGHT, eh? SS ON THE RIGHT . . . It mean something to you?'

'Not yet,' Evadne prudently replied.

'Could be anything, anything at all. Could even be some sort of a code.'

'A code? Lawks Almighty, Eustace, I never thought I'd be

the one to make such a remark, but you've been reading too many detective stories!'

'A fine thing for you to say. If this were one of your who-dunits, that piece of paper would automatically – I repeat, automatically – constitute a crucial piece of evidence. I can just see it. SS ON THE RIGHT? Why, of course. Benjamin Levey! Since Levey only just managed to escape from Nazi Germany, obviously the SS, the Gestapo – what's left of it – is hotfoot on his trail.'

She took a moment or two to boggle at the absurdity. Then: 'Eustace?'

'Yes?'

'Keep your mind on the road ahead, there's a love.'

It was just after five o'clock when they entered the Ritz Bar. He escorted her to a secluded table, ordered, together with his own whisky-and-soda, the double pink gin he assumed she would have ordered for herself, in which assumption he was entirely correct, drew out his pipe and posed it on the table's ashtray, along one of whose four narrow grooves it lay, unlit, like a tiny black odalisque.

Then, once they had been served, once her glass had been clinked against his and each had echoed the other's 'Chin chin!', she turned to him and said:

'Well now, here we are. Time to tell me what's afoot.'

'Evie,' he said, leaning towards her as though resolved to thwart any passing waiter from even fleetingly eavesdropping on him, 'I believe I've got it.'

'Got what?'

'This afternoon, as I was listening to our suspects, I was also running over the case in my mind, tabulating all the salient points in what they had to say, and I had a sudden insight, one, I fancy, that stands a jolly good chance of bringing everything to a swifter conclusion than we ever dreamt possible.'

'Aha! Been thinking behind my back, I see.'

'Oh well, if you're going to be like that . . .'

'Forgive me, just my little jest. From what I gather, then, you've uncovered some kind of a major clue?'

'I have at that,' said Trubshawe, who found it hard to conceal the sense of gratifying trepidation peculiar to anyone gearing up to astound his interlocutor with a startling piece of news. 'A clue that, as they say in the films, is liable to crack this case wide open. At the very least, it will show Calvert that we old'uns still have an ace or two up our sleeves.'

'All right,' said Evadne Mount. 'My ears are all ears. Let's hear what it is you've got for them.'

'Well,' Trubshawe began, 'you would agree that, logically, only five people could have laced Cora's champagne glass with cyanide?'

'Aren't we forgetting ourselves?'

'What do you mean, forgetting ourselves?'

'You and I were also supposed to be suspects, were we not?'

'Evie,' he asked, assuming a mock-solemn expression, 'did you kill Cora?'

'No, of course I didn't.'

'Neither did I. I repeat, then, only five people are known to us to have been aware of the change that Hanway made to the script. Only five people therefore could also have known of the moment of opportunity during which it would have been possible, unobserved, to murder Cora. And given that no one else was about to drink out of that glass, there can't be any ambiguity whatever as to the identity of the murderer's predestined victim. Right?'

'Right.'

'I repeat yet again, only five people could have murdered Cora – and yet, as we discovered when we questioned them, not one of them had a conceivable motive.'

'Hold it there, Eustace,' Evadne pointed out. 'One of them – indeed, several of them – might have had a *secret* motive. A motive of which we're still unaware and which they were naturally averse to revealing to us.'

'Yes, I thought of that,' said Trubshawe. 'Yet my own personal conviction is that they were all telling us the truth – the truth, at least, about their relationship, or lack of it, past or present, with Cora. Nearly all of them, you remember, insisted that they'd never even met her before she turned up at the studio to start shooting the picture. Only Gareth

Knight knew her from the old days, when they'd trodden the boards together, and of all of them he was ostensibly the best-disposed towards her. I say ostensibly, because of course he could have been lying – but again, don't ask me why, I believed him.

'If that were not enough, they all had a very powerful professional motive for, so to speak, *not killing her* – for, as Hanway himself put it, keeping her alive. Farjeon's death had already dealt a near-fatal blow to *If Ever They Find Me Dead* and Cora's death will probably be the *coup de grâce*. Since the future of each and every one of those suspects was tied up in that picture, the last thing any of them would have wanted was to have a second, even darker cloud hanging over it.'

'Eustace dear, it gives me no pleasure to say this, sincerely it doesn't, but you haven't told me anything yet I didn't already know.'

'Be patient with me, Evie,' said Trubshawe, making a superhuman effort not to lose his own patience. 'I long ago had to learn how with you.'

'Sorry, sorry. Go on.'

'The fact is that all the evidence we heard either took us round in circles or else led us nowhere. Yet, despite the irrelevance of most of what they had to tell us, there was something I felt for the longest time without being able to pin it down, some underlying coherence or consistency, some mysterious thread running through the testimonies of everyone we questioned.'

'Then at last – it was when Françaix told us of the theft of his script – it struck me what that consistency was. At that instant I saw, as though in a flash of lightning, what I'd been groping towards.'

'Yes? What is it you saw?' she asked, by now almost as wound up as he himself was.

'I saw that the thread running through all their evidence was Alastair Farjeon. We were interrogating them about Cora and all they wanted to talk about was Farjeon. It was as though they weren't actually that interested in Cora. As though they couldn't understand the point of being asked about her. That's why I say I believed them when they claimed they had no earthly reason to commit the crime. As we all did, I listened *to* their protestations of innocence but what I found myself increasingly listening *for* was, in every instance, the almost offhand way they made that claim. *Of course* – each of them told us – *of course* I didn't kill Cora Rutherford. Meaning, she wasn't an important enough figure in my life to be worth killing.

'And did you notice,' he went on, swept up in the tide of his own momentum, 'did you notice how not one of them seemed to be nervous or shifty-eyed? Now, Evie, that just isn't natural, even when the suspects you're dealing with are innocent. You'll always find a trace of what we used to call at the Yard the Plain-Clothes Syndrome. People are nervous when they're being questioned by the police. Why? Because they're guilty? Not necessarily. Then why? Because they're being questioned by the police, that's why. For most people a police interrogation is such an ordeal, it's enough to make anyone nervous, guilty or innocent. It's exactly like blood pressure.'

'Blood pressure?'

'A doctor can never obtain an exact measurement of a patient's blood pressure for one very elementary reason: blood pressure automatically rises when it's being measured. Which is why, during interrogations at the Yard, we were always more suspicious of those who responded calmly to being questioned than those who were sweaty and jittery and never stopped shifting about in the hot seat.'

'But, Eustace, you're contradicting yourself. If, as you say, our five suspects all responded calmly, then logically that suggests we shouldn't trust any of them.'

'That's exactly what I do say. We should and we shouldn't.'

'Explain.'

'As far as Cora's murder is concerned, we *should* trust them. It was, I repeat, as though the question – "Did you murder Cora Rutherford?" – a question, I grant you, we never did actually ask, but they all knew that it was implied in well-nigh every question we did ask – it was as though such a question was just too foolish to be dignified with a serious answer, as the saying goes, like asking them if they'd poisoned Hitler in his bunker. But we *shouldn't* trust them further than that, for the very simple reason that, when they started talking freely about Alastair Farjeon, and none of them could resist talking about him, they all revealed something about themselves that made me realise just what slippery customers they potentially were. One of them, at any rate.'

'And what was it they revealed?'

The Chief-Inspector held himself back for a few seconds in order for his response to make the greatest possible impact on his listener.

'*That, if none of them had a motive for murdering Cora Rutherford, all of them did have a motive for murdering Alastair Farjeon.*'

'Alastair Farjeon?! But Farjeon wasn't murdered.'

'Oh, Evie,' said Trubshawe, unable to resist a smile of condescension, 'you disappoint me. Don't you ever read your own books?'

'No, of course I don't. Why should I? I know who did it!' she petulantly snapped back at him, slamming the statement shut with an audible exclamation mark.

'Just let me remind you, though,' she went on. 'Your young protégé Tom Calvert – "the most promising newcomer to the Force I ever came across", if I may quote your own assessment of his quality as a police officer – issued a statement to the press that categorically excluded any suspicion of foul play in the Cookham fire. And, by the way, what have my books got to do with the price of potatoes?'

'Come now, Evie, you're being unfair. Prior to Cora's murder, young Tom had no reason to suppose that there might have been foul play. And, as far as your books are concerned, I'd just like to remind you that, if this were one of your whodunits, the so-called accidental death of a character like Farjeon would certainly be regarded as suspicious by the reader. By Alexis Baddeley, too, if not, of course, by dependable, doddery old Inspector Plodder, Plodder of the Yard.'

'Sorry, Eustace,' said Evadne, 'but this is not one of my books. It's a case of real bloody murder, the murder, you seem to forget, of a very dear friend of mine. A human heart has ceased to beat, and I can't help feeling it's tasteless of you to compare Cora's murder with the sort I write about in whodunits whose sole ambition is to entertain my readers.'

'If you would just listen to me, instead of flying off in a rage,' a flustered Trubshawe replied, 'you'd realise that what I'm saying might actually help us apprehend Cora's murderer.'

'Oh, very well,' said the novelist ungraciously, 'continue with your exposition.'

'What I deduced, then, is that all five suspects did indeed have a motive for murder, except that it was for the murder not of Cora but of Alastair Farjeon, a man few of them took the trouble to deny that they cordially detested. And, just before we left Elstree, I went off to the Gents and scribbled down a quick list so that you'd be able to see at one fell swoop what I was getting at.'

He pulled from his pocket a neatly folded sheet of lined writing-paper and handed it over to Evadne Mount.

This is what she read:

POSSIBLE SUSPECTS IN THE MURDER OF
ALASTAIR FARJEON
AND THEIR POTENTIAL MOTIVES

Rex Hanway. Farjeon's death meant that he was free at last to make a picture on his own, an ambition he himself admitted he had waited many years to satisfy.

Philippe Françaix. Farjeon plagiarised his script of If Ever They Find Me Dead.

Lettice Morley. Farjeon attempted to ravish her in his Cookham villa.

Gareth Knight. Farjeon threatened to peach on him about his having served a sentence in the Scrubs for making indecent overtures to a young policeman in a public lavatory.

Leolia Drake. She knew that only if Farjeon were out of the way would she have a chance of playing the leading role in If Ever They Find Me Dead. (Or could she have been merely Hanway's accomplice?)

Evadne laid the sheet of paper down on the table between them and was about to speak, except that Trubshawe, who would have been less than human if he hadn't experienced a certain smug satisfaction in having managed to give her a taste of her own medicine, got in first by raising his hand to silence her.

'Before you answer,' he said, 'let me just add one crucial point. If, as I believe, Alastair Farjeon was murdered, then it finally gives us something which we have all been seeking in vain from the very beginning of this case.'

'What?'

'A motive for murdering Cora.'

They both spoke at the same time.

'Because Cora had found out who murdered Farjeon!'

'Because Cora had found out who murdered Farjeon!'

'Snap!'

'Snap!'

'Now,' said Trubshawe, taking triumphant note of what he imagined was the novelist's belated conversion to the cause, 'it's time for you to tell me what you think.'

He sat comfortably back in his chair, his glass of whisky in his hand, waiting for the inevitable accolade.

But Evadne's voice, when she spoke again, was not as encouraging as he had expected.

'We-ll . . .'

'Yes?'

'. . . ?'

'What? What is it you're trying to say?'

'Nothing, nothing at all. That is, I . . .'

'Out with it, Evie.'

'Well, Eustace, frankly I don't know.'

'What in Heaven's name is the problem?'

'The problem,' she said, 'is that my bottom itches.'

Trubshawe gaped at her in disbelief.

'Your bottom itches!' he cried out so loudly that not a few of those customers who were seated at nearby tables turned their heads to stare at them both.

'Yes,' she repeated in a half-whisper, 'my bottom itches. And I have to tell you, Eustace, my bottom has never let me down.'

'What the –' he spluttered incontinently. Then:

'Even from you, Evie,' he said in a low hiss, 'this is going too far.'

'No, no, let me explain,' she replied with dignity. 'Whenever I read a whodunit by one of my rivals, my so-called rivals, and I encounter some device – I don't know, a motive, a clue, an alibi, whatever – a device I simply don't trust, even if I can't immediately articulate to myself why I don't trust it, I long ago noticed that my bottom started to itch. I repeat, it's infallible. If my bottom ever once steered me wrong, why, the universe would be meaningless.'

'How is it you never mentioned this at ffolkes Manor?'

'Really, Eustace, my bottom is scarcely something I care to bring up in mixed company. Besides, we had only just met.'

'So you're telling me, are you, that you'd put your trust in your – in your bottom before you'd ever put it in me, and I'm not just a friend, a close friend, I hope, but also a police officer who spent his professional life investigating crimes of this nature?'

'Yes, Eustace, I know how odd it must sound. Yet, close friend as you assuredly are, I'm closer still to my own bottom, after all, and I've known it far longer than I've known you.

'It works even when I'm writing my own books. It'll sometimes happen that I'm dog-tired, I desperately want to finish a chapter and I botch it by lazily employing some whiskery, second-hand plot device. Then, sure as Fate, my bottom starts itching and I realise that I've just got to go back to the drawing-board and replace it with something cleverer and more original. Which, I may say, I invariably do.'

'You could have fooled me,' muttered a sullen Trubshawe.

'I find I usually do,' she countered airily.

His face crimsoned.

'I see. Now you're being nasty – nasty and gratuitous. Have a care, Evie, have a care. Two can play at that game.'

'Look,' she said, 'I readily admit that your theory is attractive, really very attractive, and for the moment I can't quite explain – except, of course, for the itch in my bottom – why I'm ill-at-ease with it.'

'You certainly seemed to share my excitement when I proposed that it at least provided us with a clue as to why Cora had been murdered.'

'True enough. Even now, that strikes me as by far the best

argument that can be made for it. It's just that, where those five suspects are concerned, well . . .'

'What?'

'Yes, they do all appear to have had motives for wanting to murder Farjeon, I grant you that. I just can't help feeling that some of those motives are a little – let's say – weak.'

'Oh. Which ones?'

'Leolia Drake's, for example. She's a putrid little minx, to be sure, but do you really believe she'd be ready to murder Farjeon – and not only Farjeon, remember, but poor Patsy Sloots along with him – just because, in the first place, she knew, or merely expected, that Hanway would consequently be assigned to direct *If Ever They Find Me Dead* and, in the second place, because she had total confidence in his authority to cast her in the leading role? I have to say I do find that a strain on my credulity.'

'We-ell,' the Chief-Inspector defensively replied, aware as he was that, with this particular suspect, he was on shaky ground, 'I did add a rider to the effect that she might merely have acted as Hanway's accomplice.'

'Even so, Eustace, even so. And Lettice. Now, I agree, she is, as the Yanks say, a tough little cookie. But, after all, Farjeon didn't actually succeed in having his evil way with her.'

'I can't see as that makes a ha'p'orth of difference. Don't forget that, if it was Lettice, she may not actually have meant to kill Farjeon. It may just have been her intention to give him the fright of his life. I wouldn't be too surprised if we were talking of manslaughter here.'

'And Philippe? A French film critic committing murder? I mean, literally. Difficult to swallow.'

'Oh, please, let's have no truck with such tired old generalisations. Put yourself in his position. All his adult life he had lived and breathed Alastair Farjeon. Farjeon *was* his life, the only life, in a sense, he'd ever known. And now here he was, instead of having to worship him from afar, finally at his side, not just as an admirer but, so he hoped, as a colleague. He had written a script he believed would be ideal for his favourite film director. And it *was* ideal – if it hadn't been, Farjeon would never have stolen it in the first place. He does steal it, though, and all of Françaix's dreams crumble to dust. Can't you imagine how he must have felt when it dawned on him that he had wasted his whole life on someone totally unworthy of his admiration. People have killed for less, much less, in my experience.'

'Possibly so . . . Yet, you know, Eustace, as you yourself pointed out, they tended to speak quite freely and openly of their loathing of Farjeon. Why would they have done that if they suspected that they themselves were, well, suspected of having murdered him?'

'But that's just it!' Trubshawe practically shouted at her. 'They *didn't* suspect! Nor *were* they suspected! It was Cora's murder we were investigating. Not for a second did they have any cause to wonder whether it might be advisable for them to hold their tongues about their relationship with Far-jeon. Anyway, as you of all people, the Dowager Duchess of Crime, must know, the subtlest way of insinuating that you didn't kill somebody is to claim that you wished you had.'

Evadne Mount reflected on this for a moment, then said simply:

'I'm not sure, Eustace, I'm not sure.'

'Why not? Mine is the only theory which even begins to explain why one of the five might have poisoned Cora. We have nothing else to go on.'

'Not quite nothing. What about my scrap of paper?'

'Oh yes? One of those obliging scraps of paper that your whodunits are littered with? Let's be serious, Evie. It hardly stands up against what I have to offer. You recall what Sher-lock Holmes said? "When you have excluded the impossible, whatever remains, however improbable, must be the truth."'

At this she released a sharp ejaculation.

'Pshaw, Trubshawe, pshaw! Devotee as I am of Conan Doyle, I've always thought that particular apothegm to be complete drivel. There exist lots of things in the world that are theoretically not impossible but extremely unlikely ever to be "the truth". Playing a perfect round of golf, for instance, by scoring eighteen successive holes-in-one. The fact that yours is, there's no denying it, the only theory so far – *so far*, Eustace – which adequately accounts for Cora's murder doesn't mean it's true.

'Actually,' she added, 'the more I think about it, the more

221

offensive I find it. So put that in your pipe and smoke it. If you ever do actually get round to smoking that filthy old pipe of yours.'

Trubshawe ignored this unwarranted calumny on his beloved meerschaum.

'Offensive?' he queried. 'You find it offensive? Now there, Evie, you've lost me.'

'Well, just consider. What you appear to be implying is not only that one of the five suspects murdered Farjeon but that Cora subsequently discovered the identity of that murderer and threatened him or her with the prospect of taking what she knew to the police. In other words, she set about blackmailing the murderer and got murdered herself for her sins.'

'No, no, no! Now you're extrapolating, wildly extrapolating. All I said was that Cora had acquired what would turn out to be a very dangerous piece of knowledge. Just knowing that she knew may have been enough for the murderer. I never once suggested that she sought to exploit the secret.'

'Not in so many words.'

'Remember how gleeful she was when she announced to us that she'd somehow contrived to have her part "bumped up"? Remember how cagey she then became when you asked her how she'd pulled it off?'

'There you are!' cried the novelist, who visibly did remember her friend's crowing complacency. 'What is it you're implying if not blackmail? Well, I won't have it,

Eustace. I won't hear a word against poor dear dead Cora. I insist that you retract these scurrilous insinuations of yours.'

'I say, dash it all, Evie, we aren't going to fight, are we?'

'That's entirely up to you. I simply won't have you trampling over Cora's memory with your flatfoot's hob-nailed boots.'

Trubshawe, however, instead of beating a retreat, as he would once have done, elected to pursue what he saw as his advantage.

'I'm sorry. I understand how sensitive you are about Cora's death, but I wonder if you aren't letting your friendship cloud your judgement. I, on the other hand, am free to speak my mind.'

'That shouldn't take long.'

'Now listen, Evie,' said Trubshawe with steely determination, 'I know you well enough to know how you can't tolerate being upstaged, to use Gareth Knight's word. Obviously, it goes against the grain for you to acknowledge that somebody else might be right for once or simply have got there first. In your books, you make d**ned sure Alexis Baddeley always defeats poor old Inspector Plodder and you've deluded yourself that it must happen like that in life. If this were one of your whodunits –'

'I wish you wouldn't keep saying that,' the novelist testily interjected. 'It's my line, not yours.'

'I'm right. I'm right about the case and I'm right about

you, too. I know it and I think you know it, except that you can't bring yourself to admit it. And do you know why you can't bring yourself to admit it? A classic case of sour grapes. You're jealous, Evie. You're jealous because, this time around, I've come up with the goods for a change instead of you. So all you can think to do is just sit there and be mulish.'

Now it was Evadne Mount's turn to splutter.

'What – what – what bally cheek! What a royal nerve you have!'

She trained a malevolent eye on Trubshawe.

'Jealous? Of you? If I had a single jealous bone in my body, it's certainly not you I'd be jealous of! But I don't, you hear, not one.'

'Oh, really?'

'Yes, really.'

'I think not, Evie. We both know that there's at least one person in this world you're jealous of. Her very existence has you positively a-twitter with jealousy.'

'And who might that be?' she asked with as much aplomb as she could muster at short notice.

'Who might that be?' he parroted her. 'I rather think it might be Agatha –'

He got no further.

'How dare you!' she spat at him. 'How *dare* you! As I'm a lady, I won't descend to raising my voice, but I must tell you, Eustace Trubshawe, that is an atrocious calumny which I shall find hard, mighty hard, ever to forgive.'

Only when it was too late to retract what he'd said did the Chief-Inspector understand that he'd gone too far, far too far.

'Look,' he blundered on, 'there's no – I mean to say, there's no shame in being jealous of the best? Am I right?'

Silence.

'Evie?'

Silence.

'Evie, please. I didn't really – after all, I was just trying to . . .'

Realising that he was making no headway, he fell silent.

So it was that they sat there for a moment, neither of them speaking, neither of them drinking.

When the novelist eventually did answer back, her voice was calm, unnaturally calm. It was the calm that follows rather than precedes the storm.

'Very well, Eustace. I can see that you have total confidence in your theory. Are you ready to put that confidence to the test?'

'Certainly I am,' answered Trubshawe, unsure where she was leading.

'Good. Now I am not, by nature, a betting woman, but I'm willing to make a wager with you if you are willing to accept it.'

'What kind of wager?'

'I'm willing to bet you that I will solve this crime before you do.'

'And if you don't?'

'Then I swear to you that the dedication of my very next whodunit will read: "To Agatha Christie, the undisputed Queen of Crime Fiction". There – how you say? – *voilà!*'

Trubshawe drew in his breath.

'You would do that?'

'If I lose, yes. Except that I won't. Well, do you accept the wager?'

'I absolutely do,' Trubshawe replied without hesitation, adding, 'And what will I have to do if I lose? Except that I won't.'

'If you lose,' she replied, 'you must agree to marry me.'

'Marry you!!??'

Once again the Chief-Inspector had spoken so loudly that two startled waiters, both of them bearing trays heaped high with empty glasses, only just averted a collision as their paths crossed in the middle of the bar. First an itching bottom, now a proposal of marriage. These two fossilised old dears – you could almost hear the whisper buzz around the room – perhaps weren't as superannuated as they looked.

'Have you lost your mind?'

'Not at all.'

'But why on earth would you want to marry me? This very afternoon we've done nothing but quarrel like – like –'

'Like an old married couple?' said Evadne Mount, deftly completing the phrase for him.

Suddenly, quite unexpectedly, she took his hand and squeezed it in her own.

'Come clean, Eustace. You're lonely. You can come clean, you know, because you've already done so. More than once. Well, now it's my turn. I'm lonely too. Terrifyingly lonely, if you really want to know. Why do you suppose I drop into this ridiculous hotel every day? Just in the hope of finding somebody to speak to – anybody, Eustace, anybody at all. And when, all those weeks ago, it was you I found to speak to, I can't tell you how thrilled I was. So thrilled that, for days afterwards, I was hoping – hoping against hope – that you would drop in again. Really I was. It was like some girlish fantasy – that you would pretend to have dropped in by chance and I would pretend to believe you. And because it was like a girlish fantasy, it made me feel young again, almost like a girl myself.

'Well, you didn't drop in. All those days I spent sitting near the door, glancing up at everybody who passed through it, hoping, praying, that this time it might be you, all for nothing. You never did make a reappearance. It probably never crossed your mind for an instant.

'But that wasn't going to stop me. Oh no, this was my last chance and, like Cora, I was willing to do anything, abase myself if need be, to grasp it. So I waited more or less patiently for the opportunity, for the excuse I needed, to present itself. And it finally did. Out of the blue, Cora rang me up, invited me to Elstree to watch her play her big scene and I invited you.

'And now I'm grasping the chance even more tightly by

proposing this wager. My calculation is that you're so bloody cocksure you'll solve the crime I doubt you'll risk seeming a coward by refusing to pick up the gauntlet. And if you're worried about – about, you know, S-E-X – well, you needn't be. We're both much too set in our ways, not to mention too old and creaky, for any of that tomfoolery.

'So, Eustace dear, what do you say? Are we on?'

Trubshawe looked her moistly in the eye.

'We're on.'

He then momentarily turned away, pleading a cinder in one of his eyelashes – a cinder as big as the Ritz itself! – and, after feigning to have removed it, added, 'But only because I know I'm going to win.'

'At my age, love, I've learned not to be too picky. So long as you accept the wager, I really don't care why.'

She cheerily rubbed her hands together.

'So – where are you off to next in your investigation?'

'Next?' said Trubshawe, drinking down his whisky-and-soda. 'Next I believe I'll go alibi-hunting. I'll consult with Tom Calvert and, perhaps, if we both put on our thinking caps –'

'Make a nice change from that tartan terror you always wear.'

'If Tom and I put our heads together,' Trubshawe repeated between gritted teeth, 'maybe we'll find out just what those five suspects of ours were up to on the afternoon of the Cookham fire. And you?'

'Me?' said Evadne Mount. 'I'm going to the Pictures.'

Chapter Fourteen

Trubshawe spent the whole of the next day following through his hunch in the company of Tom Calvert. The younger man had been intrigued by his theory that there might after all have been foul play at Cookham, sufficiently intrigued at any event to pay a series of semi-official calls on all five suspects in Cora Rutherford's murder. The results were conclusive, to put it mildly, and it was these results that the Chief-Inspector now felt obliged to relate to the novelist. Coupled with that obligation was of course his own devouring curiosity to find out what she herself had been up to in the meantime.

Until well into the afternoon, however, Evadne was unobtainable on the telephone, and the sole hint of where she had been and what she might have been doing there had been dropped by Lettice Morley, whom he and Calvert had interviewed just after lunch in her charming bijou flat in Pimlico. It appears that Evadne had rung her up early that morning with what Lettice described as a 'self-consciously vague' enquiry about film extras, who they were and how they were hired. Needless to say, this tantalising droplet of information only intensified Trubshawe's curiosity.

Later, towards five o'clock, when he had returned home to Golders Green, settled into his favourite armchair, a freshly brewed cup of tea at his elbow, and had just begun reading Cora's obituary in the *Daily Sentinel* – no fewer than three lavishly illustrated pages were devoted to her career, her matrimonial misadventures, her untimely death and, of course, the sensational circumstances surrounding it – his own telephone finally rang. He leapt up off the armchair to take the call. It wasn't Evadne herself, though, but Calvert, who had even more tantalising news of her doings to impart. She had rung him up just half-an-hour before to ask whether it might be possible for the Police Force to persuade Benjamin Levey to set up a screening for them of the 'rushes' – the word sat as oddly on Trubshawe's ear as on Calvert's tongue – that had already been filmed of *If Ever They Find Me Dead*.

'Good grief,' muttered Trubshawe, 'what's got into Evie now?'

'No idea,' replied Calvert. 'She simply asked me if I might use my influence.'

'Did she explain why she wanted to see the stuff?'

'No. I did ask her, as you can imagine, but she played her cards very close to her chest. All she said was that it was of the utmost importance that I grant her this favour.'

'And what was your response to that?'

'Well, Mr Trubshawe, it was, you recall, Miss Mount who, on the very day of the murder, was crafty enough to deduce that there weren't forty-two suspects to be account-ed for, just five. And, during those investigations that we conducted in Hanway's office, I must say she did ask some pretty pertinent questions – brutal but pertinent. And she's written all those clever whodunits – not that I've actually read any of them myself, you know, but she never stops telling me how clever they are. And she was, after all, a close friend of Cora Rutherford and she's also, of course, your friend too. And since you and I are – let's face it – getting nowhere fast –'

An impatient Trubshawe broke in.

'What you're saying is, you agreed.'

'To be candid with you, Mr Trubshawe, I couldn't see my way to refusing. I was struck, though, by something rather queer that she said. I asked her if, as I assumed would be the case, the scene she was keenest to watch was the one during which Miss Rutherford was murdered. Well, you can't imag-ine how she replied.'

'Tell me.'

'She shuddered – when your Miss Mount shudders, my goodness me, she does audibly shudder! – anyway, she shud-dered and said tartly that she had been called many things in her life but that she was no ghoul and, if there was one piece of film she never, *ever* wanted to see, it was that. Then I said, well, what? And she breezily answered that it was all one to her! Anything the studio could show her of the picture, she'd be glad to watch! Can you believe that?'

'Of Evie,' said Trubshawe, 'I've learned to believe almost anything. But it is, as you say, queer. Yet, despite her indifference to what would be served up to her, you still agreed to hold the screening?'

'I told her I couldn't make any promises and that it was ultimately up to Levey. But, after we ended our conversation, I did get on the 'phone to him. That man's as jumpy as a scalded cat – all those years of persecution in Nazi Germany, I suppose – and at first he was fairly reluctant. Said it was quite unheard-of to screen the rushes of a film to outsiders, which, to be honest, I can well believe is the truth. He asked me what precisely was the reason behind it, since there have been no prints made yet of the footage – his word – of Cora Rutherford drinking out of the poisoned glass. I told him just what Miss Mount had told me – that it was of no importance what she was shown – and even though he was as mystified as I was myself, he finally gave way. I rather think he feared it might attract my suspicion if he didn't.

'So I've arranged for a little private show tomorrow afternoon in one of the studio's screening-rooms. I thought you might want to be there.'

'Too darn right I would!' exclaimed Trubshawe.

'Ah . . .' said Calvert. 'So you feel she might be on to something, do you?'

'Pshaw!'

'What? Would you please speak up, sir? There seems to be some interference on the line.'

'I said, no. It's just Evie. She's got a bee in her tricorne as usual. But I have to tell you, Tom, I have a very pressing reason of my own for wanting to know where her train of thought might be leading her. I'll be there all right.'

'I hoped you'd say that. Here's the plan. We'll meet at the screening-room at three o'clock. Miss Mount will need a lift down to Elstree, of course, but she told me to inform you that, if by any chance you were thinking of contacting her first by 'phone, not to bother.'

'Well, that's delightful of her, I must say.'

'Instead, she proposed that you pick her up at her flat at two on the dot. *On the dot* – those were her words and she insisted I let you know they were in italics. Said you'd understand.'

'I do,' said Trubshawe. 'Oh, I do.'

'Good. Then we'll all four meet at three o'clock.'

'All four? There's you, me and Evie. Who's the fourth? Is Levey himself going to be present?'

'Levey's still in London, apparently, trying to salvage something from the wreckage of his film. No, at Levey's suggestion, I invited Lettice Morley. I realise she's one of the five prime suspects, if we really have the right to call them that, but she's an old hand at the cinema business and she'll be able to guide us through the thickets. You don't have any objection to her being there, I suppose?'

'Not at all. I can't see the harm in it.'
'Till tomorrow then.'

It wasn't until they had left the city behind them, and were already in the green heart of the countryside, that Evadne asked Eustace how his inquiries had progressed. She seemed, despite Cora's death, in remarkable spirits, even mildly elated. Her only just dormant cloak-and-daggerish instincts had been aroused with a vengeance and you could almost see her nostrils twitch like those of a hound on the scent of a fox.

Trubshawe, too, could almost see them twitch, which is why he had elected, apart from the odd and deliberately banal aside, to remain silent.

It was Evadne who finally spoke.

'Once again, for some reason, you aren't your usual pro-lix self.'

'Me, prolix? In your company? That's a laugh.'

'But you must know,' she went on, 'how desperately keen I am to learn how you fared with your enquiries.'

'Which enquiries?'

'Please, Eustace, don't play silly games with me. You told me yourself you were planning to check the whereabouts of all our suspects on the afternoon of the fire in Alastair Farjeon's villa. And when I spoke to Tom Calvert on the blower yesterday, he confirmed that you and he had spent the day doing just that.'

'Did he also tell you whether we'd had any luck?'

'Yes, he did.'

'Then why are you asking me?'

She gave him an affectionate tap on the knee.

'Poor Eustace, I know how disappointed you must be. And far be it from me to gloat, far be it from me to say I told you so, but . . . Well, if you're honest, you have to agree that . . .'

'You told me so.'

'Precisely.'

'You know, Evie,' said Trubshawe, 'you may be right, and you certainly did tell me so, but I just can't believe there isn't something fishy somewhere.'

'What do you mean?'

'Well, look, we spent the whole day yesterday asking them, all five of them, where they'd been at the time of the fire and with whom. And every single one of them had an alibi. It's just not normal.'

'Why ever not? You call it an alibi, but that's the policeman in you talking. It's the paradox of Scotland Yard. The more unbreakable somebody's alibi, the more suspicious you coppers become. But all it means, when you say that every single one of them had an alibi, is that every single one of them was somewhere else that afternoon, just as you were somewhere else that afternoon – with me, as it happens –

and I was somewhere else – with you, natch – and my late aunt Cornelia, God rest her soul, was definitely somewhere else, and millions, no, tens of millions of people up and down the country were somewhere else. Why should an alibi be inherently an object of suspicion?'

'Evie,' Trubshawe patiently replied, 'I was forty years at the Yard and I carried out investigations into I don't know and you don't care how many criminal cases, a few of them just like this one, with five or six different suspects, and I can assure you that not once – not once, do you hear – did every single suspect have an alibi. It's not the way these things happen. People don't recall any longer where they were on a specific day or night. Or else they went shopping, except that they chose to go by themselves, and why shouldn't they? Or else they took a stroll to clear their heads before turning in for the night. Or else they were doing a crossword puzzle or I don't know what. It just isn't normal for all five stories to click, for all five suspects to be able, more than a month after the event, to account for their movements not only with total exactitude but with witnesses to back them up.

'I tell you, Evie, if I had your bottom, it would be itching now!'

Silent and thoughtful, Evadne watched the road ahead as it gently swerved through the densely forested hills.

'What were these alibis that have put you in such a state?'

'Let me see. Philippe Français was in his hotel – in

Bloomsbury, it was – writing up notes for the last chapter of his book.'

'That hardly sounds like an unbreakable alibi to me.'

'I'm afraid it is, though. He was in the hotel bar, not in his own room. It seems he's got so accustomed to writing in cafés – these frogs, I'll never understand them – he prefers to work with lots of hustle and bustle around him. The barman remembers him well. Swears he never left his table all afternoon. Served him three black coffees and a cheese-and-pickle sandwich.'

'Hanway?'

'He attended a garden-party at the Palace, no less. And who do you imagine he escorted there?'

'Leolia Drake?'

'Right first time,' said Trubshawe. 'And they weren't just seen, they were photographed. They were even presented to Their Majesties. It's true that the do lasted upward of three hours. Yet I still can't see how either of them could have sneaked out of Buckingham Palace, motored down to Cookham, set Farjeon's villa alight and returned in time for dinner at the Caprice, where they were also seen and photographed.'

'What about Gareth Knight?'

'At a club in Soho with his so-called secretary. He wore a mask and never once removed his hat – it was some kind of wide-brimmed affair that covered most of his face – but there would appear to be no question he was present.'

'Wore a mask? Just what sort of a club was it?'

'A club for single men – really ought to have been closed down years ago. It was hosting an Ivor Novello *thé-dansant*, if you can believe it. Fancy-dress affair. Guests were asked to come disguised as characters out of *The Dancing Years* and *Glamorous Night*. When the owner of the club cottoned on to who it was we were enquiring about, he was so relieved he himself wasn't the chap Calvert hoped to throw in the jug that he shopped not only our own glamorous Knight but a couple of other picture actors as well.'

'Oh yes?' said Evadne, eyes aflame with prurient curiosity. 'Who?'

'Never you mind who. Let's stick to our own business, shall we?'

'Oh, very well. I'll worm it out of you later, you silly old stick-in-the-mud. What about Lettice Morley?'

'She was in hospital.'

'What? Had she fallen ill?'

'No. Her mother had just that day gone under the surgeon's knife. Lettice was at her bedside all afternoon. Even though the nurses admit they were more or less permanently on the go, they're all ready to vouch for her.'

'So where does that leave you?'

He shook his big heavy head.

'Up the proverbial gum tree. We have five suspects in one crime for which they all had an opportunity but no motive. And we have the same five suspects in another crime – or so

I truly believe – for which they all had a motive but no opportunity. It pains me to admit it, Evie, but the only person capable of breaking one, some or all of their alibis is Alexis Baddeley.'

'Very sweet of you to say so. Don't forget, though, there is at least one advantage to being faced with five separate alibis.'

'And what might that be?'

'It takes only one of them to crack for you to have your guilty party.'

This logical notion, which had never occurred to Trubshawe, cheered him up no end as they continued the pleasant drive down to Elstree.

The cosily raked and padded screening-room held, all in all, just three rows, counting four seats to a row. When Evadne and Eustace arrived, slightly late, both Tom Calvert and Lettice Morley were already present and making perfunctory attempts at conversation. Behind them was the projectionist's box; and behind the projector itself stood the projectionist, primed to start the film as soon as he had been given the nod by Lettice. Seated alone at the very back was the inevitable, ubiquitous Sergeant Whistler.

Once everyone else had settled in the front row, Calvert said to Lettice:

'Perhaps, Miss Morley, you'd like to explain what you're going to show us?'

'Of course, Inspector.'

Lettice stood up in front of the white screen.

'What you're about to see are what we in the trade call rushes – that's to say, different takes, shots, sometimes even entire scenes, which are printed up the night after they're filmed so that they can be viewed the very next day by the director. To give him at least a rough idea of how the film is progressing. Now you must realise that very little of *If Ever They Find Me Dead* was shot before the production was closed down. And I trust that none of you is expecting to see footage of Cora Rutherford drinking from the champagne glass, because nothing of that specific scene was ever printed.'

'We do understand that, Miss Morley,' said Calvert. 'Actually, I've already requested from Mr Levey a print of the scene you just mentioned – it may well aid me in my inquiry – but we know that's not why we're here today.'

'Very well. Now, just in case any of you are still unfamiliar with it, let me quickly summarise the plot of the film. It all begins inside a West End theatre, and the very first shot is of two young women in the audience, one of whom, indicating a man sitting three or four rows in front of them – and I should point out that no more than the back of his head is visible, either to her or to the audience of the film itself – whispers to her friend, "If ever they find me dead, that's the man who did it."

'Then we immediately cut to the young woman's Belgravia flat, where the police are indeed investigating her murder. Later in the plot, when the victim's friend, the character played by Leolia Drake, decides to do a little detecting herself, she chances to meet, at a dinner party, a good-looking older man who seems to fit the bill. That's Gareth Knight, of course. She starts flirting with him and, before she knows quite what has happened to her, she has genuinely fallen in love. And so it goes from there.

'The thing is, for all kinds of practical and budgetary reasons, we in the cinema business seldom shoot pictures in chronological order. The opening scene I've just described, for example, was never filmed, since we intended to shoot it at Drury Lane and we would have had to wait for the current show to finish its run. And, in fact, the particular scene you're about to see comes right at the end of the film. It's what we call a flashback – which is to say, it flashes back to an earlier moment in the plot so that the audience can better understand the events leading up to the crime. It is, in fact, the murder scene, the one in which the young woman we already saw in the theatre is stabbed on her own doorstep by an unknown assailant. He or she then snatches the young woman's key from her, quickly opens the door and drags her body inside – except that we never actually managed to get that far in the filming.

'That is, I think, all you need to know. No, sorry, there's one other thing. As I said before, these are rushes. By that I mean, they're no more than fragments, very imperfect fragments. Extraneous noises-off, no background music, all the flaws that would be cleaned up once the shoot itself was over. The projectionist tells me that just two takes of the murder scene were printed. Rex actually shot six, but four were discarded, one because the actress began walking too fast, another because the boom shadow was visible in the shot, a third – well, I can't any longer remember what the remaining problems were. I trust, though, that two will be enough for your purposes,' she concluded, resisting the temptation to add, 'whatever they could possibly be.'

She glanced at Calvert, who nodded back at her. Then she looked up at the projectionist's box and cried, 'Okay, Fred. Ready when you are.' Then she settled down in her chair at the end of the row.

The lights dimmed.

On the small white screen, after a few seconds of assorted squeaks, squawks and squiggles, there flashed up in front of them that universal emblem of the film-making process, the clapper-board. Holding it up to the camera's eye was an only just visible crew-member, who called out, '*If Ever They Find Me Dead*, Scene 67, Take 3.' Upon which, crisply snapping its two halves together, he vanished from the screen, carrying the clapper-board with him.

What that clapper-board had been obscuring was a snowy, nocturnal, totally deserted residential street along which a young fur-coated woman started to walk. At first only her own footsteps were audible. Then, gradually, insidiously, these were juxtaposed with another, heavier set, producing an effect not unlike that of listening to two percussionists beating drums independently of one another. The young woman shot a first, furtive glance behind her, but, there being no lamp-post located in the vicinity, could see virtually nothing. As she picked up speed, though, the second set of footsteps grew louder and therefore, by implication, closer. The young woman now broke into a run. She fumbled in her handbag, presumably in search of her keys, but it was only when she had reached her own front door, lipstick and powder-puff spilling out onto the snow-blanketed pavement, that she succeeded in retrieving them. With a trembling left hand she clumsily struggled to pull off her right-hand glove, whose furry lining prevented her from getting a grip on the door-key. By then, however, it was too late. His features eclipsed by his overcoat's turned-up collar, a tall, broad-shouldered man – or what certainly seemed to be a man – had silently stolen up behind her. Clapping his own left hand over her lips, he extracted with his right an ivory-handled dagger from his overcoat pocket and drove it deep into her throat. The screen went blank.

More squeaks, more squiggles. Clapper-board. Scene 67, Take 5. The same scene, verbatim, unfolded all over again.

Throughout the first screening – the first 'rush'? – Trubshawe had been just as alert, out of the corner of his eye, to Evadne's own facial expressions as to what was happening in the film itself. He had never seen her so caught up in anything as she was in the suspenseful little drama which had played out before them. And then, during the second one, he actually heard her murmur to herself – as usual with her, murmur loud enough for her neighbours to overhear – 'I knew it!' Then again, as the sequence drew to a close, 'Of course! Of course that's how it must have been done!'

What in heaven's name was she talking about? What was this *it* that she claimed to know? That's how *what* must have been done? Cora's murder? But the actress in the picture was stabbed on her own front doorstep in a empty street, whereas Cora was poisoned on a crowded film set! What conceivable connection could there be between the two? Where was the link? What on earth had Evie seen that he hadn't? Curse the woman!

The lights were raised again. Nobody spoke. Then Calvert, no less baffled as to the purpose of the exercise than Trubshawe, said:

'Well, Miss Mount . . .'

'Well, Mr Calvert . . .'

'What I mean is, was that of any use to you?'

'Let me put it to you this way, Inspector. I was certain before. Now I *know*.'

'Now you know what?'

'Now I know,' she said calmly, 'why Cora was murdered, how Cora was murdered and by whom Cora was murdered.'

Calvert made no effort to conceal his scepticism.

'Miss Mount, with all due respect, I have been extraordinarily tolerant of your unorthodox methods and manners, but even to my patience there's a limit. If you truly believe you know the murderer's identity, then let me have it at once.'

'Ah well,' said Evadne, 'there's a slight problem.'

'Why did I think there might be?' muttered Trubshawe to himself.

'The problem is that I cannot, here and now, *prove* what I know. I repeat, what I *know*.'

'For the Law, I fear,' said Calvert coldly, 'that's not a slight problem. An insuperable one more like.'

'However,' she carried on almost as though he hadn't spoken, 'if you, Inspector, are prepared to indulge me just once more, I shall, I promise, furnish you with all the proof you could possibly want.'

'Just once more, eh?' said Calvert warily. 'Well, what is it you want of me now?'

'I want you to summon all the suspects here at the same time tomorrow. Not in this screening-room, but on the film set itself. I want you to make it clear to them why they're being summoned – that I, Evadne Mount, know who Cora's murderer is and intend to reveal his or her identity to all to them at once. By all of them, I mean Rex Hanway, Gareth Knight, Leolia Drake, Philippe Françaix and, last but not least, Lettice here.'

'Not Hattie Farjeon?'

'No, not Hattie Farjeon. Not Levey either. Better not even mention the idea to Levey. Well, will you grant me this last favour?'

Calvert turned helplessly to Trubshawe. Their eyes met. The older man's eyebrows nodded.

'Very well, Miss Mount,' agreed Calvert. 'I shall see to it that all the suspects are here again at three o'clock tomorrow. But you had better be right.'

'Oh, I am, Inspector, I am.'

Whereupon she turned to Lettice Morley.

'Just for the record, Lettice dear, does the Gareth Knight character turn out to be the murderer?'

'You have all the information you need,' the young woman coolly replied. 'You're the sleuth. Figure it out for yourself.'

Chapter Fifteen

'If there were such a thing as reincarnation, I'm convinced I should return to earth as a sheepdog.'

Evadne Mount unfurled this mock-solemn introduction like a miniature red carpet, one that Trubshawe knew was likely sooner or later to be pulled out from beneath her audience of listeners.

There they all were again, the novelist herself and, arrayed around her in a seated semi-circle (the ideal configuration, as she well knew, for having one's every word hung upon), Trubshawe, Tom Calvert and the five suspects whom the latter had summoned at her request. There they all were, once more on the set of *If Ever They Find Me Dead*, its decor now gathering dust but not yet dismantled. Like some portly Sunday-School mistress, she faced them, sitting side-saddle, as it were, on a tall three-legged bar-stool, surrounded by the empty cocktail glasses and overflowing ashtrays which had been the props for Cora's big scene – a bigger scene, as it tragically transpired, than the actress had anticipated. High over their heads was the complex lighting gantry typical of a contemporary film studio, with its criss-crossing circuitry of lights and cables, pipes and planks. And standing watch at each of the four corners of the eerily echoing hangar was a uniformed policeman, straining not to appear too obviously on duty.

Until Evadne began to speak, when beckoned to do so by Calvert, no one had addressed a word, not even a casual, passing-the-time-of-day sort of word, to his or her colleagues. What protests there were, and they were mostly formulary, had been lodged the previous day when Calvert had initially mooted the idea of a climactic gathering. Not one of the five, however, had dared to counter with a categorical refusal.

To complete the slightly macabre tableau, there could just about be heard – was it from an adjacent sound set? or else from the commissary? – the raspy strains of a gramophone recording of Vera Lynn singing 'We'll Meet Again'.

'Yes,' the novelist reiterated, 'a sheepdog. For, in truth, there's nothing I seem to thrive on more than rounding up a flock of – no, no, my dears, don't be offended, I wasn't going to say "sheep" – rounding up a flock of witnesses and herding them back onto the scene of a crime. To be honest with you, the only thing which prevents me from enjoying this present experience as I otherwise might is the fact that the victim of the particular crime I've come here to solve was one of my very oldest chums.

'But now to our onions, as our friends across the Channel whimsically have it. I'm not sure whether Inspector Calvert has already told you what's behind this little gathering of ours, but I myself am prepared to put you in the picture without any further humming or hawing. You five are here for the simple reason that we seven would appear to be the principal – indeed, the only possible – suspects in the murder of Cora Rutherford.'

Needless to say, so characteristically blunt a statement of intentions provoked an immediate outburst of protestations.

'This is outrageous, quite outrageous!' spluttered Leolia Drake. 'I've never been so insulted in all my life!'

'Inspector, I insist,' asserted Gareth Knight, 'that these farcical proceedings be brought to an end at once.'

Rex Hanway meanwhile murmured an aside to Calvert:

'Surely not the dog-eared old cliché of the detective confronting the suspects at the scene of the crime? Inspector, I know how much faith you place in Miss Mount's abilities, but really . . .'

Evadne waved a conjuror's hand over them.

'Calm yourselves, ladies and gentlemen, calm yourselves. All I ask is that you hear me out.

'As you know, Cora was poisoned from drinking out of a prop glass of champagne – more accurately, a prop glass of sham champagne. She drank out of that glass because, just as the cast and crew broke for lunch, the film's director, Rex Hanway, came up with the clever idea of adding this little piece of business to the action, a piece of business of which only eight people were aware. Mr Hanway himself, naturally, since the idea had been his. Cora, just as naturally, being the first to have been told of it. Lettice Morley, Mr Hanway's assistant, who had to know everything he decided the instant the decision was taken. You, Mr Knight, because it was you, precisely, who were due to play the scene opposite Cora. You, Miss Drake, because you happened to be conversing with Mr Knight when Lettice informed him of the last-minute change. And Monsieur Françaix, Chief-Inspector Trubshawe and myself because we all lunched with Cora, who couldn't resist telling us about it.

'Nobody else, on the face of it, knew or could have known that she was about to drink from that glass, which means that nobody else knew or could have known that there existed an opportunity of lacing it with cyanide. That's why I say, calmly and dispassionately, that you – rather, we – are the sole suspects. No matter how one looks at the case, how one turns it around in one's mind, there can be no getting away from that bedrock fact of the matter.

'Or can there? That was the question that nagged at me the longer I pursued my investigation. I am, as I think most of you are aware, the author of countless best-selling whodunits and what I'm about to say may of course be no more than professional deformation, an extreme consequence of the dexterity with which, over the years, I've had to juggle convoluted storylines, eccentric motives and ingenious last-chapter and even, on a couple of occasions, last-page twists. Yet there's one thing I've always been profoundly sceptical of – being faced, as I seem to be now, with a set of suspects not one of whom is even a tiny bit more suspicious than any other.'

Whereupon, half-sliding off her stool, she attempted to scratch her bottom, a gesture which, discreet as it was, none of them failed to notice though only Trubshawe, naturally, understood.

'It never happens like that in my own whodunits,' she went on, awkwardly righting herself, 'and somehow I can never bring myself to believe that it happens like that in life either.

'There is, of course, the old chestnut of the least likely suspect. A long time ago, however, authors of mystery fiction realised that they had to move on from that primitive device. They understood that, if they were going to continue enthralling their readers, they would all have to give their plots one or two extra turns of the screw. In short, they'd have to find an escape-route out of the vicious circle that had begun to bedevil every conventional whodunit. After all, if – as tradition dictates, or used to dictate – the murderer is the least likely suspect, and if the reader is conversant with that tradition and expects it to be upheld, then the *least* likely suspect automatically becomes the *most* likely suspect and we have all, writers and readers alike, returned to square one.'

She fell silent for a few seconds to regain her breath. The

voice of Vera Lynn had long vanished into the ether and the only sound still to be heard was a faint creaking in the gantry.

It was at that moment too that, though reluctant to cut in, an increasingly restless Calvert exchanged a fretful glance with Trubshawe, who in return merely shrugged his shoulders, as though to say, 'Yes, yes, I know, but I've been here before and, trust me, she'll get there in the end.' Whether Calvert actually did thus interpret the shrug, he nevertheless chose to give the novelist a little more leeway, while Trubshawe himself, accustomed as he was to Evadne's tendency to digress from the subject, nevertheless started to think, with scalp-scratching puzzlement, that this time she really was pushing it.

From the five suspects, meanwhile, probably relieved above all that she hadn't yet got round to pointing an accusatory finger at any of them, there came nary a peep.

'As I was saying,' she went on, 'we whodunit writers who began to feel the need to adapt to changing tastes were obliged to approach the genre from an entirely new angle.

'Consider, for example, one of my more recent efforts, *Murder Without Ease*. If you've read it, you'll doubtless recall that, rung up by some local Squire in the first chapter, the Somerset police discover a young Cockney tough lying dead in his orchard. It turns out that he and his accomplice had been caught red-handed that very morning, at the crack of dawn, in the act of burgling the house. The irate Squire had grabbed the nearest shotgun and, without really meaning to, killed the young Cockney tough, whose pockets were indeed found to be stuffed with wads of bank-notes removed from the wall-safe in the library. It was, however, the accomplice who had made off with the real prize, a priceless Gainsborough conversation piece.

'As always in my books, I'm afraid, the police are content to swallow whatever dubious evidence has been dangled in front of their noses, without even troubling to give it a good sniff, and set about questioning the usual East End riffraff. As always, too, Alexis Baddeley – she's my regular sleuth, you know – Alexis Baddeley smells a rat. So she cunningly ingratiates herself with the Squire, learns that he's been taking a number of sea-plane trips over to Le Touquet, where he's been losing heavily at baccarat, and ends by proving that there never was an accomplice.

'It was the Squire himself, you see, who had already passed the allegedly stolen Gainsborough on to a fence. It was the Squire himself who had hired the Cockney tough to *go through the motions of burgling the house*, with the promise, naturally, of divvying up the insurance payout between the two of them. And it was the Squire himself who had shot down the hapless young rascal in cold blood while he was making his so-called "escape".'

She scanned her silent, captive audience.

'Now why do I tell that story?'

'Yes, why?' Trubshawe, if not yet at the end of his tether,

then as close to the end as made no difference, couldn't help responding.

'I'll tell you why,' she boomed out to the rafters. 'Though, in my whodunit, the police, investigating what they imagined to be a straightforward case of theft, deluded themselves that they had an adequate line-up of suspects, it was Alexis Baddeley alone who came to understand that the guilty party belonged to a whole other category of suspect – just as I've also come to understand must have been the case here.'

She raised her voice a notch or two higher still, even though in the empty studio it was already more than loud enough.

'In *Murder Without Ease* the criminal was not simply the least likely suspect from among the seven or eight under investigation. He was, rather, somebody who, until the book's penultimate chapter, was not even regarded as a suspect at all. And that, I submit, has been equally true of this crime. For, in reality, you five were all no more than mere pawns – either unwitting pawns or, as I believe, in one individual case what you might call a witting pawn – in the lethal game of chess which has been played out inside this studio and over which, from the very beginning, has loomed the real mastermind.

'That said, the time has now come for me, as promised, to announce to you all the identity of that mastermind, the murderer of Cora Rutherford –'

Before she could utter another word, Lettice Morley, her coltish features livid, warped out of shape, rendered almost ugly, suddenly leapt to her feet and made a demented dash in Evadne Mount's direction. At first, the others, suspects and detectives, could do no more than goggle at her. And she seized that moment of dazed inaction to grasp Evadne by both her shoulders at once, giving her so violent a kick in the small of her back that it sent her sprawling over the wire-entangled studio floor.

A split-second later, the young assistant jerking her own body backward as swiftly as the elderly novelist's had been propelled forward, a gigantic arc-light came plummeting down from the gantry. Hitting the ground with a window-rattling crash, practically at their feet, completely crushing the stool on which the novelist had been delivering her tirade, it exploded into a thousand glinting fragments.

For a few moments nobody moved. Then, slowly picking herself up, agitatedly dusting slivers of glass and metal off her clothing, too shocked at first to react, too winded to speak, Evadne stared with disbelief at the smouldering debris.

'Great Scott Moncrieff!' she croaked. 'That was meant for me!'

She turned to face Lettice Morley. Resembling nothing so much as a half-naked infant who has just scampered out of the freezing ocean and waits to be enveloped by her mother in a thick warm towel, the latter stood pale and shivering in front of her.

'Lettice! My dear, dear girl, you saved my life!'

Without responding, Lettice pointed shakily at the gantry. 'Look! Oh my God, look!'

Gazing up, they were all confronted by a hair-raising spectacle. With a velvet fedora pulled down low over the forehead, a creature enveloped in a long black cape, a cape so voluminous it was impossible not merely to know who the creature was but to which gender it belonged, was attempting, with the coiled tensity of a trapped wild beast, to forge a path across the intricate web of cables and planks.

'There's your murderer, Inspector!' cried Evadne.

'Get going!' Calvert immediately shouted at his men. 'Now, now, now! Make sure all the doors are locked! This is one villain who won't slip through our fingers!'

And the four uniformed policemen were just about to carry out his orders when a chilling sound arrested them all at once, just as it arrested everybody else on the set.

It was a scream. A scream the like of which none of them had ever heard in their lives. An androgynous scream, paradoxically both basso and falsetto.

The individual in the black cape had caught one foot in the narrow gap between two iron girders – struggled to prise it loose – tugged at it – tugged at it again and again, more and more frantically – then gave it one last desperate tug, a tug that did finally release the foot but also caused the creature itself, for one agonising instant, to career helplessly above their raised heads – until, arms outstretched like a

256

pair of giant bat-wings, it toppled over altogether and, with a second and even more nightmarish scream, came plunging down towards them.

Everybody scrambled out of its way as it hit the cement floor with a bone-crunching splatter.

Lettice Morley screamed, Philippe Françaix blanched, Leolia Drake all but swooned into Gareth Knight's arms.

Seconds later, Calvert and Trubshawe together approached the silent, shapeless mass; but seeing Calvert momentarily hesitate, it was Trubshawe alone who knelt down in front of it. Bracing himself, he gently turned the body face upward. Even he, however, no stranger to the horrors routinely encountered in a policeman's round, couldn't help recoiling from the sight that met his eyes.

The face that he looked upon had been pulped to a bony, bloody mash by the impact of such a landing from such a height. Yet there could be no doubt at all as to whom that face had once belonged.

Chapter Sixteen

'Alastair Farjeon?!' exclaimed Trubshawe. 'Now how, Evie, how in the name of all that's holy did you know that Farjeon was the murderer? Or even that he was alive?'

Cora Rutherford's funeral had taken place that morning in Highgate Cemetery. Graced by the presence of several of the same stage and screen luminaries who had attended the Theatre Royal Charity Show with which the whole case had started, as well as by all four of Cora's ex-husbands, not excluding the Count who didn't count, it was a lavishly solemn affair, of which, dead and buried as she was, the actress herself remained somehow the life and soul. Under her veil Evadne shed copious tears, while even Trubshawe had to remove the odd cinder from his eye.

And so the novelist and the policeman had come full circle, back again at the Ivy, if now in the company of Lettice Morley, Philippe Françaix and young Tom Calvert. Rumour of Evadne Mount's triumph had already spread through London's Theatreland and she herself, on their arrival at the restaurant, had further contributed to the attention their party received by plucking her tricorne hat from her head and sending it spinning across the room straight onto one of the curlicued hooks of a tall oak-wood hat-rack. (It was a trick she had tirelessly practised at home many years before and, if she'd been challenged to perform any other such trick with the same hat, she would have been incapable of complying. In this she resembled the kind of prankster who, totally ignorant of pianism, has nevertheless mastered by rote a single Chopin Nocturne.)

Instead of answering Trubshawe's question, Evadne said only:

'First, I'd like to propose a toast.'

She raised her glass of champagne.

'To Cora.'

Then, after everyone had echoed her, the Chief-Inspector turned to the friendly nemesis who had once more outsmarted him.

'We're all waiting, Evie,' he said. 'Just how *did* you arrive at the correct solution?'

'Well . . .' the novelist hesitated, 'where should I begin?'

'At the beginning?' Lettice pointedly suggested.

'The beginning?' she mused. 'Yes, my dear, that usually is the most sensible place. But it begs the question – where *does* our story begin?

'The problem with this crime is that, unlike the one at ffolkes Manor, where there was, or appeared to be, a plethora of suspects and motives, here, for the very longest while, there were neither. It was only when Eustace and I took a few steps backward in time that we finally took our first significant step forward, if you take my meaning. It was only at that point that the case began to make any real sense.

'It's a problem that dogs numerous whodunits,' she continued, oblivious of her listeners' wistful hope that, for once, she might elect to stick to the business at hand, 'even, I confess, a few of my own. In real life, the seed of virtually every serious crime, not only murder, is sown long before the performance of the act itself. Yet it's one of the cast-iron rules of the whodunit, a crucial clause in the contract between writer and reader, that a murder be perpetrated, or at the least attempted, within the first twenty or thirty pages of the book. To leave it to the halfway mark would be a serious test of the reader's patience. In fact, were this one of my own whodunits, my readers would probably have wondered, around the hundredth page, if there was ever going to be a murder committed to justify the illustration on the book's cover.

'Moreover,' she added, 'I myself would never dream of making the victim the detective's best friend and confidante, someone with whom the reader is likely to have identified, as you critics put it.'

She turned to Philippe Françaix.

'It would be like casting a major star in a picture and having her killed off in the first half-hour of the narrative.

Not done, simply not done. That's one challenge not even Farjeon would ever have dared to set himself.

'But enough of generalities. Let's turn to Cora's murder itself. If we assume, as we all initially did, that it represented the beginning of our story, then it was a totally meaningless crime. Even though five of those present on the film set – Rex Hanway, Leolia Drake, Gareth Knight, you, Lettice, of course, and you too, Monsieur Françaix – had the opportunity of slipping poison into her champagne glass, not one of them, not one of you, had anything which bore the remotest resemblance to a motive.

'No, it was soon obvious to me – and to Eustace, too,' she hastily added, 'that Cora had, if I may put it so, entered in the middle of the *real* crime, just as we all enter a picture palace in the middle of the picture.

'It was, in fact, Eustace who first had the idea that there might exist a link between Cora's death and Farjeon's. He went even further, proposing that Cora was the *wrong victim*. In other words, if one chose to regard Farjeon's death as having not, after all, been the tragic accident everyone had always presumed it to have been, then clearly each of the same five suspects I've already mentioned had a much stronger motive for murdering him rather than her.

'Hanway, because he almost certainly knew that, once Farjeon was out of the way, he would be given the chance to take over the new picture himself. Leolia, because she was Hanway's mistress and had been promised the leading role in any film he would direct. Knight, because, as he told us himself, Farjeon was more or less blackmailing him over his unfortunate encounter with' – she couldn't resist shooting a mischievous glance at Calvert – 'an attractive young bobby. You, Lettice, because Farjeon had tried to rape you. And you, Philippe – may I call you Philippe, by the way? Given all that we've been through together.'

'But yes,' replied the critic with Gallic gallantry. 'I would be most 'onoured.'

'Thank you. I continue. You, Philippe, because Farjeon had coolly lifted your plot for *If Ever They Find Me Dead.*'

She wetted her lips with another sip of champagne.

'Simple as ABC, or so it seemed. Except that, as poor Eustace was soon to discover, every one of these suspects had an alibi for the time of Farjeon's supposed murder.

'And there you have the fundamental paradox of the case. The same five people who had an opportunity to kill Cora, but no motive, all had a motive for killing Farjeon, but no opportunity. So that led us strictly nowhere.

'Yet, misguided as it was, Eustace's ingenious insight did at least serve one useful purpose.'

'Well, thank you for that, Evie,' the Chief-Inspector neatly intercepted.

'It pointed me in what would ultimately turn out to be the right direction. For it made me realise that the beginning of this story had, as I say, occurred a long time before Cora's murder.

'As we pursued our investigation, the name which kept coming back to us was Alastair Farjeon. It was around him that everything seemed to revolve. Even more curiously, the case actually began to resemble one of his own films – especially for Eustace and me. It so happened that it was on the very night of my hoax whodunit at the Haymarket that I had the disagreeable task of breaking the news of his death to Cora – a perfect example of the "twist beginning" for which Farjeon himself had always had a penchant.

'Alastair Farjeon . . .' she murmured. 'That name, a name we barely knew before Cora spoke to us about him, would end by seeping into every vacant pocket of our lives. "Farje this", "Farje that", "Farje the other" – that's all we ever seemed to hear when we set about questioning our five suspects. As Eustace pointed out to me, they all had much more to tell us about Farjeon than about Cora, notwithstanding the fact that it was Cora, not Farjeon, whom they were suspected of having murdered.

'I felt increasingly that, if I hoped to get to the bottom of Cora's murder, it would be necessary for me to understand the psychology of this individual whom I had never met but whose name kept popping up with such astonishing regularity in our investigations. Yet, familiar as I couldn't help becoming, if only posthumously, with the man – with his obesity, his arrogance, his overweening vanity – there was one side to him of which I remained woefully ignorant. I had seen practically none of his films.

'Why did that fact strike me as so important? Well, as I know better than most, there exists no more powerful truth serum than fiction. Though novelists – and, I am certain, film directors as well – may believe that everything in their work is a pure product of their imagination, the truth, the truth about their own psyches, their own inner demons, has an insidious way of infiltrating itself into that work's textures and trappings, just as water will always find the narrowest crack in the floorboards, the tiniest of fractures, by which it can then drip down into the flat underneath.'

She herself was now thoroughly enjoying, positively basking in, her discourse. And so resonant was her voice that, even if she imagined she was communicating exclusively to her lunch companions, a number of diners at adjacent tables could already be observed, knives, forks and spoons arrested in mid-mouthful, eavesdropping on her every word. Soon the whole of the Ivy, waiters and kitchen staff included, would be following, point by point, the broad lines of her reasoning.

'So,' she went on, nobody caring or daring to interrupt her, 'when Philippe told me that the Academy Cinema had organised an all-night screening of Farjeon's films, I forthwith hot-footed it to Oxford Street with him and watched as many of them as I was capable of staying awake for.'

'And what conclusions did you draw?' enquired Tom Calvert.

'It was, I must tell you, an extremely illuminating experience. Superficially, each of Farjeon's films may seem to resemble lots of others of the same ilk. Yet detectable in all of them, like a watermark on a banknote, is what I can only describe as a self-portrait of their creator.

'And what an inventive, what an audacious creator he was! In *An American in Plaster-of-Paris*, for example, there is one terrifically flesh-creeping scene in which the hero, a young Yank who has been confined to a wheelchair, starts to wonder what his sinister upstairs neighbour might be up to. Well, what Farjeon does is have the plaster ceiling of the Yank's flat become suddenly transparent, as though it were an enormous pane of glass, so that we in the audience can actually see what he suspects his neighbour is doing.

'Or *How the Other Half Dies*, which, according to Philippe, is regarded as one of his most brilliant thrillers. I watched only one of them, but did you know that he actually filmed three separate versions of the same story? I say "separate". In reality, the three films are all identical save for the last ten minutes, at which point a totally different suspect turns out to be the murderer. And each of the three solutions makes just as much sense as the other two!

'There's a marvellous scene, too, in his espionage thriller *Remains to be Seen*, a scene that contrives to be both gruesome and funny, like a lot of his work, when I come to think of it. A half-dozen archaeologists are posing for a group photograph at the site which they're about to excavate and the photographer requests them all to say "cheese", or whatever its Egyptian equivalent might be, just before darting under – you know – that black cloak thingie draped over the tripod. And there they all stand – smiling – and smiling – and smiling – until, but only after three or four minutes, which is, I can tell you, an excruciatingly long time to wait, not just for the archaeologists on the screen but for the audience in the cinema, until the camera – tripod, cloak and all – topples over in front of them and they discover that the photographer, dead as the proverbial doornail, has a dagger stuck between his shoulder-blades!'

Whereupon she herself speared a crab-cake, deftly sliced it into four equal quarters, forked one quarter into her mouth, chewed on it for a few seconds, washed it down with champagne, swallowed hard and was ready to continue.

'After watching several of Farjeon's pictures back-to-back, I began to have an even more vivid image of the man than we had been vouchsafed by all the interviews we conducted with those who might possibly have had a motive for doing away with him. What I saw, above all, was the pleasure he took in devising ever more extreme methods of killing off his characters, methods which were almost like practical jokes, cruel, callous pranks. His brain seemed to be galvanised by evil – only then was he truly inspired. When it came to scenes of violence, murder, even torture, the scenes which were his stock-in-trade, there was absolutely no one to beat him.'

'Ah, but you have reason to say what you say, Madame!' Françaix excitedly broke in, like an actor who has just received his cue. 'It is what I call in my book "the Farjeonian touch". His camera, it is like a pen, no? Like – how we say? – a *stylo*?'

'A *stylo*?' Evadne dubiously repeated the word, with a frown of distaste for foreign phraseology. 'Well, perhaps. Though that's a bit – how we say? – far-fetched, is it not?'

'But see you, Mademoiselle,' said Françaix, shaking his head, not for the first time, at the intellectual conservatism of the English, 'all the best ideas must be fetched from afar.'

'In any event,' she went on, averse as ever to interruptions when in full flight, 'following my session at the Academy, I asked Tom here to arrange for us to be screened some rushes, as they call them, from *If Ever They Find Me Dead*. Rushes which were, as it handily turned out, of the scene in which the heroine's young female friend is murdered on the doorstep of her Belgravia flat.'

'I have to confess, Evie,' said Trubshawe, 'that that's when you had me really confused. You were watching the scene not just with your eyes but with your whole body, and I simply couldn't understand why. Cora, after all, had been poisoned on a crowded film set, while the woman in the picture was stabbed in a deserted street. I spent the whole night racking my brains to grasp what connection you were trying to draw between the two crimes. Now perhaps you'll explain.'

'There's nothing to explain,' said Evadne calmly. 'I was drawing no connection whatever.'

'But you were studying the murder so closely, so intently, as though it had just given you a clue to Cora's.'

'Nothing of the kind. I wasn't studying the murder at all. I wasn't looking at the murder. The murder was irrelevant.'

'You weren't looking at the murder?' cried Trubshawe, his brow furrowing perplexedly. 'What in heaven's name were you looking at?'

'I was looking at the camera,' came the unexpected reply.

'The camera? What camera? There was no camera.'

'No camera? Eustace dear, what are you talking about?' she answered, with a queer little titter.

'How can you possibly say,' she went on as patiently as though addressing an infant, 'that there was no camera when the picture wouldn't have existed in the first place without one?'

'Oh, as to that,' the policeman grudgingly conceded, 'I'll grant you. But, well, it's not up there on the screen. It – dash it all, it's what the pictures on the screen come out of. So, by definition, it's not something you can see.'

'Not literally, to be sure. If you learn to look at films the way I've just been doing, though, you'll certainly start to see the *presence* of the camera. It's not unlike a jigsaw puzzle. After finishing a hundred-piece puzzle, one can't help but briefly see the world too, all curvily, squirmily snippeted, as a gigantic jigsaw. Well, after watching a handful of Farjeon's films, I couldn't help seeing the world exactly the way he saw it.

'So perhaps you were right after all, Philippe. Perhaps it is appropriate to compare a film camera to a pen.'

While listening to her, the Frenchman had drawn out his own fountain pen and now frantically scribbled some cryptic notes on the linen tablecloth.

'You mean,' he said, his always moot fluency in English starting to desert him, 'ze director of a film is a kind of – how you say? – autoor? Like ze autoor of a book?'

'The author of a book? Ye-es, I suppose you could put it like that,' was the novelist's guarded response, 'though it does sound more convincing when you say it, Philippe, French as you are. But yes, indeed, the director – or, rather, this one director, the late Alastair Farjeon, both lamented and unlamented – was indeed ze autoor of his films.

'Exactly like one of your villains, Eustace, Farjeon always had recourse to the same methods, always displayed the same little tics and tropes, quirks and quiddities, whatever the subject-matter. Which is why I wasn't at all particular as to the nature and content of the rushes we were to have screened to us. And why, when I watched that one scene from *If Ever They Find Me Dead*, what I saw – what, I assure you, I simply couldn't help seeing – in fact, I'd go so far as to state that it was *all* I saw – was not the murder itself – frankly, I doubt that I could any longer offer you a detailed description of how it was committed and I am, of course, celebrated for my powers of observation – not the murder itself, I repeat, but the *style* in which it was filmed.

'Consider, for example, the manner in which the camera follows the young woman along the lonely dark street.

True, it's the sort of thing we've all seen in lots of other thrillers, except that here, subtly, almost imperceptibly, the pacing of the scene begins to change as we hear the second set of footsteps and we understand with a deliciously queasy sensation that the street is suddenly no longer quite as lonely as it was, no longer quite so reassuringly deserted. The camera, a camera as fluid and flexible as a human eye, is, before our own eyes, actually, gradually, ever so artfully, *turning into* the murderer. So that when, for the first time, the woman looks round nervously, we realise with an inward groan – and indeed, speaking for myself, with an outward groan – that it's not just the camera lens she's looking into but her future murderer's face. It's as though she *recognises the camera*, as though, ultimately, it's the camera itself that murders her.

'It was at that instant that I knew there was only one man in the world who could have directed that specific scene in that specific style – whether or not he himself had actually been on the film set when it was being shot, whether or not he himself had actually had any direct contact with the actors or the cameraman – I say again, there was only one man in the world who could have done it, and that man was Alastair Farjeon.'

'Meaning . . . ?' said Tom Calvert, speaking in a voice that was to a whisper what a whisper is to a shout.

'*Meaning that Farjeon was alive*. He had not perished in the fire at Cookham and he had certainly not been murdered.

I'm sorry, Eustace, yours was a nice, neat theory – a nice, neat theory *in theory* – but I'm afraid it simply didn't stand up. Alastair Farjeon, not Rex Hanway, was the man who directed *If Ever They Find Me Dead*. Just as Farjeon was a murderer, not the victim of a murder. It was he who killed Patsy Sloots, just as it was he who later killed Cora – by proxy, as we shall see – and yesterday afternoon tried to kill me.'

Tom Calvert was the first to speak.

'My dear Miss Mount,' he said, 'I really must congratulate you!'

'Thank you so much, young man,' replied the novelist with a smile. 'But do call me Evie.'

'Evie. But, tell me, you who know everything, did you never entertain the possibility that Hanway had simply imitated Farjeon's style?'

'Never. If there's one thing I've learned in my thirty years as a much-acclaimed author, it's that the style of an artist, an authentic artist, can never be successfully imitated by someone else. Never, never, never. Many have tried, all have failed.'

'Then who really did die in that villa in Cookham – along with Miss Sloots, I mean?'

'Oh, once I'd guessed that Farjeon was still alive, it was child's play working out how he'd managed to fake his own death.'

'Since none of us *is* a child,' muttered Trubshawe, 'you're still going to have to spell it out.'

'It was one of his doubles, of course.'

'His doubles?' queried Calvert. 'What doubles?'

'The very first thing Cora told Eustace and myself about Farjeon was that the man's ego was such, he invariably introduced into the storylines of his films a scene in which a double – I mean someone, an extra, who looked exactly like him – would make a brief cameo appearance. It became such a trademark conceit, conceit in both senses of the word, that his fans would actually start looking out for it.

'Doubles . . . Extras . . . I couldn't get those two words out of my head. I became so intrigued by the notion that there might have been a *double* Farjeon, an *extra* Farjeon, that I immediately determined to find out what I could about these stand-ins of his.

'It was from Lettice that I obtained the West End address of an agency which specialised in the hiring of film extras and, in the hope of learning whether any of those who had ever played Farjeon's doubles had lately gone AWOL, I trooped along to an insalubrious back street in Soho, one of those corkscrewy little cul-de-sacs whose houses seem to be leaning out of their own windows.

'Well, what do you know, it actually did transpire that a certain Mavis Harker, wife or ex-wife of Billy Harker, I never quite gathered which, had recently been nagging the agency for news of her husband. Not that she was pining for the poor chump, exactly, but she admitted to being on her uppers and in dire need of an influx of ready cash.

'Billy, it seems, had launched his career in the show business as a music-hall juggler. Then, before seriously putting on weight, he reinvented himself as the Great Kardomah, an Arab tumbler, whatever that is. Then, when the onset of the War led to the closure of most of the theatres on the variety-hall circuit, like many of his type he started to eke out a precarious living as a film extra. And it was then, to the teeth-gnashing chagrin of Mrs Harker, that he vanished off the face of the earth.

'The agency had a photograph of him in its files, a photograph they allowed me to take a peek at. I knew in advance, of course, pretty much what to expect. Still, when I found myself face to face with the chubby jowls, the pouty little mouth and the triple-layered chin of you know who, you could have knocked me down even without the proverbial feather. Harker was the spitting image of Farjeon, whose stand-in he'd been in *The Perfect Criminal* and *Remains to Be Seen* and who, I was informed, had been hoping for a repeat engagement in *If Ever They Find Me Dead*.'

'So,' asked Lettice, 'what do you believe happened at Cookham?'

'We'll know the whole truth only when Mrs Farjeon, who, as I shall demonstrate, was party to the scheme, is questioned at the Yard. But I imagine it went, as cocktail-bar pianists say, something like this:

'Alastair Farjeon, prominent film-maker and notorious womaniser, spots Patsy Sloots in the chorus line of the latest

Crazy Gang revue and decides to cast her in his forthcoming film. Naturally, young Patsy, a newcomer to the business, is in seventh heaven at having been selected to play the lead in a major picture by one of the most esteemed directors in the world. It's literally the chance of a lifetime and she is – this, certainly, must have been Farjeon's own presumption – supremely grateful for having had it offered to her. Intending to capitalise on that gratitude, the great director then invites the gossamer wee thing down to his Cookham villa for a dirty weekend.

'We can't any longer know exactly what occurred there, but I think it safe to suppose that he dusts down the casting couch, plies her with expensive food and wine and eventually makes his move, only to discover that his protégée's gratitude stops well short of – well, I don't have to draw you a picture, do I? He consequently works himself up into a rage, a struggle ensues and whether by accident or design – that's another part of the story which may never see the light of day – Patsy is killed.

'Aghast at what he's done, his future in ruins, prison staring him in the face, Farjeon at once telephones his wife, who as usual drops everything and comes running.

'The truth, as I see it, is that, whatever his brilliance as a film director, Farjeon had as much experience of life, of real life, as a precocious three-year-old. Right into adulthood he remained very much the child he must once literally have been, the vile kind of tot who enjoys pulling the wings off insects. And, like any child, good or bad, whenever he got himself into a scrape he instantly cried out for his mummy – or rather, his wifie, which in his case amounted to much the same thing. As for Hattie, she was, I would deduce, fairly relaxed about his roving eye because she remained confident that it posed no long-term risk to their marriage; also because, in any case, Farjeon usually came a cropper on account of his taste for women half his age and a quarter of his weight. It's true, she would turn up every day on the set to keep him relentlessly focused on the work at hand, but they were a couple, as they both knew, roped together for the duration.

'So, panic-stricken, he rings her up, she catches the first train down to Cookham and together they contemplate the wreckage of his glittering reputation. Now – I'm speculating, you understand, but it does all appear to fit together – I couldn't say which of the two came up with the idea – most likely Farjeon himself, since he'd spent his entire career, after all, devising murder scenes, so who would be better qualified? – let's say Farjeon came up with the bright idea of setting the villa alight in order to conceal the evidence of Patsy's murder.

'But, and it was a beggar of a "but", given Farjeon's caddish willingness to be photographed with his latest paramour, it must have been common knowledge on the grapevine that he'd invited Patsy down for the weekend. Thus there could be no question of hers being the only body discovered in the fire. The police – the gutter press, too – would instantly, and of course justifiably, smell a rat. And here, I suspect, it was dear, sweet, calculating Hattie who, seizing a Heaven-sent – or Hell-sent – opportunity of henceforth keeping her chubby hubby all to herself, putting an end once and for all to those adulterous dalliances of his, succeeded in persuading him that he too would have to "die" in the conflagration.'

'It's true he was in one unholy mess,' put in Trubshawe, 'but that does seem a pretty drastic solution.'

'Ah, but don't forget, if the scandal had broken, his career would have been at an end anyway and he might even have ended on the gallows. He couldn't have survived it – which is doubtless why he decided that he literally *wouldn't* survive it. So he telephones Billy Harker. Why Harker? Because, of all those whom he regularly used as his doubles, Harker had separated from his wife, lived on his own in a furnished bedsit somewhere in the East End and badly needed a pay packet. When Farjeon (as I surmise) tells Harker he wanted to discuss the "double scene" in his new picture, even proposing that he pack an overnight bag and come straight down to Cookham, poor Billy must have thought his luck had finally turned. Not just a job, one sufficiently well paid to expunge a few of his more pressing debts, but an invitation to stay with the Master. You can visualise, I'm sure, the alacrity with which he would have accepted the invitation.'

'How do you suppose he was done away with?' asked Tom Calvert.

'Well, I really couldn't say,' she replied meditatively. 'Probably something that wouldn't show, just in case the flames failed to erase the evidence as cleanly and definitively as they hoped. Poison, I should opine. Or, if no poison was to be had, then strangulation. We'll know the correct answer only when Old Ma Farjeon confesses all, as I'm positive she will.'

'Evie,' said Trubshawe, 'you've been your usual super-efficient self, I'll grant you that. I'm hanged, though, if I can understand how, as you say, Alastair Farjeon actually "directed" the film. In practical terms, I mean.'

'Well now,' said Evadne Mount, 'let us agree, shall we, that Farjeon felt obliged to accept his wife's argument that he had to "die" in the fire along with Patsy. I imagine, however, that he'd be loathe to let the new film also go up in smoke because of that "death". If nothing else, there would have been a financial imperative for ensuring that it go ahead nevertheless. So he and Hattie decided to concoct a bogus document stating that, if anything were to happen to him, Rex Hanway was to direct *If Ever They Find Me Dead* in his place.'

'This Hanway,' said Françaix, 'you are saying he also was part of the plan?'

'Absolutely. He immediately agreed to become what our detective friends here would call an accessory after the fact. Let's not forget that Hanway was so fiercely ambitious that no legalistic scruples were going to prevent him from taking over the picture. He had waited years for such a chance and he wasn't about to let Patsy Sloots' death, which Farjeon in any case probably convinced him was an accident, snatch it from his greedy little paws.

'But now,' she said, 'there arose an unexpected snag. Hattie continued to turn up on the set every single day, just as though Farjeon himself were directing the picture, to keep an eye not only on her husband's *financial* interests, as Cora conjectured, but also on his *artistic* interests. She was his spy, his mole, whose job it was to bring him back daily reports on Hanway's work. But that was precisely the problem. Hanway's work was duff. Farjeon's script was followed to the letter, but what he himself had forgotten was that most of his best ideas, certainly the most original ones, had always come to him at the last minute, generally once he was on the set. And Hanway just didn't have it. He may have been a competent craftsman, but he didn't possess an ounce of his mentor's genius. There came a point – you remember, Eustace, what Cora told us? – there came a point when it was touch-and-go whether the production would actually proceed.

'For Farjeon that wouldn't do at all. He was a vain, arrogant narcissist who couldn't accept, who *wouldn't* accept, that he might be denied the chance of once more flaunting his brilliance to a suitably awe-struck world, even if only by proxy. Already, just as he himself had been about to start shooting the film, a stupid mishap – which is no doubt how he rationalised Patsy's passing – had prevented it from going ahead. To have his cherished project aborted a second time, because of another man's incompetence, no, no, that would have been intolerable to somebody of his type.

'So this film-maker, this artist, this genius, who had taken on one outlandish challenge after another – having one of his protagonists go to bed in Clerkenwell and wake up in the Rocky Mountains, having another confined to a wheelchair throughout the entire picture, setting yet another of his pictures inside a cramped lift – decided that he would accept the supreme challenge. Like the lovers who kissed each other through a little girl in the one scene of *If Ever They Find Me Dead* which Eustace and I watched being shot, he would direct the film *through somebody else*.

'And so it was that, all of a sudden, Hanway miraculously found his creative feet. Nobody could understand how, like Farjeon before him, he began to have these wonderful ideas right there on the set – ideas worthy, for a reason you will now all understand, of Alastair Farjeon himself.

'The modus operandi was actually, unwittingly, revealed to us by Hanway in Levey's office the day after Cora's murder. You recall that, when I asked him to explain how he'd abruptly regained his confidence on the set, his reply was that he no longer asked himself what Farje would have done. He was being more honest than we knew. If he no longer had to ask himself what Farje would have done, it was because Farje, precisely, was now telling him what to do! Farjeon, in fact, was using Hattie as a secret conduit to Hanway of all the last-minute ideas and eleventh-hour changes which had always made his films so unique.'

'Why didn't he just telephone Hanway?' asked Lettice.

'Too risky. His voice, that plummy, lugubrious voice of his, would certainly have been recognised by the studio's telephonist, who had doubtless heard it many times before. No, it was safer by far if Hattie were discreetly to take her "late" husband's detailed notes to Hanway's office where, once he had read them, they would instantly be destroyed. Which they were, save for this one singed scrap of paper that I rescued from his waste-basket.'

So saying, she dipped her two hands into her handbag, located the memo and ironed it out on the table before them. 'Though I realised, naturally, that it could have been any one of a thousand-and-one memos unrelated to the case, what I found especially suggestive was the fact that it had been set alight as well as torn into strips. Patently, it was a piece of paper whose recipient wanted nobody else to read and, thinking about why that should be so, I began to wonder, for the first time, whether this so-called *wunderkind* might not after all be little more than a ventriloquist's dummy.

'As you see, since most of the paper has been burnt, all we have left to work on are these twelve surviving letters: SS **ON THE RIGHT**. And Eustace, ever on the *qui vive*, at once came up with the theory that "SS" might somehow be related to Benjamin Levey's eleventh-hour flight from Nazi Germany.'

'Oh, come now, Evie,' said Trubshawe, flushing, 'you know quite well I was only joking.'

'I, on the other hand,' she continued, 'and despite my reputation as an incorrigible romancer, immediately let my mind run along more practical lines. Unearthing my old rhyming dictionary, I inspected a column of words ending in "ss" until I came to a pensive halt at "kiss". Why? Because it at once reminded me of the scene from *If Ever They Find Me Dead* that I mentioned just a few minutes ago, the one in which Gareth Knight and Leolia Drake simultaneously kissed a little girl's left and right cheeks.

'Now just think of it. Couldn't SS ON THE RIGHT once have been part of a sentence that read in toto: DRAKE GIVES HER A KISS ON THE RIGHT CHEEK, KNIGHT ON THE LEFT?'

They all stared at her. The world, which three-quarters of an hour ago had been upside-down, had now slowly revolved until it was once more positioned the right way up.

''Pon my word!' grunted Trubshawe.

'Good grief,' cried Lettice, 'you're the cat's pyjamas all right!'

'What an imbecile that I am!' Françaix effused. 'Why, it leaps to the eye! It is pure Farjeon!'

'My dear Evie,' said Calvert admiringly, 'in the Middle Ages you would have been burnt as a witch.'

'Thank you, Tom. So kind.'

'There is, though, one crucial question you still haven't answered.'

'Which is what?'

'Why did Farjeon kill Cora Rutherford? Or, as you seemed to imply a moment ago, why did he have her killed?'

Up to this point, the novelist had been so intoxicated by her own powers of ratiocination she had almost forgotten that at the heart of the case, after all, was the murder of a very dear old friend.

'Ah yes,' she said sadly. 'Cora, poor Cora . . . I'm afraid she must have thought she was being awfully cunning. The Achilles' heel of so many cunning people, though, is that they tend blithely to ignore the fact that others can also be cunning, even more than they are themselves.

'As Eustace will confirm, she announced to us one day that her role in the film, a minor one to start with, had unexpectedly got much larger and juicier. It had been mysteriously "bumped up", as she put it. To know the whole truth we'll again have to wait for Hattie Farjeon's confession, but I'd bet my bottom dollar that Cora, who never lost the atrocious habit of barging into her acquaintances' private affairs, had gone to have a word with Hanway, had found his office unoccupied, had started nosing about, as was her natural wont, and had eventually laid her hands on one of Farjeon's memos.

'She instantly recognised his handwriting, handwriting

that she would have known, even in block capitals, from all those brutal rejections she'd received from him before he consented to give her the part. And, just as instantly realising the most significant implication of the text itself, she understood that what she held in her hands was a major bargaining chip.'

'So in that at least I was right,' crowed Trubshawe. 'What you're saying is that she blackmailed Hanway?'

'Oh,' replied Evadne Mount evasively, 'blackmail is such an ugly word, don't you think?'

'Not half as ugly as the crime itself.'

Declining to be drawn, she continued:

'Let's just say that she put it to Hanway that there seemed no good reason why she shouldn't take such a damning piece of evidence to the police. Let's also say that Hanway, thinking on his feet, actually did come up with the one good reason for which she herself was angling. And let's end by saying that, if he were indeed to have proposed that her part in the picture be fleshed out, or bumped up, I fear that Cora, desperate as she was for a comeback, would simply not have been able to resist making a pact with the Devil.

'What she did was wrong, terribly wrong, and God knows she paid for it. But she was my oldest friend, and I've always stood by my friends, and I'm not about to desert her now, even though she's dead.'

'Bravo, Evie,' said Tom Calvert.

'Thank you, Tom,' she replied. Then, in a voice that was

becoming a trifle hoarse, so unduly long and wordy, even for her, had been her monologue, she went on:

'Yes, poor old Cora, it just didn't dawn on her that she had set herself against an individual as evil as any of the characters in his films. And she never was what anybody would call the soul of discretion. Farjeon and Hanway knew that they couldn't trust her. Excactly as a blackmailer will always come back for more, what was to stop her – I can almost hear them ask themselves – demanding a leading role in Hanway's second picture? And his third? And his fourth? No, no, no, she had to be silenced at once.

'The murder method almost certainly emerged from Farjeon's own diseased brain. Having already fed his protégé several last-minute alterations to the script, he must have calculated that the introduction of this new idea of his – Cora drinking from the half-filled champagne glass – would arouse no suspicion whatever on the set. Hanway would be garlanded with praise and Cora would meanwhile have been disposed of.

'As for who actually did the dirty by filching poison from the laboratory and spiking the lemonade, well, it wouldn't surprise me at all to learn that it was Hattie, our Madonna of the knitting-needles, to whom no one ever paid too much attention.'

'Evie,' said Trubshawe after a moment of silence, 'you are unquestionably right in all these suppositions of yours, but yesterday you were nearly murdered yourself, which would have been devastating for us all. Me more than anyone,' he couldn't prevent himself adding.

'Why, Eustace, I'd begun to wonder if you really cared.'

'None of that, none of that!' he riposted gruffly. 'You know what I mean – and what I *don't* mean. But, damn it all, why didn't you share your suspicions with the rest of us, instead of exposing yourself alone to the risk?'

'Don't you see, my dear, I couldn't, I just couldn't. Everything I knew, or thought I knew, was a mere hypothesis, a house of cards which wouldn't for a second have stood up in a court of law. It was all based on a single fact – at least, I regarded it as a fact, though no one else did – the fact, as I say, that Farjeon was still alive. A fact, however, which I absolutely could not prove.

'Can you imagine me at the Old Bailey, requesting the judge to screen the murder sequence from *If Ever You Find Me Dead*, then pleading with him, "M'Lud, I submit that the visual style of the scene we have all just watched constitutes conclusive proof not only that Alastair Farjeon did not die in the fire which destroyed his villa but also that he was responsible for the deaths of Patsy Sloots, Billy Harker and Cora Rutherford"? 'Pshaw! I'd be thrown out of court on my rear end!

'No, I had to produce the only evidence which would prove me right – Alastair Farjeon himself. I had to flush him out, and the only way I could do that was to set myself up as a decoy. Which is why I insisted that everybody be present on the set for yesterday afternoon's session, even the one suspect, Rex Hanway, whom I'd already guessed had been an accomplice. Why, too, I promised to reveal the murderer's identity. I had to be certain that everybody would be there so that, if anybody was going to try and prevent me from making my announcement, it could only be Farjeon himself. And, if I was confident that he *would* try to stop me, it was because he had, after all, the perfect alibi. He was dead!'

'I'll be for ever in your debt, Evie,' said Calvert, adding, 'Yours too, of course, Mr Trubshawe.'

'Oh, me,' said Trubshawe. 'Don't feel you have to thank me. As usual, I was just Inspector Plodder, the hapless butt of all the amateur sleuth's jokes.'

'Please, no false modesty. You two formed a great team. And, talking of teams, I gather from Evie here that I'll be offering you congratulations of a very different order before not too much time has passed, eh, Eustace?'

'Tush tush!' growled the Chief-Inspector. 'You're getting a touch too big for your breeches.'

'In any case, my dear,' Evadne piped up, 'you may or may not be relieved to know that you're going to have a breathing space before we eventually tie the knot.'

'Oh, and why would that be?' asked Trubshawe.

'I've got to write my new whodunit first.'

'You're going to write a new whodunit?' asked Lettice.

'I most certainly am. It will be dedicated to Cora's memory,

286

not' – she glanced meaningfully in her future husband's direction – 'repeat *not*, to Agatha Christie.'

'But that's terribly exciting news, Evie. Dare one ask what it's about?'

'Why, what do you suppose?' she replied as though the answer were obvious. 'The story we've all just lived through. We authors are a thrifty race, you know. We never waste anything, never throw anything away.'

'Great Scott Moncrieff!' cried an incredulous Trubshawe. 'You mean you're planning to write about Cora and Farjeon and Hattie and the rest of them and put them all in a book?'

'That I am. Naturally, I won't use their real names. I'm a novelist, after all, an artist. I'll have to invent lots of new ones. But don't you worry, Eustace, don't go snapping your cummerbund. You're going to be in it too. As a matter of fact, you're all going to be in it.'

'*Sacre bleu!*' exclaimed Philippe Françaix, his eyes swimming heavenwards. 'This is – how you say? – the end!'